ELI

ELI

A Ranger's Tale
Part One

MARC ALAN EDELHEIT

Eli: A Ranger's Tale
First Edition
Copyright © 2021 by Marc Edelheit. WGA Registration: #2132236
I wish to thank my agent, Andrea Hurst, for her invaluable support and assistance. I would also like to thank my beta readers, who suffered through several early drafts. My betas: Jon Cockes, Nicolas Weiss, Melinda VALLEM, Paul Klebaur, James Doak, David Cheever, Bruce Heaven, Erin Penny, April Faas, Rodney Gigone, Tim Adams, Paul Bersoux, Phillip Broom, David Houston, Sheldon Levy, Michael Hetts, Walker Graham, Bill Schnippert, Jan McClintock, Jonathan Parkin, Spencer Morris, Jimmy McAfee, Rusty Juban, Joel M. Rainey, Jeremy Craig, Nathan Halliday, Ed Speight, Joseph Hall, Michael Berry, Tom Trudeau, Sally Tingley-Walker, James H. Bjorum, Franklin Johnson, Marshall Clowers. I would also like to take a moment to thank my loving wife, who sacrificed many an evening and weekends to allow me to work on my writing.
Editorial Assistance: Hannah Streetman, Audrey Mackaman, Brandon Purcell
Cover Art by Piero Mng (Gianpiero Mangialardi)
Cover Formatting by Telemachus Press
Agented by Andrea Hurst & Associates, LLC www.andreahurst.com
Marc's Website: http://maenovels.com/

MARC'S NOTE:

For clarification purposes, this book takes place years before Eli meets Stiger in Tales of the Seventh. If you have not yet read Tales or Chronicles, you may wish to begin there first. As a side note, this story was outlined and planned around the time that I wrote *Stiger's Tigers*. Unfortunately, I could not write it until I had finished *The Tiger's Imperium* and *The First Compact*. Once those books were done, I then needed to find the time. Starting the book on Patreon as a serial helped make this one a reality. I would like to offer a big thank you to my Patreon Legion.

You may wish to sign up to my newsletter to get the latest updates on my writing.

http://maenovels.com/

Reviews keep us motivated and also help to drive sales. I make a point to read each and every one, so please continue to post them.

I hope you enjoy *Eli: A Ranger's Tale* and would like to offer a sincere thank you for your purchase and support.

Best regards,
Marc Alan Edelheit, author and your tour guide to the worlds of Tannis and Istros

TABLE OF CONTENTS

CHAPTER ONE

Eli lowered himself to a knee beside the marker tree and stared at the ground before him, studying it closely. He breathed in slowly through his nose, inhaling the scent of the forest, and let it out through his mouth. Wet bark and moss were on the air, as was the decay of the previous season's leaves. All of it smelled good to him, right, as it should.

Just as there was nothing out of the ordinary on the wind, there was not a mark or track on the forest floor, at least not any that a normal person might notice. Eli, however, was far from normal when it came to observation and tracking.

He glanced up at his companion, Mae'Cara. She was scanning the trees around them, searching for any sign of a threat, which was unlikely given their current location. Still, elven rangers were always cautious and on guard.

For an elf, Mae was pleasant to look upon. She had striking brown eyes and hair, brushed straight, which she wore loosely down to her shoulders. She was athletic in build and had a serious air about her, as well as a piercing gaze. She carried a light traveling pack on her back.

Mae wore the green and brown leathers of a ranger, the Guardians of the Forest. She held her bow loosely in a hand, and like his, her arrows were wrapped in a leather bundle. These had been secured to her pack, as were her cloak and a blanket to lay upon the ground or wrap around oneself for warmth. She carried a narrow sword in a leather sheath belted to her side and a dagger, which was concealed in her boot.

"What do you think, Eli?" she asked, without looking over. "They came this way, didn't they?"

"I believe so." Eli leaned forward and touched a partially decomposed leaf. It had been disturbed recently and was not resting where it had originally fallen. He could tell by the faint outline in the forest floor where it had been before being moved, a few inches to the side. He shifted the leaf aside and saw what he expected to find underneath, moss that had been disturbed when someone had trod upon it.

"The tracks have been erased, and those that are left are concealed well with leaves." Eli straightened and pointed at the marker tree. "Someone even brushed up against it and accidently removed some of the bark—see that strip there? Probably when they leaned upon it or, more likely, placed a pack against the trunk as they were resting."

"Hah. I see it. I knew I was correct," Mae'Cara said. "They are following the old road to Lysen'Dale. I told you. It's the quickest way out of our lands."

Eli stood and glanced over at the marker tree. Its base had been intentionally shaped to point west, before being allowed to grow straight up. Those who did not know what to look for would simply see a misshapen tree and think nothing of it, for such things happened with nature. However, to elven eyes, the tree was so much more.

His people had shaped its growth and others like it to mark trails, paths, and hidden roads within and outside their lands. Every half mile along the road, there would be such a tree, indicating the proper direction for the traveler.

All one needed was a starting point, and then they followed the trees.

"If we get to the next marker tree and find similar evidence," Eli said, "then it is likely as you say."

Mae'Cara was new to being a ranger and had been part of the Corps for less than five years. She was overly eager, with an enthusiasm Eli found not only tiring but at times trying. There was a lack of patience there, at least to elven sensibilities—really his own. And yet, oddly, there were moments he found it refreshing. How strange.

Though she had found her calling, Mae had yet to completely find her balance in life. It was an elven thing, something that came with the passing of many years. Eli knew she would discover it. Given time, all elves did, and time was something his people had in great abundance.

Turning his mind from her, he scanned the forest around them. They were on the border of his people's territory, in a region that was mostly uninhabited. Once, it had not been so. The lands about them had been the heart of a thriving kingdom, with rolling grasslands, pastures, and farms. Back then, humans had lived in these parts.

That had been long before his people had claimed this land for their own, more than fourteen hundred years prior.

Eli had not had the opportunity to meet and study the people who had once lived here. They had passed on before he'd even been born. That made him slightly regretful, for one of the joys in his life was seeing new things, learning, and, most importantly, finding some excitement to help stave off the monotony. And humans always seemed to provide the excitement.

He wondered what this region had looked like before his people had allowed the forest to reclaim the land. He supposed it had appeared similar to other human lands he'd seen in his travels.

Humans were curious creatures. They had such short lives, yet they lived life to the fullest, or so it had always seemed to him. They held nothing back and made the most of the years that were given to them. In a way, Eli envied them for that.

A gentle wind blew through the tops of the trees, rustling the leaves and setting several free from their branches. Under the shade of the trees, it was a pleasant enough day, not too warm and not too cold. Fall was only days away. The nights were becoming crisp. Soon enough, the great cold would descend upon the north and then would come the snows. Eli liked snow.

Leaves fluttered to the ground around them. He watched them fall, feeling a sense of serenity in their movements. The forest's heart was strong, healthy, and loving. When he closed his eyes, he could feel her song, her voice, something that never ceased to invigorate his spirit. This was one of the reasons he loved being a ranger, the connection to the Great Mother of the forest.

"I always enjoy the change in seasons," Eli said, picking up a newly fallen oak leaf that had come to rest on the ground before him. It had already turned yellow, but it was golden perfection in his eyes, a piece of natural art the tree had worked hard at growing.

"Getting distracted again?" Mae asked. "Have the falling leaves caught your interest?"

"No more than usual." Eli turned the leaf over in his hand and examined it. The leaf was part of the never-ending lifecycle of the forest. In time, it would become one with the soil, returning from whence it came.

The change of seasons taught much and so too did elven eyes, which marked the passage of time. He had long since learned nothing in life was permanent. He looked back at Mae as he set the leaf down upon the forest floor. She was eyeing him, as if amused.

"Everything changes, given time," Eli said.

"How far ahead do you think Mik'Las is?" Mae asked, refusing to be distracted.

His thoughts darkening, Eli considered the question. "I'm guessing no more than a week, maybe less since he's working so hard to cover his tracks."

"I do not see why he bothers," Mae said. "He had to know we would come after him."

"He bothers because he does not wish to be caught. He well knows we will kill him for what he's done."

"Death is too easy an escape." Mae's voice became hard and cold. Any amusement she had felt vanished in a flash. "He earned what's coming."

"Yes," Eli said, feeling some regret that circumstances were propelling them in that direction. "He has certainly earned his fate."

Eli removed his bow from his back and leaned it against the marker tree. He had made the bow himself. It was the ultimate mark of a ranger and was his one true pride and joy. He had carried it with him for more than a hundred years now.

Not only had he made it, but he had also grown the tree from which he had harvested the wood. The weapon was a work of art, smooth, balanced, highly polished, and incredibly strong. The wood came from the heart of the tree and, like all such bows, was one of a kind. So too was Mae's. Crafting one's bow was a rite of passage and a final test before one could be named a full-fledged Guardian of the Forest.

Eli shrugged off his pack, untied the flap, and pulled out his waterskin and a cloth-wrapped bundle of food. Inside the pack, he had a few personal possessions, as well as a flint, a small flask of oil, a single change of clothes, and some food. Of the latter, their supply was dwindling. A small axe was strapped to the outside of the pack. He always traveled light.

He also carried two daggers, one quite normal and the other curved, a gift from his mentor. It was a work of near perfection and a reminder of their friendship.

"Water?" Eli offered up the skin to Mae.

She gave a nod and took the skin, uncorking it. Tipping it back, she drank deeply, while Eli unwrapped the bundle of food, revealing thick strips of dried and seasoned river fish. He took a piece and began chewing on it. The fish was tasty, but hard and without moisture. Though not his favorite of foods, it would keep him going and that was what mattered.

"We're going to need some real food, fresh food." Mae eyed the fish unhappily as she handed the waterskin back to him. "We have been traveling for a week straight now. I have grown tired of dried meat and hard bread."

"That's right," Eli said, without looking over at her. "We will have to hunt tonight, do some gathering from the forest, then push on."

They had been traveling hard, working to catch up to their quarry, who had gotten a head start on them. Eli glanced up at the sky, which peeked through the tree canopy. It was midday.

He thought on the direction they were traveling. It had been several years since he had been through these parts, but he knew them like the back of his hand, for Eli had spent significant time in this forest. That Mik'Las had come this way with such a grim purpose saddened him to a degree.

"There's a shelter ahead, the Task'Umaul Holdout," Eli said. "I doubt he knows of it. In fact, he shouldn't."

"The Task'Umaul Holdout?" Mae repeated. "I've never heard of it."

"Not many have," Eli said. "It is infrequently used. We will find plenty of game around it, as well as a river-fed lake that should be rich with fish."

"Sounds a pleasant spot."

"It's not on our land. We will have to be watchful."

"The Castol?" Mae asked.

"We're on their border, aren't we?"

Mae gave a disgusted grunt. "Humans."

"Most will have no idea the shelter's there." Eli glanced up at the sky again. "Only a select few are so blessed."

"Are you certain?" Mae asked.

"Nothing in this life is certain, which is why we will be watchful. You need to keep that in mind."

Her mouth tightened slightly, but she did not reply.

"We should be able to make it there before dusk," Eli said. "It will be a good place to stop. We can spend the night, get some hunting in, gather some edibles, maybe even fish a bit. We can rest a day or more before pushing on."

"I really do not like the idea of giving him time to gain ground on us," Mae said. "Not after all that he's done."

"There is no need to rush. No matter how long it takes, we will find him. That is our mission, and I might add, we will not return until we have completed what we set out to do."

Mae was silent a moment.

"Why send us both?" Mae asked, looking over at him. Eli offered her some meat, which she accepted, taking two thick strips. "You are a senior ranger, and I was just ranked into the Corps. Why us both? Why make us a team?"

"Are you disappointed in your partner?" Eli asked. "Or do you think this mission is beneath you?"

"No, it is not that," Mae said and then seemed slightly embarrassed. "I mean no offense. I am just curious, is all." She paused and regarded him with serious eyes. "You know the reason, don't you?"

Eli chose not to answer. He suspected she knew too. His father had a hand in setting the events in motion that had seen his pairing with Mae for this job. Once again, his father was interfering, working to control his son's life. No matter how far Eli went or how hard he pushed him away, Tenya'Far was always there, waiting to pounce.

"You are not going to answer me?" Mae tapped an impatient, almost demanding foot on the ground. "Are you?"

"You are just full of questions." Eli had been hoping to avoid this subject. But he knew that would not happen. She was too smart for that, and perhaps that was the root of the problem. Mae was very much like her mother and refused to accept things as they were or appeared to be.

"It is political," Mae said.

"Perhaps."

"My mother is the warden. Everything with my family is a political consideration, even pushing me into the Corps."

"That is certainly one possibility," Eli admitted.

There was another, a more sinister one, and he found that personally troubling. It was a possibility he felt he was not ready for. Eli was surprised she had not yet considered it. He wondered how long it would be before she pieced it together. When she did, it would not be a pretty scene, for Mae'Cara had a temper.

He decided instead to deflect. "It could also be as simple as us being the only rangers available. Generally, the simplest explanation is the correct one."

He offered her the bundle of dried fish again. She took another piece and popped it into her mouth, chewing slowly as she eyed him, somewhat suspiciously. After a moment, she swallowed.

"You are nothing like your father," Mae said.

"I try not to be." He really did not want to discuss his familial relations with her, especially when it came to Tenya'Far. She was, after all, the warden's daughter. Secrets needed to be kept, especially those that involved family.

"I've heard it said your father had ambitious plans for you, until you ran them aground."

Eli considered his response. "Were these whispers at court? How scandalous. What would your mother think of you spreading gossip?"

She shot him an unhappy scowl, for he'd intentionally touched a nerve and she knew it. Eli wanted nothing to do with politics. That was one of the reasons he had defied his father's wishes and entered himself into ranger training. His father had almost disowned him for that betrayal to the family's interests. Eli wished Tenya'Far had cast him out. In a way, it would have made things simpler.

Few amongst his people ever managed to complete the training, but Eli had wanted nothing more in his life than to be a ranger. The Corps was a small, elite group, unlike any other. Entering the Corps had meant escape from the clutches of family obligations. So, he had thrown himself headlong into the training, aiming and working to become the best he could be. He had pushed himself hard and then some. Though Mae had been pushed into the Corps, Eli suspected they had more in common than perhaps either realized.

"Do you enjoy being difficult?" Mae asked, a note of irritation creeping into her voice. "Are you always like this?"

"Well," Eli said as he wrapped the fish back up, "when we return, you can ask my sister. She knows me well enough and loves gossip too. I am sure she will tell you everything you desire to know—in confidence, of course."

"I'll take that as a yes, because you don't have a sister." Mae tilted her head to one side and crossed her arms, signaling her displeasure with him.

"I don't?" Eli asked, pretending to be surprised. "Has anyone told my father? He will be quite shocked when he discovers the truth. Imagine that, I don't have a sister and he doesn't have a daughter. Wow, just wow."

"You have to be one of the most maddening people I know. There are times when you want to make me scream with frustration or maybe even hit you, teach you a lesson. I think I might enjoy that."

"And I think I'd enjoy you trying." Eli flashed her a grin, then returned the bundle of fish and the waterskin to his pack before tying it closed. He stood and shrugged the pack back on, settling it into a comfortable position. He picked up his bow and looked in the direction they would be traveling. "The border is only a mile distant. There is a small river we will have to cross. It is a good thing I know a shallow ford, and there's a perk."

"Oh?" she asked. "What is that?"

"It's not the rainy season, so we will only get our legs wet. You won't have to worry about your hair." Eli paused as she glared at him. "You know... my sister loves washing and brushing her hair."

"Tell me," Mae said wearily, as they started walking, "how did I get stuck with you again?"

He looked back at her and felt the grin begin to spread across his face. "Because I'm the best at this sort of thing, you know—being a ranger and all that goes with it." He showed her his teeth. "You still have a lot to learn, warden's daughter, and I'm your instructor."

Before she could lash out at him, he increased his pace to a near jog. Behind him, Mae matched his stride, and once again, they began to make good time, for Eli knew they had a lot of ground to cover if they wanted to make the holdout before dusk.

"Humble," she called ahead to him, "aren't you?"

"I don't even know the word," he shot back and increased his pace even more.

CHAPTER TWO

"I thought you said no one knew about this place?" It was more of a statement than a question.

Even though he wasn't looking at her, Eli could sense Mae's intense satisfaction.

"I'd say it certainly looks like someone was here before us," Mae continued. "They made a camp, and not too long ago either."

Eli gazed around and fought off a scowl. He felt a stab of frustration. There were footprints everywhere, hundreds of them, many leading right up to the holdout's entrance. It was one of those places that was out of the way and difficult to not only reach, but find, which was what made it such a perfect refuge and sanctuary.

That was what he found so maddening. He and Mae were in the middle of nowhere. Eli knew it could not be a coincidence. He was certain of that fact. He believed in fortune, but not in coincidences, especially considering their mission.

Why bother to stop here?

When he spoke, it was more a whisper to himself than anything else. "I guess nowhere is always someone's somewhere."

"What was that?" Mae asked, looking over at him, her brow furrowing slightly. "What did you say?"

"Occasionally," Eli said rather grudgingly, "I have been known to be wrong."

"I wish I had something for you to write that down for me with," Mae said. "I'd like to memorialize this moment. I really would. Eli, the famed ranger, finally acknowledges that he's wrong and, dare I say, fallible like the rest of us."

"Fallible?" Eli gave a soft grunt as he glanced over at her. He added a tinge of hurt to his tone. "You really think I'm fallible?"

"That's right," Mae said. "Fallible."

"That hurts. It strikes me to the core, like an arrow shot through the heart."

"You are also a terrible liar," Mae said.

Eli chewed his lip and turned away from her. They were standing on the edge of a steep forested ridge, with aggressive terrain that became more rugged the higher one climbed. Through the trees, the top of the ridge seemed to hang over them. The slope above was intimidating. Eli estimated it was another thousand feet to the summit.

A cave was to their immediate right. Its entrance was nearly twelve feet wide and rose to ten in height. In the fading light of the day, it appeared to be a yawning maw that led only to a place of sinister darkness.

Mae seemed to tire of her amusement. She knelt by the charred ashes of what had once been a good-sized fire. It had been set just before the entrance to the cave. She fingered a partially burned log, rubbed the ash between her fingers, and then touched it to her tongue. She looked over at him.

"Maybe a week old, surely not much more than that," Mae said. "I can't say for certain how long they were here, though. Judging by the evidence they left behind, maybe a day or two at most."

As he slowly ran his gaze around the forested hillside, soaking in every detail, Eli agreed with that assessment. Mae was one of the more gifted rangers in the Corps, and like him, a natural. Though he would never admit it to her. Then again, he considered, knowing her mother, that wasn't much of a surprise. The warden would have accepted nothing less from her only daughter.

Despite there being plenty of fallen trees and branches lying about from which to gather wood for a fire, several nearby trees had been cut down. All that remained were their axe-chopped stumps, wood chips, and branches that had been shorn from the tree, visible scars that would blight the forest for years to come. There was also a stacked pile of chopped wood that had not been burned. He felt a pang of sadness at such thoughtlessness, the senseless ending of life when there were alternatives.

There was even an old fallen tree, a snag, no more than thirty yards off in the forest. Instead of harvesting that and breaking it up for the fire, they'd gone for the living trees. The dead wood of the snag would have burned better, easier. He could almost feel the Great Mother's pain at what had been done here.

The carcasses of several deer lay a few yards from him, in a pile. From what he could see, only the best bits of meat had been taken. The rest had been left to rot, including the pelts. That irritated him even more, for there was a responsibility to use as much as possible when taking a forest creature, at least in elven eyes.

Traditionally, elves left little to go to waste. Then again, humans were not elves. They thought differently. Eli had learned that lesson the hard way, and yet sometimes he found it surprised him.

"It looks like they sheltered in the cave, likely from the recent rains that passed through the region." Mae glanced into the cave. "They left behind plenty of trash. Humans have no respect for the forest."

Eli did not say anything. It rained a lot in this forest, especially at this time of year. He took several steps downslope toward a pit, or really a trench, that had been dug. It was several feet long. A freshly cut tree of intermediate years had been felled, stripped of its branches along with the bark, and laid along the side of the pit for sitting, almost on the edge and in danger of falling in. He wrinkled his nose as he approached. A cloud of flies buzzed around the makeshift latrine. They had not even bothered to fill it in before leaving.

The forest floor before the latrine showed signs of excessive use and rain, which had turned the ground to mud. It had since mostly dried. The excavated soil from the trench was piled up on the backside of the latrine. Eli focused in on several boot prints that were much clearer and easier to read than most of the others. He knelt and examined them closely.

"Anything interesting?" Mae asked, stepping nearer.

"Hobnails," Eli said. "They wore boots too, not sandals. Judging by the other tracks, the type of boot seems fairly uniform."

"Soldiers, then," Mae said. "That would certainly explain all the tracks. Despite those deer carcasses, I think we can safely rule out a hunting party."

"Seems that way," Eli said. "I'd hazard a Castol light infantry company, perhaps fifty men in total."

"Sixty miles to the south is an imperial garrison," Mae said. "How can you be sure they're Castol?"

"I can't. The imperial protectorate is just too distant for them to bother with the Castol in this area. They have enough issues pacifying and keeping the peace in the protectorate. Besides, there is not much out this way and no reason to come north, at least none that I can think of. Also, I've heard of no recent flare-ups between the Castol and Mal'Zeel."

"I guess that makes sense, then. You have more experience in these parts than I do. Still, it would be nice to know for certain who came this way."

"Well, it seems I've been wrong before." Eli came to his feet. "You said so yourself, so who knows."

"And I am pleased to be here to see it happen," Mae said. "The gods have surely favored me this day."

"Some are more favored than others." Eli moved toward the cave entrance. "Such is the way of life."

"If it is the Castol, this place is only a few miles from the border. Our patrols out this way are infrequent. Besides the obvious implications of their presence here, the Castol could be regularly trespassing on our lands. If they are, such behavior cannot be tolerated. We let them do it once and it will happen again. Allow it to occur too many times and they'll be settling on our lands. Then, we will have a real fight on our hands. Best to discourage them before they put down roots."

"Is that your mother speaking for you?" Eli asked. It was a struggle not to grin at her. He knew the barb would strike deep.

Mae turned a hard look on him. "When we return this way, we must check to be certain the Castol are staying on their side of the border."

"I suspect they are, for the most part. The Castol have not troubled us for at least a century. I don't think they will start now."

"Then what were they doing here?"

Eli had already surmised the answer and knew she was likely thinking the same. He could see it in her gaze. She was just looking to test his thinking. But she'd been right on the border. When this mess was all over, they needed to be certain the Castol were not trespassing, especially since they were already out this way. There was no telling how many years would pass before another ranger team came by.

"Now that is a good question," Eli said. "You already know the answer."

"Mik'Las. They were here to meet him."

"That is a strong possibility," Eli said, "and likely the correct answer. This means his actions were planned in advance and not spontaneous as we had assumed."

"He is working with the Castol, then."

"We don't know that, yet." Eli felt troubled by that thought. What had Mik'Las been thinking? That had bothered him to begin with. Now, it seemed there was a strong likelihood he was coordinating with the Castol. That was not good and reinforced the need to check the border lands.

"Before we turned for the holdout, his trail was going to the south toward imperial lands," Mae said. "It did not appear he was headed here, to the holdout."

"No, it is clear from his direction of travel that he wasn't. I believe it possible the soldiers that stayed in this place"— he glanced up through the leaves at the darkening sky— "did not meet up with him here."

"You mean they were just passing through? Their rendezvous was elsewhere?" Mae asked.

Eli nodded his affirmation.

"How far is the nearest town?"

"Mickalene is at least forty miles to the north," Eli said. "It is not the easiest of hikes, say a two-, maybe three-day trek.

The ground in this region is rugged and filled with steep hills and ridges. There is a Castol garrison in Mickalene too. I am thinking that is where the soldiers came from."

"We can verify that easily enough. We just need to find their tracks and direction of travel."

"We can also follow their path after they left," Eli said. "If we're correct, and I believe we are, they will link up with Mik'Las and his party a few miles from here." Eli paused and glanced up at the darkening sky again. "We can do that in the morning, when there is more light. I think I'd like to settle in for the night."

Mae glanced at the cave and a look of disgust came over her. "I do not wish to stay here tonight, not in a cave. I do not enjoy being underground."

"Neither do I," Eli said.

"The humans have also contaminated this place. I'd rather sleep under the stars." Mae paused and looked around them. "Even though this is not our land, we should rightly clean it up and remove all evidence of their stay here. The forest deserves to be restored to how it was."

Eli agreed. He felt the same urge too, the desire to clean up. Unfortunately, it would remain as the humans had left it.

"We do not have the time for that," Eli said. "It would take significant effort. Things remain as they are, at least until we run Mik'Las down and deal with him. We cannot allow him to get too much of a lead on us. If we do, we risk his trail going cold, and then the hunt becomes more difficult."

She gave an unhappy nod of understanding.

Eli turned toward the cave. He moved up to the entrance and looked inside. It was littered with refuse, bones with vestiges of meat, leather scraps, a discarded canvas bag, and some other items, even small pieces of wood whittled into various shapes. Eli saw a figurine of some kind, likely an idol, and a carved bird had been left behind. He had no idea their meaning. Had they been an offering to the gods, or just a way to pass the time? The artist, for a human, had been quite good.

Mae had followed him and, at his side, was looking on with plain disgust.

Eli glanced behind them. The light was dying, and fast. In another half hour it would be dark. He studied the trees, scanning them carefully. There was no hint of movement or sign they were being watched. Mae was watching him curiously, clearly wondering what he was up to. Eli ignored her and, satisfied that they were not being directly observed, stepped into the cave and the darkness.

The interior of the cave was large and ran twenty feet back. The air was colder. Mold, dampness, and the stench of bat droppings were on the air. It all tickled at Eli's nose and he resisted a sneeze. Several bats hung overhead. One of the little creatures, disturbed by their presence, took to flight. It fluttered between them and out of the cave.

There was a jumble of boulders at the far end. Part of the cave had collapsed long ago, blocking whatever had been on the other side. With Mae following, Eli moved up to the rockfall. He took a long moment to study what was before him.

"What are you doing?" Mae asked. Her curiosity was clearly getting the better of her and so too was her impatience. It was yet another sign of her youthful impetuousness. In time, she would learn patience.

In truth, Eli wasn't sure he was looking forward to that. There were times he fully enjoyed the spark of her spirit and spunk. Then again, sometimes... her zeal and fervor wearied him.

"Help me," Eli said as he crouched down next to a large slab of stone that appeared as if it had fallen vertically from the ceiling. He gripped the left side and pulled as hard as he could.

Without question, Mae moved over and found a grip. She pulled with him. At first, nothing happened as they strained. Then, with a screech of rusted and ancient hinges, the slab began to move, first slowly and then quicker.

"That's good enough," Eli said, when the opening was wide enough for them to enter one at a time. He and Mae peered into the opening. Before them stretched out a dark tunnel carved through the rock. At the far end, there was a faint hint of natural light.

Mae did not say anything. She tilted her head to the side curiously, then looked at him in question.

"Come on," Eli said. "There's something I believe you will want to see. It's a treat."

"A treat?" She sounded dubious.

"Trust me."

Without waiting for an answer, he stepped into the tunnel that was barely wide enough for the two of them. Mae followed him in. He moved past her, back toward the stone door. A rusted iron crossbar had been hammered into the back side of the stone. Eli gripped the iron handle and swung the door closed. It screeched the entire time, until it made a deep booming sound as it came back into its original position. The sound echoed up and down the tunnel.

Eli waited a moment for his eyes to adjust to the darkness and then started forward down the tunnel. The floor was smooth, with no obstacles to worry about tripping over. Mae said nothing. She just followed. He could almost sense her intense curiosity and excitement at experiencing something new. That was something Eli could appreciate.

After six hundred yards, they came to the end of the tunnel and emerged out onto a forested hillside that overlooked a small valley. Mae took several steps forward, past him, her eyes scanning everything in sight, soaking it all up.

The valley was no more than a mile wide and two long. In the growing darkness, it was heavily shadowed. A lake was at the bottom of the valley, with a forested island at its center. A series of steep ridges hemmed everything in. To the north was a slender waterfall that fed the lake. The last rays of sunlight shone against the top, lighting up the falling water in an orange, almost fiery glow.

Everything looked pristine and unexplored, as if no one had ever come here. There were no tracks anywhere around where they had emerged—none but those that animals had made. Eli saw fresh rabbit and deer prints.

There was a peacefulness to this place. Eli had always enjoyed the valley. He had made a point of stopping by every time he came this way, which was sadly an infrequent occurrence.

"Welcome to the Task'Umaul Holdout," Eli said and looked over at Mae. He felt a sense of triumph as understanding flooded her gaze. "And it seems I was right after all. Those soldiers did not discover the holdout. They only camped on the doorstep of the refuge. So, if I'm right, that makes you—" He paused dramatically. "Come on, you can say it…"

Her gaze locked on the valley, Mae opened her mouth as if to speak, but she did not.

"I believe the word you are looking for is *wrong*," Eli said.

Mae glanced at him with wide eyes before turning her gaze back to the valley. Refusing to take the bait, she shook her head slowly, in awe at the sight before them both.

"It's beautiful."

"Yes," Eli said and let out a heavy breath of resignation, giving up on the teasing. He knew what she was feeling. He had felt it himself the first time he'd set eyes on Task'Umaul. "It is most certainly that. We will be safe here. No one will disturb us. You can be assured of that."

"This place is calming to the soul," Mae said, her voice barely audible. "It has its own voice, an old one, ancient. I can feel it singing to me, welcoming us."

"Yes," Eli said, "Task'Umaul is a special place."

"I could spend years in peace here."

"The caretaker would not like that very much." Eli started walking down the slope toward the lake below. The island would be their ultimate destination this day. "He gets a little grumpy when guests overstay their welcome. Trust me on that."

"Caretaker?" Mae looked over at him in surprise. She scrambled to catch up. "Someone lives here?"

"He's more of a hermit than anything else and prefers his solitude, guards it even. Had those soldiers found their way in here, they would not have left to tell the tale." He looked back at her. "This is his valley, and make no mistake, he already knows we are here. Let us hope he's in a welcoming mood."

CHAPTER THREE

The bottom of the canoe made a scraping sound as it slid easily up onto the island's shore, just yards from the tree line. Eli placed the paddle down at his feet and hopped out, his boots splashing into the calf-high water of the lake. The water was cold. From the front of the canoe, Mae was able to step directly onto dry land.

Without speaking a word, the two of them hauled the canoe completely out of the water, pulling it farther onto the shore. Eli had guided them to a specific point on the island, just before the head of a trail that led through the trees. At the end of that trail was their destination.

The sky overhead was almost completely dark. It was also starting to cloud over. Eli thought the clouds looked ominous. The moon had yet to rise above the ridges that tightly ringed the valley. As a result, the land around them was heavily shadowed, and yet to elven eyes, the growing darkness was not an issue. Elven eyes could see easily enough in low light conditions, better than most other races on Istros.

Somewhere off in the distance, thunder rumbled. It sounded like someone was beating discordantly on a drum. After several heartbeats it died off.

Reaching into the canoe, Eli pulled out his pack and shrugged it on. He took his bundle of arrows and set them on the ground at his feet, along with his bow. Mae had removed her pack, bow, and arrows. She set those on the ground next to his. Eli reached in and pulled out both paddles. He moved them farther up onto the shore and out of the way and then returned to the canoe.

"Let's flip it over," Eli said, "in the event there is rain."

As if to emphasize the point, thunder growled again off in the distance. The sky briefly flashed with lightning.

"Your powers of observation are impressive, oh master ranger," Mae said. "Care to tell me your first clue on that?"

"Come on. Let's get this done before the rain arrives." Eli bent down and gripped the side of the canoe. Together, they turned it over. He regarded the upturned canoe for a moment. It had been carved from a single fallen tree and was exquisitely made. It was clearly his people's work. And yet, the last time he had come this way, the canoe had not been here. Ten years had passed since Eli had been to the refuge.

He straightened and turned to look out over the water lapping gently up against the shore. Eli wondered who had made the canoe. Perhaps a passing ranger, perhaps not.

To his knowledge, a few others knew of this place, but not many. After a moment, he decided it did not much matter. The canoe was simply evidence others had come here, which wasn't particularly surprising. It had probably been left as a thank you to the caretaker.

Presaging the coming storm, a cool, gentle breeze gusted around them. The far shore was over a hundred yards distant. There were small wind-driven waves on the surface of the lake that lapped up against the shore of the island. The sound was calming, relaxing even. An owl glided across the water. Eli followed its graceful flight and, with it, his heart swelled.

This valley was one of his favorite places to visit. Not only was it beautiful, but it brought him a sense of profound peace, something he felt nowhere else, at least not so fully. Simply put, he loved it here and always had.

Eli closed his eyes and allowed the Mother to pervade his spirit as she greeted him, welcomed him to her home. He breathed in through his nose and then out slowly through his mouth. He was already beginning to relax. A faint hint of woodsmoke was on the air.

"Someone has a fire going," Mae said.

"I am impressed." Eli glanced toward the path and then over at Mae. "Such powers of observation are most worthy of a ranger."

Mae gave an amused grunt.

"It seems we are being welcomed, our visit anticipated."

"Welcomed?" Mae asked, looking over at him. "By the caretaker?"

"Yes. He has laid a fire for us." Eli picked up his bundle of arrows, pack, and bow. He was tired and looking forward to some rest.

Lightning illuminated the sky in a flash. Thunder followed a few moments later, rumbling deeply once again. It sounded closer, louder. Eli knew it was only a matter of time until it began to rain.

"It has been a long day," he said to Mae. "There is a warm fire waiting for us and, dare I say, shelter from the coming rain." Eli sniffed at the air again. "It seems like a meal has been prepared too. Venison, if I am not mistaken." He gestured toward the trail. "Come on."

He started for the trees and the trail ahead that led deeper into the island. At the tree line, he took a moment to glance back. Mae had shrugged her pack on. Bow and bundle of arrows in hand, she followed a few feet behind. He continued down the path and then after ten feet came to a stop. He turned and looked back at her again. She stopped too, studying him curiously.

"What?" Mae asked.

"While on the island…" Eli glanced around into the trees and paused as he considered them. After several heartbeats, he turned his attention back to her and started again. "While on the island, do not leave the trail. Under no circumstances are you to venture into the trees. It is dangerous to do so, deadly in fact."

"Dangerous?" Mae asked, her brow furrowing. It was her turn to glance around them, peering into the trees. "How so? I sense nothing wrong about us." She fell silent, her eyes scanning the trees more closely. "I—I don't hear anything either. That is—odd."

Her gaze returned to his, and without saying a word, Eli took a step nearer to the edge of the trail and reached out his left hand to the nearest tree, which was less than a foot away.

Before he could touch it, a blue shimmering formed around his outstretched hand. It felt like he had plunged his hand into a bucket of ice-cold water. A deep soul-stealing cold began invading his spirit, seeming to crawl from his hand up to his arm and shoulder. It was slowly leeching the lifeforce from him, drawing it away, one tiny measure at a time. The sensation was agonizing. It took difficulty to not cry out. Had he not prepared himself, he might have screamed. Instead, Eli remained silent and gritted his teeth, bearing the pain as it came.

Mae gave a start and took a step back. Having made his point, Eli pulled his hand away from the field and broke contact with it. The cold subsided, but his hand ached painfully as the warmth—or, really, the life—began to return to it.

"What was that?" Mae asked, clearly alarmed and troubled. "Some sort of magic?"

"This island is a unique place. What you saw is the Task'Umaul."

"I do not understand."

"In another tongue, an ancient one, I am told it translates roughly to, *the Border.*"

"The border to what?" Mae asked, peering suspiciously into the trees around them. "And in what language?"

"As to the language, I am not entirely sure," Eli admitted. "It is my suspicion this island is a Gray Field."

Mae stilled and looked at him as if she had difficulty believing his words. "You brought us to a Gray Field? This island is a place of death?"

"I did," Eli said gravely. "Step off the path and you leave the world of the living ..." Eli did not finish his sentence. He fell silent, his eyes going to the trees. He still sensed not only the peacefulness of the valley, but also a deep sadness from the Mother, as if she had been wounded, hurt terribly. The sadness, the hurt ... was centered on the island.

"And step into the world of the dead," Mae finished quietly.

"I would not recommend deviating from the trail. The experience is overrated"—he glanced at his left hand—"and, dare I say, painful."

"You have stepped off the path of life?" Mae asked. He could read the shock in her gaze. "Willingly? You walked into the world of the dead?"

"Yes," Eli said quietly and suppressed a shudder at the memory. "I have no desire to do it again." He let go a slow breath through his teeth. "I almost did not return."

"And this caretaker, he watches, cares for this Gray Field?"

"I am—not sure about that either," Eli admitted. "No one really knows his purpose or reason for living in this valley. He is here and has always been here. This place is his home. Though I've heard it said, a rumor really, he came to this world with our people from Tannis."

"But you do not know for certain?"

"No one I've met who was around during that time will speak on it, and that includes both the caretaker himself and my father."

Mae was silent for several heartbeats as she considered his words.

"My mother would know the truth of the matter," Mae said.

"She's not here," Eli said, "is she?"

"When we return home, I will ask her."

"It is a mystery I have long sought the answer to. If she answers you, I would know the truth." Eli glanced up the trail. "The caretaker has never been known to leave this refuge. The important thing to remember is that he is a friend to elvenkind. He has proven that repeatedly. Rest assured, we are safe in this place."

"As long as you don't step off the path." Mae gazed off into the trees.

Eli could sense her unease. "As I said, I would not recommend the experience."

"Thank you for the warning. I will do as you say."

Satisfied that she understood the danger, Eli turned away and continued onward. With Mae close behind, he followed the trail as it led a winding path deeper into the island's interior.

The forest around them was silent and, for lack of a better word, dead-sounding. There was not even the buzz of insects on the air, let alone birds calling to one another as they settled in for the evening. There was nothing, no hint that anything living was about them.

Eli did not know if the trees on the island were even real. They might be an illusion or somehow immune to the Gray Field...to the world of the dead. How that was possible, he had no idea. Whatever the cause, a powerful magic was clearly at work in this place.

The path was some sort of barrier—at least Eli thought so. He did not fully understand how it worked, just that it did. No one he had met knew either. And when he had asked, the caretaker had refused to answer. Task'Umaul was not only a unique place, but one of mystery.

A short walk brought them to a clearing. In the center of the clearing was a single-room log cabin. Smoke drifted upward from a chimney and yellowed light spilled outward from two windows that faced the trail. The shutters had been thrown open. The smell of roasting meat was strong on the air, as was woodsmoke. Eli's stomach rumbled with hunger at the anticipation of a hot meal. Mae had come to a stop beside him and was studying the cabin.

Eli turned to her as a solitary drop of rain fell upon his arm. "As I said, we are welcomed."

"The caretaker lives here?" Mae asked, eyeing the cabin warily.

"No. This cabin is meant for guests, us specifically, and anyone else who happens along. In short, friends may come and stay here."

"Friends?" Mae asked. "Like us?"

Eli gave a nod. "I am a friend to this place, and now so too are you. As I said, friends, those who have a need, may come and stay."

"For a short time," Mae added.

"Yes. That is correct." Eli stepped up to the door and opened it. On well-oiled hinges, the door swung easily. He glanced inside. As he had expected, the cabin was empty and clean. It consisted of a single room with a stone fireplace. There was a table, two chairs, and two cots. An oil lamp burned brightly on the table, filling the single room with a dull yellow light.

The last time he had come this way there had only been one cot. Somehow, the caretaker had known he was coming with a traveling companion. How he had known that, Eli had no idea. It was one more mystery to add to the list.

The cabin was warm from a low fire that crackled in the hearth. Several dozen chopped pieces of wood lay stacked next to the stone fireplace. Over the fire, a hunk of venison, enough for two, roasted on a spit. It smelled delicious and caused his stomach to rumble again.

By the looks of the meat, it was nearly finished roasting. On the table lay several wrapped bundles of varying sizes, along with two wooden plates, a pitcher, and two mugs. Eli set his pack, bow, and bundle of arrows down to the left of the door on the floorboards.

He moved over to the table and glanced into the pitcher. He picked it up and sniffed the contents. It looked and smelled like red wine. Eli wondered how the caretaker had come by it, for there were no vineyards in the valley.

Setting the pitcher down, he picked up one of the wrapped bundles. Mae had followed him in and was gazing around the interior of the cabin with curiosity.

"He was expecting us." Mae set her pack down, placing it against the wall. She closed the door, then leaned her bow against the wall in the corner.

"It seems that way." Eli unwrapped one of the bundles. Inside was dried meat. It looked like salted pork. He showed her. "There are also provisions for our journey, enough for a week or more."

"While we are here, we will not need to do any hunting, then." Mae ran her gaze around the small cabin, clearly appraising it.

"It does seem so." Eli felt a little disappointed. He enjoyed fishing and found the activity calming to the mind. More importantly, the lake was filled with fish. He glanced around the cabin. In the far corner, he saw a fishing rod. Eli smiled. The caretaker had anticipated that need too.

"This is human construction." Mae patted the wall with a hand.

"Yes, this is a human design," Eli confirmed. "Some humans are surely friends of the valley."

"That surprises me."

"Not me," Eli said as the rain began to patter against the roof, the sound calming to his spirit. He loved falling asleep to the sound of rain, just as long as he wasn't being personally rained upon.

"Well," Mae said, "the cabin is certainly cozy at least."

"I prefer to think of it as shelter from the coming rain. I think we should both be grateful for that."

"And yet, the canoe was elven. Others of our kind have come this way." Mae glanced over at him. "Who is this caretaker? How did he know we were coming and more importantly"—she gestured at the table—"what we would need?"

"No one knows how he knows what he knows." Eli wrapped the dried meat back up and returned it to the rest of the provisions on the table. "But I'd say it is clear he does not wish us to linger. The supplies are proof of that."

"How much time do we have?" Mae asked.

Eli was silent for several long moments as he considered the question. "I'd say no more than a day before we wear out our welcome. Tomorrow we will rest. I could use a swim in the lake. Bathing sounds nice too." He paused and looked over at her. "You can explore the valley and get to know the Mother here. In fact, I would recommend it. That way, if at some point in the future you ever have the need to return, you will be recognized and welcomed."

Mae gave a nod. She was silent for several heartbeats. "The valley is safe, then?"

"Safe is a relative term. But for the most part, the answer is yes, the valley is harmless. All except the island, of course. You must exercise caution."

"You advise caution… and here we will be staying in a cabin surrounded by a Gray Field. The world of the dead is just yards away."

"The cabin is safe ground. The trees are not."

Mae did not reply to that.

"We will depart the day after tomorrow," Eli said, "and pick up the hunt where we left off."

"I feel uncomfortable delaying our pursuit," Mae said. "Perhaps we should consider departing at first light. The caretaker has replenished our supplies. We have what we need."

"We have all we need except rest. You and I have been traveling hard for more than a week. Rest is in order, and if Mik'Las is traveling in the company of soldiers of the Castol, his pace will be slowed by them. We should be able to easily gain ground on him."

"We do need rest," Mae agreed, sounding suddenly weary.

Eli moved over to the fire and held out his hands for warmth. His left hand still ached from coming in contact with the Gray Field. He had not wanted to do that, but a demonstration of the dangers about them had been in order. Mae needed to understand, without any question, the true nature of the Task'Umaul. She needed to see it with her own eyes.

"Will we meet the caretaker?" Mae asked.

"I do not know." Eli paused for a long moment as he considered his next words. "With luck, we won't. For when he does show himself, there is always a reason. And I have found I do not much enjoy his reasons."

CHAPTER FOUR

Carefully, Eli unhooked the trout. Trapped in his hand, it wriggled furiously, trying to break free of his grip. It was a good-sized fish, at least ten inches from tip to tail. He could feel the powerful muscles straining as it struggled, waging a futile battle against his hands. He considered the animal for a long moment. It was a beautiful fish, magnificent in its own way, perfect.

The sun was hanging directly overhead, shining its midday warmth down upon the lake and surrounding valley. A gentle breeze gusted around him, tugging at his hair and clothes. Small rippling waves on the lake's surface sparkled brilliantly as they caught and reflected the sunlight.

The fish gave another strong wriggle. He returned his attention to it. Had he needed sustenance, he would have kept the fish.

"This is your lucky day," Eli said to the fish. "Good travels, friend."

He tossed the animal back into the lake. It landed with a splash a few feet from where he stood upon the partially submerged boulder on the lake's edge. He watched the fish as it shot away under the surface, until it disappeared into the murky depths of the lake.

Eli sucked in a deep breath and let it out slowly. After the rain had blown through the night before, the day had turned magnificent and warm. High above, just barely a speck in the sky, an eagle soared. His heart ached at the sheer beauty and lushness surrounding him.

He sat back down upon the boulder. It was smooth and warm from the sun's touch. White lichen dotted its surface. The rock jutted out from the shore into the water almost six feet. Small waves lapped up against its edge, making a soft pattering sound that Eli thought quite pleasant.

He could smell the water, the moist dirt of the shore just a few feet away, flowers, and the most pleasant of all, trees of the nearby forest. This was his favorite spot in the entire valley, even if a Gray Field was nearby.

The fishing rod lay next to him. He considered making another cast, then decided his day of fishing was at an end. He was out of worms and did not feel like digging for more. He had also caught a near perfect fish, held the living thing in his hands, and then returned it back to its domain. He wrapped the line around the rod and safely tucked the hook into the line, then set the rod back down on the rock to his right.

Eli gazed back out over the water and wondered what it was like living in the fish's world, not breathing air. It must be so alien, so different. Swimming as opposed to walking for one's entire life. How strange... how interesting. Eli tried to imagine it.

Fishing had always been a pleasant diversion. It gave him time to relax and reflect, to think. Perhaps, he thought suddenly, fishing was not as relaxing for the fish? The experience must surely be traumatic. He had not thought on the fish's perspective. Had he just been terribly cruel, needlessly so? Was the fish aware of what had occurred? Could it think and remember the experience of being caught? Eli decided he did not know.

It was an interesting subject and one that bore more reflection. Thankfully, he was in the right place to begin weighing such deep thoughts. Still, it might be years before he came to a determination on such a serious matter.

The day was also quite beautiful. Why ruin it with serious thinking? No, now was certainly not the time to start that sort of thing. Eli decided to just enjoy the moment, along with the sense of peace brought on by the valley.

Yep, that's what he would do.

"What are your thoughts?" The voice came from behind. It was neutral, and male. The words were spoken in fluent Elven.

Eli closed his eyes. He had not heard the caretaker's approach. That was no surprise. No one ever did. One moment the caretaker was not there and the next he was, as if he had just popped into existence. That was just the way of things in this valley. Eli had long since given up on trying to figure out his secret. He supposed some mysteries would always remain mysteries, perhaps even whether a fish could remember.

"Tell me, friend," the caretaker said, when he did not answer, "what are your thoughts?"

"I am at peace here," Eli said. "This valley is nearly the perfect place ..."

"But?"

The question hung on the air. Eli found he was hesitant to answer. His thoughts returned to the lake. The fish's domain and entire world was beneath the surface. The Gray Field was the boundary between the domain of the dead and living. It was kind of like the surface of the lake for the fish. Leave the water for too long and the fish dies.

"But?" the caretaker prompted.

"You know the answer to that question."

"I would still hear it."

"This valley is nearly the perfect place, but for the Gray Field," Eli said with a heavy breath. "I do not enjoy its proximity or even the thought of such a place existing."

"The world of the dead makes you elves uncomfortable. It brings up thoughts of your own mortality, something the High Born do not enjoy contemplating. I have news for you, Eli. All sentient races do not much like the idea of dying. Some just fight the concept a little harder than others."

Eli opened his eyes, as the scuff of stone told him the caretaker was joining him on the rock. He glanced over and saw a young man, cleanly shaven. Outwardly, the caretaker appeared human. Eli knew he was not. He could feel it, a sort of power or really a presence of mind radiating outward, pressing against his own. He had heard the caretaker took different forms for different people. The caretaker was something else, something different, an unknown. What, Eli had no idea.

"You are correct," Eli said. "All things change. Even we, the High Born, grow old with the passage of years and eventually move from this world to the next, the world of the dead."

"That is the natural progression of the life cycle."

The caretaker sat down next to him, cross-legged. He had short brown hair and wore a simple gray robe cinched at the waist by a coarse rope. The ends of the rope were knotted and frayed, old-looking. He had the appearance of a simple monk or human priest.

Gazing across the lake, the caretaker was silent for several heartbeats. "This valley *is* the perfect place, because of the Gray Field."

"Not for me," Eli said. "I want nothing to do with the world of the dead."

"Just as the fish wants nothing to do with the world of air and land. You have no curiosity? This I find surprising for one of the High Born."

"Not for the Gray Field," Eli said, without looking over, "not anymore."

"The Field is so much more than what you think it is." The caretaker's tone held a hint of sadness. "And one day, it will mean more to you than you can possibly imagine."

Eli looked over at the caretaker and adopted a slight mocking tone. "Oh, great oracle, are you telling me of my future?"

The caretaker gave a grunt of amusement.

"My days of foretelling are long since done." The caretaker's gaze became distant as he stared out across the water. The silence between them grew. Then he sucked in a deep breath, and when he spoke next, his tone was grave. "I once interfered in events, tried to turn back the tide, stem the advancing darkness. I became directly involved, when I should have stood apart. I broke the rules."

"Tannis," Eli surmised, looking over.

The caretaker gave a curt nod. "I will not make that mistake again."

Eli had so many questions. His curiosity was burning like an uncut wick on a candle. He knew if he pushed too hard, there would be no answers, no revelations. So, he decided to remain patient and refrain from questions, for the caretaker had come here for a purpose.

"Never again will I interfere so directly."

The caretaker sat there and gazed out upon the lake for what seemed like a long time.

"Thank you for the use of the cabin," Eli said, instead of pressing. He wanted to keep the caretaker talking. If he continued talking, Eli would learn more, unravel more of the puzzle.

"You are always welcome here," the caretaker said. "So, too, is your friend."

"Has she met you yet?" Eli asked.

"No, and she won't, at least not this visit."

"I see."

"Do you?" The caretaker glanced over at him curiously. There was depth to his gaze that Eli felt chilling.

"Does it matter if I do?" Eli countered.

"I suppose not. Let her know she is welcome to return. Will you pass that on? The Mother likes her and she gets few visitors these days."

"I will," Eli said.

"Did you tell her about the waterfall?"

"Only that she should visit it. Why do you ask?"

"She's there now," the caretaker said, "experiencing the Pool of Reflection."

Despite the warmth of the sun, Eli felt a chill move down his back. "That was something I was not prepared for."

"Few are." The caretaker looked over at him. "I am curious—what did you learn when you gazed into its depths?"

Eli did not immediately respond, as his memories went back to that fateful day. He recalled the beauty of the waterfall and the pool at its base, being drawn to it, almost sucked in. He shook himself.

"Fallibility," Eli said. "Not that I'd willingly admit it to anyone else."

"So, you think you failed the test at the pool?"

"Yes." Eli's voice was barely a whisper. "I...I was not strong enough."

"You learned more about yourself, a greater insight and understanding in that moment, than you did in your first hundred years of life. I would not call that a failure, but experience. The Pool of Reflection is meant as a tool."

"It is a harsh one, then," Eli said. "To see one's past and present, desires, flaws, imperfections and be tested by them …"

"Everyone who gazes into those enchanted waters sees something different. You saw what you needed to see. No more, no less. That is the nature of the trial."

"I did not enjoy my test," Eli said.

"Not many do."

"What do you think she will learn?"

"I will turn that question back upon you," the caretaker said. "Tell me."

"I am not entirely sure. Regardless of what she experiences, Mae will come away knowing more about herself. And that, I will admit, can be useful. I found it useful."

"Is that why you brought her here?"

"Not entirely," Eli said. "We are after someone."

"Mik'Las. You seek a reckoning for wrongs visited upon your people."

Eli glanced sharply at the caretaker.

"Yes, I know of your mission."

"He took something he was not entitled to. We will retrieve it. He will pay for his crimes."

"Maybe, maybe not. Only time will tell."

Eli fought off a scowl.

"Mae'Cara's mother thought you might bring her here."

Now that surprised Eli. He had no idea the caretaker had spoken with the warden. How was that even possible? The warden was hundreds of miles away. To his knowledge, the caretaker never left the valley. How often did they speak? What magical means did they use?

"Does that surprise you?"

"It does," Eli admitted.

"The warden has taken an interest in you, Eli." The caretaker looked back out across the lake. "Did you know that also?"

Eli became concerned at such a thing. Crossing the warden did not much appeal to him. He rather enjoyed being in the Ranger Corps and the freedom that came with it. Should she think poorly of him, there was no telling what might happen.

"It is not your father's doing," the caretaker said, "not another attempt to control you, if you are worried about that."

"It's not?" Again, Eli found himself surprised. His father seemed to interfere in everything involving his son. At times, Eli thought it might be his mission in life.

"No." The caretaker glanced back over at him and smiled slightly. There was something sad about that smile. "It's my fault alone."

"Why? Why does the caretaker meddle with my life?"

"Something is on the wind," the caretaker said and turned his gaze away toward the sky, "something elves do not much enjoy. Your people fight against it."

"Change," Eli surmised.

"Powers long since dormant are stirring upon this world, preparing for the struggle to come. The conflict that is coming, even your people cannot ignore, the return of the Last War."

Eli knew of the Last War. It was why his people had come to Istros, to escape. They had built a home here, a refuge, a sanctuary that they guarded dearly. That the Last War was coming to Istros was not welcome news.

"That is why you speak with the warden," Eli said.

"Yes. She knows what is coming and is powerless to stop it. So, instead, she is taking steps to meet it and prepare your people for the trials and challenges ahead."

"She speaks to you about such things?" Even though the answer was obvious, Eli had not been able to help himself. The question just sort of popped out.

"She values my counsel," the caretaker said. "We speak from time to time on such matters. Soon a dark tide will threaten to consume this world."

"Didn't you just tell me you would not interfere again?"

"Did I?" The caretaker gave an amused chuckle. "Perhaps you misheard me."

Eli did not reply. Once before the caretaker had given him some inkling of what was coming in his near future. The result had not been an enjoyable experience. Yes, it had been exciting, but in the end, Eli had been left wanting and hurting.

"You and Mae'Cara have a potential future together," the caretaker said after a few moments of silence. "I see that current, the flow in time, the string knitting its way between you both." The caretaker paused and let out a long breath through his nose. "It is one flow amongst many."

Though he was surprised, Eli did not reply. The caretaker looked over at him. Their gazes met. Eli found something timeless about the caretaker's eyes, a sort of vastness and depth he had not noticed before. It spoke of seeing more than the mundane world around them.

"Tell me, are you prepared for that eventuality?"

"I—I am ..." Eli hesitated, then decided to admit the truth. "I am not sure. But you know that."

The caretaker gave another nod. "It is why you brought her here."

"One of the reasons. She should know of this place."

"Elves complicate things more than they need be."

"There is some truth in that statement," Eli admitted grudgingly.

"And that is an understatement," the caretaker said.

Eli gave a shrug of his shoulders.

The silence between them grew again. Eli turned his gaze out to the water and watched the waves glitter with reflected sunlight. The peacefulness he had felt a short while before, the tranquility, had vanished like a morning mist burned away by the newborn sun.

"I like you, Eli," the caretaker said. "I always have. Do not deny yourself a measure of happiness. Life, even an elf's, is too short. I have seen others like you come and go too soon, too quickly, their lifeforce burning brilliantly until it is extinguished."

"How old are you?" Eli asked, looking over. This line of conversation was deeply troubling to him.

"I do not measure years the way you do. My answer to that question would be meaningless."

Receiving no satisfactory answer, Eli decided to return to the topic at hand. "Her mother put you up to this, playing matchmaker?"

"No," the caretaker said. "The warden is most definitely against such a union. Even though it would tie the Far and Cara families closer together in union, I do believe she disapproves of your father, if that is any consolation."

"He will certainly not approve either, which usually is reason enough for me to do it. He does not like the warden and openly opposes some of her policies."

"You would marry for spite?" The caretaker seemed surprised.

"If I did, it would likely come back to haunt me. When roused, Mae has a sharp tongue. If she discovered the truth behind such a motive, she would make me pay. Then again, there is the warden. Angering her can prove just as unhealthy. She is not known for forgiveness. I don't much enjoy the idea of irritating Mae's mother."

"Be honest, Eli," the caretaker said, "you love irritating people."

"If I chose to marry, it would be for love, with no other considerations. I would not allow anyone to interfere. As you say, life is too short."

"That is the correct answer."

"I am not sure I am ready for such things," Eli admitted after a moment, "or to even seriously contemplate it. There are others that would make suitable matches as well, others that I might find love with."

"True. I see those flows too."

Eli turned his gaze back to the water. Again, the silence grew between them. Eli closed his eyes and tried to enjoy the warm sun on his face, the wind tussling his hair, but could not. The caretaker had given him much to think on.

"Well." The caretaker stood. "My time here is at an end. I find your visits a pleasant diversion."

Eli prepared to stand, but the caretaker motioned him to remain where he was.

"Stay, please. I get little enough time here in this pleasant place. Even if I am unable, I would rather have someone enjoy it." The caretaker turned and moved away a few steps, then stopped, looking back at Eli. "What you were sent to retrieve…" The caretaker trailed off.

"What about it?" Eli was suddenly on guard. Had the warden told him?

"Even though the warden wants it back, it is meant for another."

Eli went still as he stared at the caretaker. "Another?"

"Yes. When it is time...if you are smart...you will let it go. Take vengeance if you are able, but let it go."

"And if I don't?" Eli asked. "The warden can be unforgiving."

"Then there will be serious repercussions for not only your people but others as well. Every action is followed by a reaction, cause, effect. Trust me on this, Eli, you don't want to see the effect."

"I wish you would tell me what you see."

"If I did, things would turn out different." The caretaker fell silent for a heartbeat. "As I said, powers are stirring. There is still time, but it is beginning to grow short."

Eli turned his gaze back to the lake. He hated these visits with the caretaker. They ruined the peace he found in the valley.

"Don't tell me any more of my future," Eli said. "I do not wish to know."

There was no response. When he looked around, the caretaker had gone. It was as if he had vanished into thin air. Eli let out an unhappy breath and returned his gaze to the lake, staring vacantly at its beauty.

"It never gets any easier," Eli said aloud to himself.

"No," the caretaker's voice came from the air around him, "it doesn't."

CHAPTER FIVE

Eli sank to a knee and examined the ground closely. Just feet away and to his right was a good-sized creek that cut a meandering path through the forest.

The creek could easily have been described as a small river. In fact, Eli would have called it that himself, only whenever he came through these parts, anyone he met called it a creek. So, it was a creek. Perhaps, he thought, the locals had just never seen a real river?

Normally, the creek was easily crossed, but today it was swollen from the recent rains and had overflowed its banks. He eyed the brown water warily. There were thick branches and entire tree trunks traveling downstream, almost rushing, as if they had somewhere to be. Despite being a good swimmer, he had no desire to attempt a crossing under such conditions, not with the debris in the water. It would surely prove dangerous in the extreme.

Eli wondered how the fish managed to survive. Did they find a place to hide until the flooding eased? He turned his attention back to the ground and the tracks before him. After a moment, he looked up at Mae.

"They crossed at this spot here."

"Probably before the storms. It doesn't look passable now." Mae was standing on a small granite boulder a few feet away, gazing at the water running by just inches from her boots. She had not turned to look at him. Her gaze was distant for a moment, as if she were seeing something else and not the creek. She sucked in a deep breath. "The prospect of crossing does not much appeal to me."

"I'm not too keen about it either." Eli came to his feet. He looked up the creek and then down it. "The forest is old in these parts. Perhaps we can find another way across."

"Oh?"

"There is a chance, with the recent rains, a tree fell across the creek."

"I guess that is possible." Mae sounded skeptical. "The question for us—which way do we go? Upstream or down?"

"How about downstream?" Eli said.

"Why downstream?"

"It seems easier."

She gave a snort and turned to look upon him. There was skepticism in her gaze. As she regarded him, it only seemed to grow. After a moment, she placed her hands upon her hips and tilted her head to the side. "Is that the only reason?"

Eli paused for a heartbeat. "No." He gestured downstream. "There is a small bridge ten miles to the south, near a forest village." He turned his gaze back to the swollen creek. "Well, last time I was through this way, there used to be."

"You could have just told me that right off," Mae said, "saved us both some time."

"Where is the fun in that? You've been less than talkative all day. At least I got you talking."

She gave a grunt but did not reply.

"With any luck," Eli continued, "the bridge has not been swamped by the flooding. Let us hope it's still there or that we're fortunate enough to come across a tree that has fallen across the river."

Mae spared him an unhappy look as she hopped off the boulder. "There's only one way to find out. I guess downstream it is."

She glanced at the river once more, then started off at a good pace. Eli felt himself grin slightly. He hesitated a moment, watching her. He had to admit, Mae did have a fine figure.

Content to let Mae blaze a trail, he followed. For some time, neither said a word as they moved silently through the forest. A few yards from the creek's edge, the trees were tall and old. The undergrowth was sparse, which made travel easy. The forest floor was covered in last season's leaves and carpets of moss.

They kept up a good pace, with the miles moving by rapidly. The late morning air was crisp, and the sun was bright. Somewhat occluded by the canopy of leaves hanging overhead, the sun did not provide much warmth. Still, Eli felt himself perspiring with their exertions.

It had been two days since they had left the valley. Since then, Mae had been uncharacteristically quiet, troubled, almost brooding. More than once he had caught her covertly staring at him, her gaze contemplative, perhaps even speculative. Her behavior was clearly a side effect of the Pool of Reflection.

What was going on in her head?

He had no idea. More importantly, Eli had not pried either. He felt uncomfortable doing so. In fact, he had no desire to know what she had been through as she had gazed into those enchanted waters. The Pool of Reflection was a deeply personal experience. That much was clear to him after his own experience with the pool. Whatever she had experienced had nothing to do with him—at least he hoped not.

After six miles, Mae came to an abrupt halt. She pulled out her waterskin and took a drink, then offered it to him. Eli shook his head. Mae gave a shrug of her shoulders, took another sip, then stopped it and returned the skin to her pack.

"Beautiful day," Eli said.

Mae glanced up at the sky. At first, she did not say anything. Then a slight, almost unhappy scowl settled upon her face.

"I suppose it is."

Eli looked in the direction they were headed. The creek continued to rush by a few feet to their right, making a pleasant and relaxing sound. Eyeing the water, Eli wondered what kind of fish resided in the creek. He wished they had some time. He would have loved to cast a line. Then again, with the debris in the water, fishing was likely impossible. That thought depressed him slightly.

"Shall we continue?" Mae asked.

"Yes." Deciding to lead the way, Eli started off. He felt like a short jog, so he picked up the pace, weaving his way effortlessly through the trees and what little brush grew up under their shade. Mae easily kept pace.

After a mile, feeling the burn in his legs, Eli slowed his pace to a walk. He was perspiring more heavily. The jog had felt good, invigorating. Eli loved running. When traveling long distances alone, he'd frequently run a mile, then walk a mile, repeating the process over and over again. A ranger had to have their wind, stamina, call it what you will, to travel great distances rapidly.

A few more steps brought them to a ledge, over which the stream became a waterfall, dropping two hundred feet to the forest below. The water roared as it went over the ledge and fell into a good-sized pool below them.

Eli stepped out onto the rock ledge that ran alongside the creek at the waterfall's edge. The rock was slick underfoot, covered with lichen and patches of moss. A misstep would easily mean a deadly fall.

He looked over the side and gazed downward. Two old tree trunks that were surprisingly large had washed down into the pool below. They lay at awkward angles. From experience, Eli knew the pool was deep, at least thirty feet. White froth bubbled on its surface. It was choked with debris, leaves, limbs, broken tree trunks. Farther downstream, the creek became rocky and the water turned white.

He enjoyed coming to this place. It provided a nice view of the forest that stretched far southward, as far as the eye could see.

He crouched down just before the edge. Below them the creek continued onward, cutting a meandering flow through the forest. He followed its path with his eyes, then pointed at a spot several miles distant.

"The bridge should be about there," Eli said.

Mae took a knee beside him and followed his finger. "I don't see it. The trees are hiding it." Chewing her lower lip, she looked over at him. "That is, if your bridge is still there." She paused a heartbeat. "How long has it been since you came this way?"

"Long enough that there's the chance the bridge is no longer there," Eli admitted, "possibly the village too now that I think on it. Who can say with humans…?"

The wind shifted, bringing smoke their way. He began scanning the forest below, searching for evidence of the fire. It smelled stronger than an average campfire.

"There." Mae pointed. "That's where the smoke is coming from."

Eli looked and saw a thin veil of smoke rising from what he judged to be a wide area about five miles off in the forest. With the brightness of the sun, the white smoke was hard to see. It was in the direction of the village, but it did not seem quite right to his eyes. The smoke appeared more dispersed than it should be, almost as if something or somethings were smoldering after having nearly burned themselves out.

"We should be seeing smoke from several fires," Mae said. "It's much too diffused."

Eli agreed. What were they seeing? He did not know, but suspected it was bad, at least bad for the settlement. Motion near the base of the falls below caught his attention. A girl had emerged from the trees, stepping onto the water-smoothed stone at the edge of the pool. She was wearing a brown tunic and pants, along with leather boots. She was also carrying a bow, with a sword belted to her back.

Mae had spotted her as well and was leaning forward curiously, hand on the stone of the ledge as she studied the human. The girl below stepped up to the edge of the creek, where it left the pool under the falls, and knelt by its side. Cupping her hands, she took a quick drink, then splashed some on her face.

She straightened and glanced back, almost nervously, the way she'd come. It was as if she had heard something. Picking up her bow, she stood, then turned back to the swollen creek.

She seemed to be contemplating the fast-moving water. There was a series of large rocks and boulders across the far edge of the pool that over the years had either fallen from the cliff or had been washed over the waterfall during severe floods. Each was separated by several feet. A crossing was possible but, with the flood level up, perilous. Even he would have hesitated.

What was she thinking?

A hound bayed somewhere off in the distance. The human's head whipped around, looking back the way she had come again. Then without further hesitation, she jumped onto the first rock. She hopped from one to the next, until she was in the middle of the creek.

"She's in trouble," Mae said as the girl below made the next jump, which was a much longer distance than the others. She landed awkwardly on the edge of the rock. For a moment, her arms windmilled. Eli held his breath. The girl managed to regain her balance. She jumped to the next rock.

"Yes," Eli said quietly, "that seems evident."

There was more baying, clearly coming from multiple dogs. They sounded nearer, just inside the trees. She reached the other side, and as she did, several leashed dogs appeared, along with a dozen armed men. The dogs, having sighted their prey, began barking and baying wildly.

"Castol soldiers," Eli said. "Judging by their uniforms they are light infantry, not militia."

One of the soldiers had a bow. Arrow ready, he knelt, drew back, and rapidly loosed a shot. The girl ducked. The arrow went wide, missing her by a couple of feet. He took another arrow from his quiver and began nocking it. The girl had already nocked her own arrow. She calmly aimed down her bow for a heartbeat and loosed. The arrow flew true and hit hard, taking the man with the bow in the chest and punching through his gray leather armor. He gave out a surprised cry and fell back to the ground.

The wounded soldier rolled back and forth on the stone, clearly in great pain, as his blood spread out around him. The arrow had gone clean through to the other side, the point emerging from his back. Two of the Castol soldiers moved to help him.

"She's good with that bow," Mae said. There was no admiration in her tone. It was a simple statement of fact.

"Yes, she is." Eli found himself intrigued by the scene playing out below them.

"Bastards," the human girl shouted in the common tongue, back across the river at her pursuers.

"Get her," came the harsh reply from one of the soldiers. Eli could not tell if he was an officer or sergeant. "I want that bitch dead. Do you hear me? I want her dead. A gold piece for whoever brings me her head."

The offer of gold told Eli he was an officer.

The soldiers, one at a time, moved forward and began jumping from rock to rock. The girl watched them for a moment before turning and plunging into the woods. Though an elf would never have done it, she had left her bow behind. It was not hard to understand why. She was out of arrows.

"I think we should help her," Mae said.

Eli glanced over at Mae. "It's not our quarrel. Why pick a fight when we don't need to be doing so?"

"You are more than right," Mae said. "This is not our fight. But then again, it might be."

"What do you mean?" Eli resisted a frown.

"We've been following Castol soldiers. From their tracks, Mik'Las joined up with them. I would say the two groups are in league with each other, which makes them our enemy and this our problem."

"That is a bit of a stretch, even for you," Eli said. "We are in Castol lands. These soldiers could be from a completely different company. We don't know that they are the same ones we're following."

"We will not know for certain," Mae said, "until we cross the river and backtrack to the ford. Still, I am thinking, helping this girl will give us valuable intelligence."

"You are just looking for someone to save again."

"Maybe I am," Mae said. "What of it?"

Eli was silent for a moment as he considered her and the girl who was running for her life.

"If we're caught," Eli said, "or detected, it could create an issue with the Castol."

"We won't be."

Eli allowed himself a frown. He glanced back down below. Most of the soldiers had made it across the swollen creek and were moving into the trees. He did not like the odds the girl faced. It seemed rather unfair. Then again, Eli never liked to fight fair. Still, his sense of injustice, like Mae's, had reared its head, and he hated when that happened.

"All right," Eli said, "we will help her escape. If we can do it without killing any of the Castol, all the better."

"Good." Mae took several steps back from the edge of the waterfall. "I suppose you know a way down?"

Eli drew back out of view from the soldiers below before standing and coming to his feet.

"There's a trail off to the left that leads down." Eli slipped his bow from his back. He drew an arrow from his bundle, then looked over at Mae. "Let's get to it, then."

CHAPTER SIX

With a look of distaste, Mae paused, looking down. She was studying the body that was facedown amidst the previous season's leaves. Holding his bow and two arrows lightly with a hand, Eli sank to a knee. He took a moment to gaze around the small clearing, carefully scanning the area about them. He could detect no one lurking in the shadows of the trees.

His gaze shifted to the forest floor. There were dog prints all about the clearing. The soldiers had clearly carried the hounds across the creek. Occasionally, off in the distance, one of the animals bayed, which meant the pursuit was still on and the girl yet lived.

"Who is this human girl?" Mae asked, looking up from the body.

Eli raised an eyebrow but said nothing as he studied the dead man. He sucked in a deep breath. The scent of copper was strong. The man's lifeblood had spilled out onto the forest floor. Eli looked up at the sky. Dusk was approaching and would be upon them within the next hour and a half.

"He's been taken from behind," Mae said, drawing his attention, "which means she came up on him unawares and stabbed him in the back. She also slit his throat so he could not cry out."

Eli glanced down at the soldier. This was the second body they had come across in the last forty feet. Over the long years, Eli had seen plenty of death. And yet, he had never seen anything like this, at least from a human. The girl, who could not be more than twenty, had efficiently killed a man of greater size and strength. From how he had been killed and the way he was lying on the forest floor, Eli was certain the soldier had never even heard her coming.

Eli was becoming more intrigued by the moment. The girl represented a mystery, one he was keen on unraveling.

One of the hounds gave a long howl in the distance.

"Is she the hunted or the hunter?" Eli whispered to himself, his eyes roving over the body again.

"What?" Mae asked, glancing over. "What did you say?"

Eli looked back over at her. "You have to wonder if she is the hunted or the one doing the hunting."

"You are suggesting she wanted them to follow her?" Mae cocked her head to the side.

"I am." Eli turned and pointed to a tree to his left, an old oak with a thick and age-gnarled trunk. "She waited behind that tree. You can see her tracks there." He moved his finger, aiming at the ground. "He was likely a straggler. Once he passed by the tree, she emerged from hiding and stole up on him."

In his mind, Eli could see the act as it had happened, the girl silent, determined as she stalked her victim. She was a killer for certain, but there was much more to her story, and Eli wanted to learn it.

A dog squealed painfully, the sound ringing out from amongst the trees. The animal went silent.

"She has forest training," Mae said.

"Yes," Eli said, simply.

"A human ranger perhaps?" Mae sounded dubious about the possibility. "I did not think the Castol had any rangers."

"She is no ranger and the Castol do not have any. Were she a ranger, her tracks would be better concealed, at least the ones she does not wish her enemy to see. She has done just enough to fool these soldiers, but not us." Eli breathed in deeply and let it out. "But yes, she has training."

"We need to find her and learn more," Mae said.

"Agreed."

"She has potential," Mae said. "If possible, we must help her."

Eli stood, took one more look around, and began moving, rapidly leaving the clearing behind them. He had given up on following the girl's tracks. She was good, and though he could have tracked her, it was much easier to follow the soldiers, who were not interested in concealment. Besides, the soldiers were following the girl, and she had no intention of escaping. She wanted to be followed. After what they had come across, he was certain of it.

Eli and Mae moved through the forest, silent, alert, ready for danger, to react to the unexpected. After a quarter mile, they came upon another body. Eli knelt beside the man. The dead man's eyes were open and impossibly wide as they stared toward the sky. His sword lay several feet away. His nose was broken, and a knife was lodged deeply in his left side, just above the hip. The blade had punched right through the leather armor. It had taken some force to do that.

Still and unmoving, a dog, one of the shaggy hounds, lay a few feet away. Its brown fur was matted with dark blood. Eli turned his gaze back to the body.

"She used his own weapon against him." He gestured at the man's empty knife sheath. "See?"

"This kill looks personal," Mae said. "First she dealt with the dog, then she disarmed him and, if I am reading matters right, beat him a little." Mae paused a moment, clearly considering. "Perhaps they fought, then she disarmed him and, as you said, killed him with his own blade." Mae crouched down, studying the disturbed forest floor. In places, it was badly torn up, clearly indicative of a struggle. Mae moved back over to the body. "I think she waited as he bled out and watched him die."

"You may be right," Eli said. "This was a very personal killing. She might not need our help."

"Still, she's outnumbered," Mae said. "I can't help but feel this is tied somehow to our mission."

Eli's curiosity had been fired up. What was going on here? Was it really their problem? He did not believe in coincidences and was starting to suspect that Mae was correct.

"Let's see what we can do." He stood and started off again. Mae followed close behind. They continued to follow the soldiers' tracks. Another quarter mile and they discovered a fourth body, lying next to a stream. This one's throat had been efficiently slit. Though only a trickle, the blood was still flowing from the gruesome wound at the neck. It had drained into the stream and given the water a coppery tinge.

Eli reached down and felt the man's cheek.

"He's still warm."

"She's close," Mae said and then, as if to emphasize that point, there was a burst of excited shouting a short distance off.

"We've got her," a voice called louder than the others. "Come on, boys."

Eli scanned the forest ahead. He did not see anything. He nocked an arrow and began moving forward through the trees. He was silent, an unseen ghost. A few feet to his right, bow held at the ready, Mae moved with him.

Forty yards brought them within sight of another clearing ahead. This one was artificial. The stumps of old trees littered the ground. Normally, that would irritate Eli, but not today. He was focused on what lay ahead.

Eli could see figures just beyond the edge of the tree line, five men and the girl. The harsh clash of steel on steel rang through the forest as one of the men traded sword blows with her. It was followed shortly by a curse, then another solid clang as swords met yet again.

"Bitch," her opponent spat at her.

"Come get some more," the girl taunted. "Perhaps next, I will take more than a finger, maybe your manhood."

The man she was speaking to had fallen back and away from her. He was cradling his sword hand, eyeing her coldly. Blood was running down his arm.

The men had formed a half-ring about the girl. It was clear they were working to move around and behind her. She backed up a couple of steps to keep that from happening.

Nothing about her indicated she was panicked or frightened. In fact, she appeared cool, collected, grim even, and completely under control. Her blonde hair had been tied into a ponytail. Several strands had come loose and hung down her tunic. A trickle of blood from her scalp ran down her forehead.

She took another step back, and as she did, she moved the sword out before her, slicing the air for her opponents to see. It was a smooth swing and spoke of not only training in how to use the weapon, but control and competence. The muscles of her arm flexed powerfully with the movement.

She settled into a crouch as she prepared for an attack. Eli had never seen anyone like her, at least when it came to humans.

One of the men lunged at her, stabbing out lightning fast. She crossed swords with him, blocked and turned the blade away and toward the ground. Then, before he could fully recover, she lunged back, going over to the attack. Her opponent barely managed to jump away before her sword would have cut him in the belly. The others who had been attempting to move around her took an uncertain, unsteady step backward.

"Come on, you cowards," she snarled at them in the common tongue. "Here I am. You want me, come and get me."

No matter how good she was, the odds were decidedly against her. The time to act had come. Eli glanced over at Mae as they closed the last few feet to the edge of the clearing. He flashed her a series of signs, telling her to move to the right and that he would go left.

She gave a firm nod, and they went into motion.

"All right, boys," one of the men said as Eli worked his way around to the left. "There's only one of her and five of us. On three, we rush her and end this farce. Let's make the captain happy and claim some gold, eh? We can all split it."

There was a grumble of agreement to that.

"We all go together," another man said.

"One..."

Eli came to a stop beside a thick oak tree, knelt, and raised his bow, aiming at the nearest Castol soldier. There was a small bush between him and the clearing.

"Two..."

Eli released. His arrow hissed away. He was already reaching for the next as the first one hit, taking his target right in the side of the neck. The arrow punched clean through before coming to a stop. Eli's victim stood there, shocked, looking down at the arrow that had magically appeared out of his neck. He opened his mouth to scream, but no sound came out. A fountain of blood began to flow from his mouth instead. As he began to sink to his knees, there was a meaty-sounding thwack as Mae's first shot hammered home into another soldier's back. He gave a deep grunt.

"Three!"

Arrow nocked, Eli was already aiming at his next target. He released. The bow twanged, and a heartbeat later, his arrow smacked into a soldier's side. Mae loosed her next shot a fraction of a moment later and took a fourth man, the one who had lost the finger, square in the back.

That left only the speaker, who had rushed forward to attack, but then hesitated as he realized something was not quite right. He turned, staring at his companions in shock as they almost simultaneously dropped to the ground. Then realization seemed to sink home. His gaze moved out into the forest, probing its depths, eyes searching fearfully.

He had made a mistake taking his attention off the girl. She did not give him time to recover. She rushed forward to attack. Half turned, he brought his sword up in a hasty defense, but it was too late. She beat his sword easily aside, then rammed the tip of her weapon into his stomach and thrust it deep. He gave a heavy grunt that became part strangled scream. His sword dropped to the forest floor and with both hands he clutched her sword arm. He moaned as she gave the sword a savage twist. They stood there a moment, seemingly both frozen, then he began to lose his strength. She stared into his eyes, her gaze cold and hard.

"And now, Arvens, you get what you deserve, a well-earned death." She gave him a shove off her blade. The blade came away bloodied, with scraps of flesh hanging from it. He crumpled, falling, his intestines spilling out onto the ground around him.

Chest heaving, she regarded him for a long moment before spitting upon her dying opponent. Mouth working silently, he stared up at her in what was clearly shock. She stabbed down and tore open his throat. He gagged, choking on his own blood, then went into convulsions, before rolling over onto his side and falling still.

She was silent for a prolonged moment. "You deserved worse than that," she said.

Bow in hand, Mae stepped from cover. Eli stood and moved out and into the open as well. The girl's eyes fell first on Mae, then flicked to Eli. There was a deep, burning anger in her gaze, a malignant thing, but he detected surprise lurking there too as she took them both in.

"Elves," she said, then swung her gaze around the clearing before returning her attention to Mae and Eli. "I had them right where I wanted them."

Eli stared at her. Here she was, confronted by two elven rangers, who had just saved her. There was not a hint of fear or even, for that matter, any measure of gratitude.

"Why did you interfere?" she demanded, heat in her tone. "They were mine to kill."

"We thought you needed help," Mae said.

The girl shot Mae a hard look that spoke volumes as she pulled a small dagger from her boot. She walked up to one of the Castol soldiers who was still alive. He had an arrow through his chest and, whimpering like a baby, was attempting without success to pull it free.

"Oh gods, no." He looked up at her as she approached. He held out a pleading hand. "No, please."

Ignoring him, she brushed the hand aside and efficiently slit his throat. Then, without waiting for him to expire, moved back to the one she had just disemboweled.

She stared down at Arvens for several heartbeats before crouching next to him. She wiped her dagger clean on his leather armor before sliding it back into her boot. She cleaned her sword next, then returned the weapon to the sheath on her back. Again, it was a practiced move, something she had clearly done many times before. The sword was crude, but well maintained. It could be used as either a one – or two-handed weapon. It was designed for slashing more than stabbing and was not from these parts. Eli wondered where she had gotten it.

"I did not need your help," the girl said firmly. She looked up at them as both Eli and Mae moved a few steps nearer. "This bunch were dead the moment they made the decision to chase me."

"Who are you?" Eli asked. His curiosity was fully aflame.

"Does it matter?" she asked, her tone suddenly weary.

Eli could only imagine how tired she was. She was doing her best to conceal it from them.

Eli placed a hand to his chest. "I am Eli, and this is Mae."

"Two rangers," she said. "You're a little far from home, aren't you?"

"We are," Mae answered. "And who are you?"

"I'm Jitanthra," she said. "Most people call me Jit."

Jit turned her attention back to Arvens and began rifling through the man's things. After looking in a small pack, she pulled a purse off him and shook it. The coins inside jingled. She opened the purse and then let out a dissatisfied breath.

"Not even a gold or half-silver." She pulled a roll of bread from the pack, took a bite, and began chewing as she moved onto the next man. She did not find a purse on him, but instead, after a rapid search, tore off a bit of fabric, which had been sown over the inside of the man's tunic. Several coppers had been concealed inside. She deposited them into the purse she had acquired from Arvens, then moved onto the next man.

"We are after someone," Mae said, taking a half-step nearer. "Perhaps you know him?"

Jit looked up at that as she swallowed the portion of bread she had been chewing. "Who?"

"Mik'Las," Mae said. "He might have come through this way in the last few days. Do you know him?"

Taking another bite of the roll, Jit shook her head at the name and began rifling through the next man's possessions. Like Arvens, he had been carrying a small pack too.

"Is he an elf?" Jit asked through a full mouth as she worked.

"Yes."

"Then," Jit said, swallowing, "I've not seen him, nor heard of him."

"You have encountered the High Born before," Eli surmised, "haven't you?"

"Yes," Jit admitted after a moment, then popped the last of the roll into her mouth. While she chewed, she searched the next body. She deposited two more coppers into her newly acquired purse as she moved on to the last man. She efficiently searched him but came up empty.

"Who?" Eli pressed, when Jit stood.

"Rivun'Cur," Jit said.

Mae sucked in a startled breath that was barely detectable. She had gone still. Eli knew the girl could have said nothing that would have caught Mae's attention more.

"He trained you," Eli surmised, with a sidelong glance over at Mae.

"No." Jit looked off into the woods, with a distant expression. "I wish he had. No, Rivun'Cur was just kind to me." She paused, looking back at them, suddenly seeming hesitant. A moment later, she continued. "I guess you could say we are good friends, after a fashion. Though I am unsure whether he would admit that to anyone."

Mae glanced over at Eli, her look intense and hard, grim even. "Do you know where Rivun'Cur is?"

"Yes." Jit jerked a thumb at one of the bodies. "They took him."

Eli felt a stab of alarm. Mae had been right. This had just become their business, and in a big way too. Eli understood, without a doubt, he would be forced to resolve this mess before continuing after Mik'Las. Eli cursed their luck. Fortuna had clearly stirred the pot and it may have just changed everything.

Why couldn't things ever be simple?

"Who exactly took him?" Mae asked intently, taking a step forward.

"Lord Edgun," Jit said, a hard look settling into her gaze.

"I've never heard of him," Eli said.

"He's the local lord in these parts," Jit said. "The king charged him with securing this region of the kingdom or something like that. It was given to him last season as a reward for some great service rendered. At least, that's what I was told. People don't much like him."

"Why?" Mae asked. "Why did he take Rivun'Cur?"

"I don't know," Jit said. "The soldiers came the day before yesterday. They took him prisoner and brought him back to the castle that's being built a few miles from here."

Mae glanced over at Eli. Rivun'Cur was a different matter altogether. If he had been mistreated or, worse, killed, it might lead to war between the High Born and the Castol, for surely the warden would not take the matter lightly.

"That was just before they took all the able-bodied men and slaughtered everyone else in the village," Jit added bitterly. "I … I wasn't here when it happened, the killing."

Eli glanced around at the bodies. His gaze returned to Jit.

"So, that's why you wanted to kill them?"

"They've earned it," Jit said. "These bastards were the ones left behind to loot."

"They killed your family?" Mae asked. "Burned your village?"

"The village was not our home. Rivun'Cur and I had stopped there for a spell." Jit paused. "It was a pleasant place, with nice people."

Eli felt his heart quicken. He was becoming more intrigued by the moment. She traveled with Rivun'Cur. That marked her as important, unique, someone special, even if she did not see it herself.

"So now," Eli said, "you will go and kill Edgun?"

"Will you try to stop me?" Jit had gone still.

"If this Lord Edgun took Rivun'Cur prisoner," Mae said firmly, "then our interests align. We will help you free him."

Jit was silent for a long moment as she considered them. "Why would you care about one exiled elf, a castoff?"

Mae took another step closer. "We, my people, owe him a debt that can never be fully repaid. That is why we will help you."

CHAPTER SEVEN

As they walked down what had been the main street, Eli ran his gaze slowly over the remains of the village that spread out around them. The stench of smoke was overpowering. It made his eyes water and tickled at his nose. The sweet, sickening, and cloying smell of burned and charred flesh was also quite heavy on the air.

The destruction was so complete, it was as if a dragon had come and, in a fit of uncontrolled rage, burned down the small village. All that was left were the stone foundations of homes, piles of ash, and charred beams that had not been fully consumed by the fire. Wisps of smoke rose from the nearest structures. No bodies were in evidence.

The forest around the village had been cut back several hundred yards. Farm fields had replaced the trees. Most of the fields had already been or were in the process of being harvested. That was likely the only reason the fire had not spread. A forest fire would have only compounded the tragedy.

He came to a stop. At his feet, in the middle of the dirt street, lay a child's ragdoll. The doll was covered over in a thin layer of gray ash. He bent down and picked it up, shaking it, so the ash fell free. The doll was small, barely larger than his hand. As close as he could tell, it was stuffed with horsehair or something similar. Made out of canvas, the doll had been patched many times over. It had a well-used and loved look about it. He could almost picture a child holding it tight.

A deep sadness welled up within him. The doll's owner was most likely dead. A life cut prematurely short, yet another tragedy amongst many in this forsaken place.

Looking up from the doll, Eli had the sudden desire to turn around, leave, and never come back. Only, he could not and would not do that. He almost felt bound to witness what had happened here, if only for those departed souls who had suffered so needlessly. He started moving again.

Jit was just ahead of them. Her gaze roved the ruins as she walked down the street, moving forward, deeper into the remnants of the village. She seemed almost dazed.

By a mutual, unspoken consent, he and Mae held back, allowing the human space. Eli could well sympathize with the feelings she was experiencing. Jit had known the people who had called this place home, friends and acquaintances alike.

"The village of Taibor," he said quietly, "is no more."

"That's this place's name?" Mae asked, looking over.

"Taibor started as a single farm," Eli said, "cut right out of the forest. Buck Taibor was the human who first put down roots here. He was not the most honest of men, but he was hardworking, determined, and I liked him. He was also handy with a sword and swore good too. As I recall, when it came to profanity, he was rather proud of his wide-ranging vocabulary."

Eli paused, thinking back to the man who had died so long ago. It seemed like a lifetime had passed. Eli's gaze went to Jit. Humans were so short-lived.

"I helped him build his house." Eli turned his gaze back to Mae. "It wasn't much, a single-room cabin, but Buck loved it. You know, I miss sharing a fire with him and talking long into the night. He was a fascinating fellow." Eli ran his gaze over to the nearest ruins and let out an unhappy breath. "Knowing what would become of this village, I wonder if old Buck would have still settled here … Somehow, I doubt it."

Eli glanced once more at the doll before tucking it into one of his leather belts, which crisscrossed his chest. Why he decided to keep it, he was not quite sure. It somehow seemed important. He picked up his pace, working his way farther down the street, between the burned and smoking structures. Mae kept up with him.

The village had stood here for almost a hundred and fifty years. After Buck's death, Eli had visited Taibor a couple of times. Though it was mean and the people poor, the village had been a happy place. At least, he had thought so when he'd come here last. But without his friend Buck, it had not been the same.

"Now this is a place of death," Eli said to himself as he reached the village square. It was a small green oasis of mountain grass, set amongst the desolation. The villagers had kept it neatly cut, groomed even. Another ranger, Garus'Teel, had given the grass as a gift to the village for some minor service. It had been Garus's way of thanking them.

As the years passed, the village square had become a common place for all to enjoy. There would no longer be anyone left to tend the grass. Eli found that disheartening.

At the far end of the green, three thick stakes had been driven into the ground before what had once been the longhouse where the headman lived and held court.

A man was strapped to each stake and was facing away from them, toward the longhouse. Though he could not yet see, Eli knew what they would find in its ruins, for the stench of death and burned flesh had grown more powerful with each passing step. Birds hopped around the remains of the still-smoking longhouse, squawking loudly amongst themselves as they fought for the best bits of flesh.

Jit continued across the green. She stopped at the stakes. Turning to stare at them for a long moment, she regarded each body in turn. After several heartbeats, she turned away, moving past the bodies and toward the longhouse. She took four more wooden steps before stopping again. Jit slowly sank to her knees.

On the edge of the green, Eli had stopped. Face troubled, Mae looked over at him. Though far from having lived a sheltered life, he knew she had never seen anything like this. Eli, however, had, all too many times. That also saddened him.

"What kind of monsters would do this?" she demanded of him.

Eli looked upon the scene before them, just beyond the stakes. Like the other buildings in the village, all that remained of the longhouse was ash and charred timbers. None of the walls had survived the fire. He was near enough to see the blackened bodies, and there were a lot of them, mostly grouped, almost huddled together toward the center of the longhouse. The fire had not been strong enough to turn the dead to ash. The smoke had probably overcome them long before the flames.

"The worst monsters walk on two legs," Eli said quietly.

"They locked them inside and burned the building." The horror in her tone was plain and it was growing by the moment. "Do you think they burned the children too?"

As if to soothe the child's departed soul, Eli reached up and touched the doll, absently caressing it. Mae's eyes went to the doll, and with sudden understanding, her expression hardened. He had made his point.

"Humans are cruel," she said.

Eli looked away for a moment, then glanced over at her. What she said was, beyond a doubt, true. They could be cruel.

"Have you met very many humans?" Eli asked.

"No," she replied, "only a handful, mostly diplomats come to pay respect to my mother. They were—nice to me, respectful." She waved a hand out before them. "There was no hint of this barbarity within them."

"I see," Eli said.

"And what is that supposed to mean?" Mae asked of him.

"The world outside the boundaries of our lands can be a hard one," Eli said. "And yet, humans are not so different than our own people. There is good within them."

"How can you say that?" Mae asked him. "Especially after this mindless atrocity?"

"I have seen it and others like it," Eli said. "Do not blind yourself to the obvious. Humans are not all bad. Most would never think of doing what was done here. They would view such an act just as you do, barbarous, abhorrent in the extreme."

She did not reply. Eli got the impression she was skeptical.

"We can be just as cruel as those who perpetrated this abomination," Eli added.

"I doubt that." Mae looked over at him.

"Oh?" Eli asked, meeting her gaze. "Think of who we are pursuing."

Mae held his gaze for a long moment. He could see the dawning comprehension in her eyes. Eli hated himself for what he had just done. Her rose-colored vision of the world was no longer so rosy. It was something she would not ever be able to reclaim.

Mae turned away, and as she did, Eli started forward again, moving across the green, which stood in harsh contrast to the ugliness surrounding them.

He had given her a lot to think about. It was likely one of the reasons the warden had assigned Mae to this mission with him. Her mother had wanted her daughter to get a better understanding of the harsh realities of the outside world. And who better to give that education than him?

The three men who had been tied to the stakes were, for humans, elderly. Eli suspected they had likely been the village elders and they had been beaten and tortured. It was clear to him they had also been left to die a slow death, watching their families and friends burn alive and choke on the smoke in the longhouse. Such cruelty bothered Eli. It always had and he knew always would.

Just beyond the stakes, Jit was still kneeling. Her head was bowed, and her hands were clasped before her. She was not crying as he had expected, but instead appeared to be muttering something with her eyes closed. He could not make out what she was saying.

Was she praying?

He turned his gaze from her to the longhouse. Amidst the ruin were dozens of burned bodies half buried in ash. The birds were busily feasting away, worrying at the charred flesh. They made a garish noise and an even worse sight.

When night fell, the forest animals would arrive. In a few days, there would be nothing left but bone and ruin. A dozen years from now, the forest would move in and reclaim everything. A hundred years on and there would be little evidence that the village had ever existed, let alone of the people who had been massacred. Only those skilled enough to know what to look for would be able to read the signs of past settlement.

"Taibor," he said under his breath, as if doing so would commit the name of this place to his memory, searing it in. "I will remember you."

Unlike Mae, Eli knew this had not been a mindless act. An example had been made here, a lesson for others. It was likely directed at the other peoples that lived out in the forest and in the surrounding region.

Edgun would make certain that word of what had occurred here spread. The villages and settlements in his domain would know fear soon enough, for if Lord Edgun could do this to Taibor, he could easily do the same to them. In fear, they would buckle under and do whatever was asked and required. Such was the way of things, especially human kingdoms, like the Castol. Rarely did the people rise up.

Eli felt the child's doll tucked into his belt. Two hundred years from now, even less would be left of the village. Only a handful would recall Taibor, mostly elves. Of those few, Eli would be one.

Standing, Jit glanced over at him briefly. Her gaze went to the ragdoll, lingered there a heartbeat, and then traveled back to Eli's face. She had stiffened at its sight. After a moment, she let out a soft sigh of breath.

"Her name was Destina," Jit said, gesturing with a hand, "the little girl who owned that doll. She was five. I believe she called it Inna."

With that, Jit turned away and stalked off to the left. Eli glanced down at the doll. Jit had just given him much, much more than he had expected.

"Destina," he said, trying out the name. He decided he liked it. Inna was a good name too, for the doll.

Eli looked back upon the longhouse. Had he been destined to come here, to see this place? To bear witness to the horror? He decided he had. This was not some random whim of Fortuna.

He turned around, eyeing the bodies of the old men, the village elders. Mae was right. The people who had done this were monsters. It told him they were capable of much worse. It was not Eli's place to put a stop to such things. This was the Castol king's responsibility. It was, after all, their land and their people. Still, by taking Rivun'Cur, Lord Edgun had made it Eli's problem.

He let out an unhappy breath. The departed deserved to be buried, as was custom in these parts. Only, Eli knew he did not have the time to do that.

"I am sorry," Eli told the dead men.

Motion drew his attention. Mae was moving after Jit. Leaving the dead behind, he decided to follow, to see where the human was going.

On the edge of the village, sitting alongside a road that ran between the fields, were two parked wagons and three carts. Six horses were picketed a few feet off. The wagons and carts were heavily loaded with furniture, sacks, and tools of all kinds, along with an assortment of other items. Likely everything that could be looted had been taken and loaded onto the transport before Lord Edgun's men had fired the village.

There were no livestock present. Eli looked around and saw pens for keeping animals. They had probably been driven off already. The men who had been chasing Jit had likely been left behind to clean up. There had been no one left to resist, so why bother leaving a stronger force?

Eli's gaze followed the road. Beyond the fields, it cut into the forest. It was no more than a trail, but it connected Taibor with the neighboring villages.

Jit regarded the wagons. She looked over at Mae.

"I had hoped Captain Jesset and the rest of his men were still here." Jit sounded deeply disappointed. Her gaze slid to the horses. She walked up to the animals, then stopped and looked back at Eli and Mae. Dusk was fully upon them. The sky had begun to grow dark. "Do you want them?" Jit asked. "I have no need of horses, not in this forest."

"No," Eli said. "Best to free them. There is plenty of forage for them to eat out there, and they will find a herd of wild forest horses soon enough."

She gave a nod and began removing the tack. The freed horses milled around as she quickly worked, moving from one to the next. When done, she stood back. The animals remained where they were, seemingly oblivious of the fact that they had just been freed.

"Haa," she shouted, waving her hands in the air. "Get gone." Still the animals did not move. Jit slapped one of the horses hard on the rump, causing it to start. Another gave an unsettled whinny. She shouted even louder and stomped her feet. "Haa!"

The horses broke into a slow gallop across the nearest field before moving into the forest. Jit watched them go and then turned back toward one of the carts. It was loaded with packs and bags of various sizes. She began rummaging around in it. After several moments of work, she pulled out a brown traveling pack that had a well-worn look to it.

"Ha," Jit exclaimed, "mine."

She knelt next to the cart wheel, opening the pack. She examined the contents a moment before pulling out what was inside: a change of tunic identical to the one she had, a pair of pants, two pairs of socks, an old brush, toiletries, a flint and fire-starting kit, a stained canvas roll for a tent, a wool blanket, some rope that was neatly tied, and a well-worn leather-bound book. She laid a hand on the book, almost reverently, and seemed relieved that it was still there.

From around her neck, Jit pulled out a silver pendant. Eli could not see the face of the pendant. She brought it to her lips and kissed it, then returned it from whence it came.

He eyed the book carefully but could not tell to which god she paid homage. The book was unmarked. Eli was anything if not patient. He supposed he would find out in due course.

Amongst her things on the ground, Eli saw a rolled line for fishing. It had been secured with a hook. There was also an old towel and an iron ring, the kind that went around the necks of slaves in the empire. The ring had been sawed open.

"Are you missing anything?" Mae asked.

"They took my money," Jit said, unhappily. "But I got some of it back. A few other things are not here." She waved a hand at the carts and wagons. "Feel free to help yourselves to anything you might want. The people who owned it no longer have a use for it."

"We have all that we need," Mae said firmly, with a glance thrown to Eli.

Jit gave a half shrug of her shoulders, then set about replacing everything back into her pack, storing it away neatly. She stood and returned to rummaging around the cart. Several moments later, she came away with a crude hand axe, along with a leather belt. She tied the belt around her waist and then secured the axe there, twisting the belt so it made a loop for the shaft.

She found some food next, two loaves of bread, a chunk of salted meat, a cut of white cheese, and a small bag heavy with flour. She grabbed a smaller rough spun bag, emptied it of its contents, and then placed the food inside. She put this newly acquired haversack into her pack, along with an empty waterskin she had discovered, then cinched it closed and stood.

"Do you want to retrieve your bow?" Mae asked.

"My bow?" Jit seemed confused for a moment. "You were watching me as I crossed the creek." It was not phrased as a question, but as a statement.

"Yes, we were," Eli admitted, "from above the falls. We decided to help after we saw the odds you faced."

"The bow was not mine," Jit said. "I took it from one of the bastards chasing me. It was poorly made. The range was terrible."

"It was good enough," Eli said.

"Yes, it was." Jit patted the axe secured at her hip. "Besides, I have a new friend now, and you both are armed with bows. I reckon, like Rivun'Cur, you are better shots too."

She eyed them for a long moment, then, as if growing tired of the conversation, Jit looked away. She ran her gaze over the village once more. Eli saw Jit's jaw clench.

"I believe you both wanted to see this castle?" Jit's expression was a hard one as she turned to look back at them. Her tone was even harder, as if forged from steel. "The place where they've taken Rivun'Cur?"

"Very much so," Eli said. "How far is it?"

"At least thirty miles to the west," Jit said. "Are you serious about freeing him? You mean him no harm?"

"We are," Eli said, "and we only seek to help. We will go to his aid with or without you."

"That's what I thought," Jit said. "He is my friend, and I won't leave him there, not with the likes of the bastards who would do this to Taibor. I will go with you."

"And I would not have it any other way," Eli said.

Mae shot him a surprised look. Clearly, no matter how capable Jit was, Mae did not approve of the human going with them. Eli could understand Mae's reasoning. This was a High Born matter, best solved by the High Born.

But then again, it was also now a human problem too. Jit owned a portion of it, for she had traveled in the company of Rivun'Cur. In Eli's eyes, she deserved as much a hand in his rescue as they did. And, most important of all, Eli did not intend to let her out of his sight, not for a heartbeat. She was a mystery, one he was dearly looking forward to unraveling. Jit was coming with them, and that was final.

Eli had always liked humans. Their lives were so short, and a select few really lived life to the fullest. And when he found one like that, excitement tended to follow them around. And where there was excitement, interesting things happened. Eli liked it when things became interesting.

Was that why Rivun'Cur allowed her to travel with him? Or had it been something else that had brought their paths together?

Mae looked about to protest. Eli decided to beat her to it.

"She comes," he said in Elven.

"Of course I am coming," Jit replied in fluent Elven. "I thought we had already decided that."

Eli almost grinned at her. "We just did."

Mae studied Jit for a long moment, then took a step forward. "It's getting dark, and you need some sleep." Mae looked over at Eli. Her eyes were slightly widened and it seemed she now understood Jit was special. "As do we. It has been a long day."

Jit gave a weary nod before glancing up at the rapidly darkening sky and then to the village. "I have no wish to stay here. We can find someplace along the road, somewhere out of sight, if that is agreeable."

"It works," Eli said.

Without another word, Jit hoisted up her pack, shrugged into it, and then started off. She turned onto the road that led into the forest, traveling westward. Setting a brisk pace, she quickly left them behind.

Mae spared Eli a troubled glance. "Are you certain about this?"

"Having her come with us?"

Mae gave a nod. "There's something about her..."

"Yes," Eli agreed, "something that Rivun'Cur saw too."

"Let us hope this is a good thing that he saw in her," Mae said in a grave tone. She started after Jit.

Eli watched Mae and Jit for a long moment. He turned back and looked out onto the village. His hand once again sought out the child's doll still tucked into his belt. Eli felt a stab of anger. Though he had never met Destina, he would see justice delivered in her name, even if his actions ultimately caused complications between the Castol king and the warden.

Lord Edgun's days amongst the living were numbered, for either Eli or Jit would kill him. Of that, he was certain. Sparing the village a last look, he turned his back on the devastation and started after Jit and Mae.

CHAPTER EIGHT

Eli tossed a piece of wood onto the fire. The small blaze flared and sparks cascaded upward into the night's sky, burning themselves out, one after another. He moved back to his original position and sat down cross-legged. The fire created a pool of light in the surrounding darkness and pushed back against the growing coolness of the night.

Knees drawn up against her body, with arms wrapped around them, Mae sat to his left. A waterskin lay at her feet. She was staring with a distant look into the flaming depths of the fire and had barely spoken a handful of words since they had left Taibor. He knew it was only a matter of time until she broke the silence. After Taibor, Eli did not much feel like talking either. The sights, sounds, and smells of the place were too fresh. So, he bided his time.

It came sooner than he expected.

"How did you find this place?" Mae asked him finally, without looking up from the fire. The question seemed more an excuse to break the uncomfortable silence than anything else.

Eli sucked in a long breath and glanced idly around. They were in a sheltered glade, with thick, seemingly impenetrable pines all around. The trees grew in a near complete circle. To their left was a small lake bordered by similar pines.

Under the pale light of a half-moon, which hung high overhead, Jit had slipped into the cold water to bathe. He could see her. She was standing in waist-deep water, her back to them, and washing her hair. Eli knew the water of the lake was cold, especially at this time of year, but that did not seem to bother her in the slightest.

"A while back, Garus introduced me to this place," Eli said finally, turning his gaze to Mae. "Though I suspect he had a hand in planting the pines to create a sheltered campsite, he never explained how he found it or why it was chosen."

"You weren't curious?" Mae asked.

"I did not say that," Eli said. "I chose not to ask."

The silence between them returned. The last time Eli had stayed in this glade, it had not been a happy time either. He resisted an involuntary shiver, for he did not much enjoy dredging those memories up.

"Wasn't Garus your first partner," Mae said, looking up from the fire, "like you are mine?"

"That's right. He showed me what it was to be a ranger." Eli paused, thinking back to those days. They had begun so simple, things had seemed so straightforward, his motivation plain. Only years later had things grown complicated and difficult. Perhaps that was just the way of life. Everything moved from simple to complex.

"That must have been an experience," Mae said, "having Garus'Teel as your mentor."

"He was an unforgiving teacher," Eli responded quietly.

"Was he as good as I've heard?" Mae asked as a burning piece of wood cracked loudly, sending a shower of sparks upward.

"Probably better," Eli admitted. "When he set his mind to doing something, he was a veritable force of nature until

81

it was done." Eli paused, thinking back, recalling his teacher and mentor. The memories were far from fond. Garus had expected and tolerated only excellence. "Without him, I would not be the ranger I am today. There is no doubt in my mind about that."

Mae gave a nod as she lifted her skin of water and drank a little. "I met him once, only briefly. As head of the Ranger Corps, he had come for a meeting with my mother. I was young and found him not only reserved, but—intimidating."

Eli gave a dark chuckle. "I found him intimidating as well, until I got to know him. Then he really frightened me."

"He scared you?" Mae asked.

"That is an understatement," Eli said, then decided to give a little more. "I never thought I would measure up to his standards."

The silence returned again. It seemed they were dancing around what they had seen in Taibor. Only, Eli had the feeling there was more to this line of questioning than Mae had let on.

"It is a shame he retired from the service," Mae said. "I always thought that a great loss for our people."

"He grew weary of the outside world." Eli's thoughts went back to their last mission together. To say it had been a horrific experience was gravely understating things. It had almost cost them both of their lives and had seen Garus seriously wounded. Shortly after that, Eli's mentor had retired.

A priest of Avaya had been involved. And where Avaya went, there were spiders, big ones too. Eli did not care for spiders, not anymore.

"After today..." Mae said, and hesitated a moment, her gaze going distant. "With the razing of Taibor, I can well understand why he would willingly turn his back upon things. Before, it was not so clear. I couldn't fathom his reasoning."

Eli gave an absent nod and returned his gaze to the fire.

"He must have seen much in his time as a ranger," Mae said.

"All rangers do," Eli replied. "We are the first line of defense for our people. Upon us falls many unpleasant a task. Such work wears on one. There comes a day when it becomes evident it is time to step aside, that one has done and seen enough. Those who begrudge such a decision have not fully walked in the boots of a ranger."

They both fell silent with that, listening to the fire crackle and the forest leaves rustle as the wind gusted lightly around them. The smoke of the fire swirled like a mini tornado and blew in Mae's direction. She moved closer to him to get away from the smoke, her arm brushing lightly against his. The wind shifted after several heartbeats and carried the smoke in a different direction, away from them.

"I did not much like what I saw in Taibor." Mae lightly pressed into him, clearly upset. "Will there be more such unpleasantness? More of that sort of thing?"

"Our work is mostly done within the borders of our lands," Eli said as he met her gaze. He would not lessen the truth of their job. "Occasionally, we must venture out into the wider world. It is usually then that we encounter such unpleasantness." She was about to say something, when Eli held up a hand, forestalling her. "However, there are other things that we get to experience, some exciting, some fascinating, and some terribly interesting mysteries. They tend to counterbalance the ugliness. At least, I believe they do."

Eli shifted his gaze to the lake. Mae followed, twisting slightly to look. Up to her neck, Jit was still in the water.

"Like her?" Mae asked.

"Yes," Eli said, "just like her."

Mae returned her gaze back to the fire. Again, the silence returned.

"Why did you not take it, when it was offered?" Mae asked.

Eli knew to what she referred. "Take what?"

"Don't play games with me," Mae said. "Why did you spurn my mother? I know you were offered command of the Ranger Corps, given an opportunity to step into Garus's boots. Everyone thought you the logical choice as his replacement."

"Everyone, except me."

"Why would you not want it?" Mae seemed perplexed. "The position comes with so much, a seat on the council even."

Eli did not reply. He just stared into the flames.

"She wanted it for you," Mae pressed.

"Did she?" Eli asked, looking up. His father had even wanted it for his son. It would have meant father and son would have sat on the council, together, two of the warden's six closest advisors.

"What do you mean by that?" Mae snapped back, leaning away from him.

The cool night air touching his warmed skin where Mae had been before she withdrew from him made her distance from him seem more pronounced.

"I did not view being ranger commander as an honor. It was not something I desired."

"Why?"

"One day you will know." Eli looked beyond her. "One day, there will come a time when you fully understand, like you now do with Garus's decision to step aside."

Jit returned to the fire. She had dressed in a change of clothing. The tunic and pants she had worn earlier had been washed and wrung as dry as she could get them. The human eyed them as she moved over to a small tree that had begun growing within the confines of the glade. Jit hung the tunic and pants from a branch that was shoulder height. Her blonde hair, which glistened from reflected firelight, had been tied back into a single ponytail.

"Rivun'Cur and I once stopped here for a few days," Jit said, speaking to them in Elven. "It is a peaceful place, calming to the spirit. I like it very much. Being several miles from the only road in these parts, there's no one to bother you. I never much cared for other people."

"Solitude's Rest should be this place's name," Eli said.

"Does it have an actual name?" Mae asked curiously.

"Yes," Eli said. "I just gave it to you."

She shot him an unhappy scowl. "And here I thought you were showing your creative side."

"I've learned elves have such places all over," Jit said. "Some are nice, others not so much, but they are all private."

Eli had to admit her grasp of their language was quite good. She spoke the High Born tongue almost like she'd been born to it though she still had an accent. Mae shifted, as if uncomfortable. Eli suspected she was having similar thoughts.

"We prefer not to be bothered when we travel," Eli said. "It makes things less complicated."

"You want to move about without attracting too much attention," Jit said. "That's what I think."

"There is truth in what you say," Eli said.

"Of course there is."

Jit moved over to her pack. She pulled it closer to the fire before opening it and taking out the haversack she had recently acquired. She removed the hunk of cheese from inside. With her dagger, she cut a piece off and popped it into her mouth as she sat down before the fire.

"Hidden roads and paths deep in the forest," Jit said, "along with marker trees and no one knows. Heck, I never knew."

Eli and Mae shared a look. Rivun'Cur must have shown her what to look for. That was unexpected, for it was an unwritten rule that such things were not revealed to outsiders. Then again, Rivun'Cur was an outsider.

"Can you tell us more about this Lord Edgun?" Mae asked.

"Not much more than I already said." Jit chewed thoughtfully on the cheese. "He's not liked in these parts, and his word is the law, the only law, I think."

"This is his domain," Mae said, "especially if the king of the Castol granted it to him. His word would be law."

Jit gave a shrug, as if the matter of law did not bother her too much. She was silent for a few heartbeats before she spoke. "He came here from the capital with several hundred soldiers, among them a mercenary company. Or perhaps it was that it was Edgun's own private company. He might be the mercenary. At the time, I wasn't really paying attention to the conversation. I was more focused on getting a hot bowl of fresh stew in my stomach. Now, I wish I had listened closer." She finished chewing and swallowed. "He's raised taxes and has begun bleeding people dry."

"Was Rivun'Cur interested in the conversation you are speaking about?" Eli probed.

"He was," Jit said as she took another bite. "We were in a tavern. I thought it a bad idea to stop there, as we'd attract attention. We always attract far too much attention when we stop in a town. But he wanted information. I think that's when we ran afoul of Lord Edgun. He must have had ears listening in on the conversation."

Eli did not like the sound of that. It meant there were likely spies in each settlement.

"Why did he want Rivun'Cur?" Mae asked.

"I don't know," Jit said, "our business had nothing to do with him."

"What's the castle like?" Eli asked, deciding to change the subject. He wanted to move things along and get a sense for what they faced. "Have you seen it?"

"I have," Jit said. "It's not much of a castle, not yet anyway. He chose an old stone keep atop a hill and rebuilt it. Each town and village is required to send people for labor to help construct its defensive walls. They rotate in and out at certain times of the year. No one's really too happy about that. The levy angered a lot of people, especially those in Taibor."

Eli had heard of such a practice before. It ensured that there was a constant pool of labor available to keep construction going. However, in practice, the human peasants sent to work typically were not always so motivated. Frequently they would shirk, or simply not show up, or perform their work in an overly slow manner. Had that been the real reason Taibor had been sacked? Had Edgun been looking to set an example so that the other towns and villages made sure to send workers? To motivate them?

"There are four outer walls," Jit continued. She picked up a thin branch and poked absently at the fire. "The walls are made of wood, though they're working at replacing that with stone. It overlooks the town of Brek."

"I know the town." Eli vaguely recalled the keep too. It had been a crumbling and overgrown structure, at least a century old, that had been abandoned shortly after its construction. He could not remember why the humans had abandoned it. "If I recall, the keep is on the hill on the south side of the town. The big one, right?"

"Yes," Jit said. "I would assume he's keeping Rivun'Cur there. People say Edgun rarely comes out of that keep. It is also said that people taken there don't come out either." Jit paused as a hard look came over her. "I intend to get him."

Eli shared a worried glance with Mae. He knew it was really the first place to start looking. If Rivun'Cur was not there, then they might get answers on where he was being held.

"How did you meet Rivun'Cur?" Mae asked.

Jit stiffened, then, with seeming effort, forced herself to relax.

"It's all right," Mae said. "We're just curious."

"I don't want to talk about it." Jit's tone was hard and unbending. She looked back down at the fire and then up at them before swallowing the cheese she'd been chewing. "If you must know, we've been traveling together for three years now. The beginning of summer, we came up from the south."

"Why?" Mae asked.

"It is a private matter," Jit said, sounding almost defensive.

"Fair enough." Eli exchanged another brief look with Mae.

"This Mik'Las." Jit looked between them. "The one you're hunting, who is he?"

It was Mae's turn to shift uncomfortably.

"A criminal," Eli said. "We have been sent to bring him back to be judged or, if that proves impossible, to send him on to the next life."

"He must really be a bad person," Jit said. "I've come to learn that elves treasure life. It is one of the things I like about your people."

"For the most part, we do treasure life," Eli said, "though Mik'Las does not."

The thought of what they might have to do pulled at Eli's heart and saddened him. Feelings aside, if push came to shove, Eli intended to shove. He would end Mik'Las's life in a heartbeat. Then, he would feel bad about it later. Eventually, Eli knew, with time, he would get over such an act, for Mik'Las had proven himself to be a detestable person.

"Mik'Las is a murderer," Mae said. "He killed fellow High Born. There is no greater crime amongst our people, nothing more heinous."

Jit seemed surprised as she looked between them. "Why would he do that? Why would he commit murder?"

"There was something he coveted," Mae said in a hard tone. "It was not his to take."

"And yet he did it anyway," Jit said.

"Yes," Mae said.

"A murderer, a thief," Jit said, "and an elf too. I guess his apple fell off the cart."

"What you say is not far off the mark," Eli said. "Mik'Las is a bad egg."

"There are a lot of bastards like him out there," Jit said, before yawning powerfully, then recovered. "I've run into more than my fair share and sent those I could on to see the ferryman."

That last statement told Eli that Jit was imperial.

Jit yawned again.

"Well, we've talked enough," Eli said, slapping his thighs lightly. "Get some rest. You look like you could use it. Mae and I will stand watch tonight."

"Are you certain?" Jit asked. "I don't mind taking a turn."

"We are," Mae said.

"All right," Jit said, giving in. "Thank you."

"I've got first watch." Eli stood. He moved over to where he had left his bow and picked it up, along with a handful of arrows. He doubted he would need them. They were far enough off the beaten track that it was unlikely anyone was out in the woods, especially at night. No one was looking for them either. No one knew they were out here. Still, Eli had long since learned it was far better to be safe than sorry. "I will have a look around. Both of you, get some rest."

With that, Eli stepped away from the fire and the light, moving between the pine trees and out into the forest. Several yards away, he stopped. Eli waited, allowing his eyes to adjust to the darkness around him. He counted to four hundred, all the while resisting the urge to glance back at the fire. He could not help thinking about Mae leaning into him and how natural it felt. Forcing the thought down, he turned his mind to Jit and whatever Rivun'Cur was after. That was certainly a mystery.

An owl hooted somewhere off in the darkness to his left. Eli looked, but could not see the creature. It was concealed amongst the trees. He smiled slightly. Eli loved the forest, especially at night, for it was a lively place. Moving out into the forest, he became one with the night, a ghost in the darkness.

CHAPTER NINE

"There it is." Jit waved before them. Hand on the pommel of her sword, she gave a disgusted snort as she crouched next to a boulder. "The town of Brek and Lord Edgun's castle."

Resting his bow upon the lichen-covered rock underfoot, Eli sank to a knee next to Jit and wiped perspiration from his brow with the back of his forearm. A few feet away on his left, Mae dropped to a knee as well.

They were on a rocky ridge overlooking a small valley, within which lay the town, about two miles away. There was a scattering of trees along the ridgetop, with scrub brush growing amongst the rocks and boulders around them. Directly below was a steep drop-off with thick forest. The climb up the reverse slope of the ridge had required not only effort but some scrambling. Eli had found it invigorating.

Bright and brilliant, the sun hung directly overhead. There was not even a hint of a cloud. The sky was as blue as could be and the air was not too hot nor too cold. The day was, for lack of a better word, perfect. At least Eli thought so.

Motion overhead caught his attention. He squinted to see better. Barely visible, a speck amongst the blue, a hawk was soaring high above, on the hunt. For a fleeting moment, Eli forgot why they had come to the ridge. He wondered what it would be like to fly so high. He tried to imagine it, seeing the world as a bird does, no worries other than getting one's next meal. It must be wonderful, he thought.

"It stinks," Mae commented. "They must be living in their own filth down in that town."

Almost regretfully, Eli turned his attention away from the hawk and to the town. His mood clouded slightly. They had business to attend to, for down there somewhere was Rivun'Cur and Lord Edgun.

"It does smell," Eli agreed, sniffing lightly at the wind, which carried the stench of civilization, a mixture of smoke, waste, and decay.

Nestled in the small valley, next to a river, lay Brek. From their vantage, the town was a jumble of buildings pressed closely together, with unpaved streets and alleys. Despite a gentle wind blowing and occasionally gusting in their faces, an ugly gray haze of smoke hung sullenly over the town, as if it refused to be budged. The smoke was undoubtedly from numerous cookfires and hearths. Smoke was always an indicator of settlement, whether that be human or High Born.

Farms surrounded the town on all sides but the river, where buildings ran right up to the edge of the water. The fields were extensive and mainly dedicated to crops, but there were also several fenced-in pastures for small herds of sheep, cows, goats, and a handful of horses, likely draft animals for hauling and plowing.

Brek had grown large since Eli's last visit, which had been some years before. He could not remember when exactly he'd been here last, only that it was a while. He found it frustrating that he could not recall how long it had been. That was a problem with a long life. Over time, memory tended to fail. Eli had always found that painful, especially when it came to people he cared about.

Had it been twenty-five years? Or longer?

From the looks of things, the settlement was still expanding. Several buildings were under construction on the north side of the town. The forest was actively being cleared beyond the fields that bordered those structures. In his mind, Eli could envision the town in fifty or sixty years becoming a small city. That was a matter for concern, because, as a bird flew, Brek was not all that distant from his people's lands. Still, that was a problem for the warden and another day.

Across the river, a large, sloping hill dominated the terrain all around. There were no others as tall within the confines of the valley. Both on the hill and around it, the forest had been completely cut back. A scattering of sheep grazed along the slopes. Eli could not see a human watching over them.

A stone keep, four stories in height and capped with battlements, sat atop the hill's crest. When Eli had last been through these parts, the keep had been an ivy-covered ruin falling apart, crumbling one stone block at a time. It had been rebuilt and looked new. Plaster had also been applied to the outside of the keep and then painted, or more likely whitewashed with a lime base. The end result was a white so brilliant that the keep shone under the sunlight.

For a moment, Eli wondered why the humans had bothered. Then understanding dawned. Lord Edgun wanted everyone to see the keep and seat of his power. No one below could miss it, which meant nobody could mistake his authority.

Around the keep was an impressive defensive wall made almost entirely of tree trunks and topped with a covered barricade. The barricade in places was still in the process of being constructed. Eli gave a low whistle. Whoever had overseen the wall's construction knew how to build fortifications and had turned the keep into a veritable castle.

A wooden bridge and road connected the town with the castle. From what he could see, a guard detail stood at the bridge, granting access to only those authorized to pass.

"I am no expert on human fortifications," Mae said, "but even I can see that castle is formidable."

"For an organized force, those walls would be a difficult obstacle to overcome," Jit said, "but not an impossible one."

"I don't know why he's bothering to build such a castle around these parts." Eli's gaze sought out the sentries posted strategically on the wall. They were walking along the barricade and, he supposed, gazing watchfully out at the town and surrounding terrain. At this distance, they were little bigger than ants. He counted at least ten on the side facing them. "The nearest threats are only the locals. What he's constructing here looks designed to hold off an army, and he's been at it for more than a year at the very least."

"Whose army?" Mae asked.

"That is the question which begs to be answered," Eli said, studying the castle critically. Three of the corners of the castle's wall had been rebuilt from wood into stone towers. Two of the towers were already complete. The third was nearly finished, with a wooden crane looming over it. Large piles of shaped stone had been stacked before the tower. A dozen workers busied themselves around it. Once the corner towers were completed, it was likely the walls would be next to be converted.

"Give it a few years," Eli said, "and the castle will be entirely surrounded by stone walls."

"Could Edgun be concerned the empire will march north and threaten his position here?" Mae looked over at

Eli in question. She sounded doubtful. "Did the king send Edgun to fortify his southern border?"

Eli rubbed the back of his neck as he considered his answer. "I've heard of no recent tensions between the empire and the Castol. As far as I know, the empire is engaged in a war to the southwest and has no interest in pushing north, at least not while they are hotly engaged. Were circumstances otherwise, our rangers embedded with the imperial legions would have sent word, our ambassador too."

"We recently came up through the occupied provinces," Jit said, joining the conversation. "The only garrison forces near the border were auxiliaries. Most of those were third-rate and engaged in nothing more than supporting the imperial tax agents and keeping the roads clear of bandits. Their kit was so poorly maintained, honestly, I thought them a sad lot."

Eli glanced over at the human. The fact that she knew the differences in the quality of military formations told him a lot. That and her assessment of the castle being an obstacle that could still be overcome. How could she know all this when the empire did not send their women to war?

"What does it mean then?" Mae asked, drawing his attention and his thoughts away from Jit. "Why build such a castle then? Out in the middle of nowhere? Surely he can't be too concerned about our people. Could he?"

Eli turned his gaze back to the town as he considered the questions Mae had posed. Two main roads made the town a strategic point. One traveled from the north to the south, moving all the way to the imperial provinces. South of Brek, the road was of poor quality and not suited to an army's movement, which meant it would make a poor invasion route for the empire. The other road moved east from Brek, almost to Rivan territory. It too was not the best quality.

Those main roadways, despite their deficiencies, made the town important and a minor hub for regional trade. Still, they did not explain the need for such a fortified position. All the Castol really required was a small garrison and a fort to project power throughout the region, not a full-blown castle for defense.

"I don't know," Eli admitted after several moments. His gaze was drawn to two covered wagons trundling away from the town, heading northward along the road. The distance made it look like both wagons were crawling along at a painfully slow pace. Eli knew that to be deceptive.

Trailing behind the wagons was a small herd of sheep being shepherded by an individual. A group of at least two dozen people shambled along a few yards behind the animals. The group was clearly under a guard detail. The guards walked to either side. Were they slaves, criminals? The distance made it impossible to tell.

"He's concerned about something." Eli shifted his gaze back to the hill. "You don't go to that much effort to construct such a formidable castle."

Eli glanced over at Mae. Her gaze was focused on the town, eyes flicking about. This was the first human town she had ever set eyes upon. Despite their grave purpose, he understood the excitement likely coursing through her, for he had once felt it himself. She wanted to explore the town, to see everything, to experience a different culture. That much was clear to him.

Eli caught her attention and pointed toward a dark column of smoke to the north. It was a smudge on the horizon just above the low ridges that surrounded the valley. At first glance, it was easily missed.

"That is the mine," Eli said.

She followed his finger, and her eyes narrowed as she studied the smoke. She looked back at him. "As in underground, and digging?"

Eli gave a nod.

"Out in the middle of the forest?"

"It's why the town is here," Eli said, "at least why they decided to originally settle in these parts."

"What kind of mine?" Mae asked, clearly curious now. "And why is the town so far away from it? Surely the distance reduces productivity. That has to be more than six, maybe even seven miles distant and well outside of the valley."

"Copper," Eli answered. "The smoke is from the smelting process. And as to why they settled so far away... once you leave the valley, the terrain becomes quite rugged to the north. Lots of hills with little good land for cultivation. When they first came to these parts, there were a few hovels close to the mine. As the population grew with the mine's output, the owner needed to feed the people he brought in to work, and that included their families. Hunting alone could not do that, hence settling this valley and carving fields for farming out of the forest. The river also provides irrigation for the farms, fish, and a little commerce. The town grew out of the mining effort. Now it has become much more than a source for labor. It is the focal point for the region."

Mae gave a nod of understanding, then looked over at Jit. "Have you seen the mine?"

Jit shook her head. "Just the town, and only for a few hours. Once Rivun'Cur got what he needed, we moved on. We didn't feel like staying longer than we had to. The people down there are on edge, an unhappy lot. They seemed... desperate."

"Lord Edgun's fault, no doubt," Mae said.

"I thought so," Jit said. "Perhaps by building the castle, he wants to secure the copper mine, making sure no one can take it from him."

"That is a possibility," Eli said, then after a moment's reflection, decided against that being the reason. If the mine was pulling silver or gold out of the ground, which humans valued and craved more than copper, that would be cause enough for a castle or some fortified structure. Copper, not so much, for the metal was plentiful in the region.

"Or," Jit added, "he might have just wanted to better guard his hide. Rivun felt the people in these parts were close to rising up against Lord Edgun."

Eli nodded absently as his gaze sought out the castle again. A formation of soldiers was marching out of the gate and down toward the bridge. Eli estimated there were around fifty soldiers. Lord Edgun clearly had the muscle to dominate the town and region.

"How do we go about this?" Mae said. "It's not like we can walk right down there and ask where they are holding Rivun'Cur."

"No," Eli said. "That would not be the wisest course of action. The moment we show our faces, Lord Edgun and his people would see us as an immediate threat, especially after having seized Rivun'Cur."

"I could go," Jit said. "Ask about, see what I can learn. I'm human after all."

"Are there people down there who would recognize you?" Eli asked. He suspected there were.

"Some of Edgun's men would," Jit said, "but not many. I am good at stealing about. They'd not notice me, and if they did, I'd make them wish they had looked the other way."

Eli regarded her for a long moment. Jit seemed certain. After what he had seen her do, he knew she could handle herself. But still, she might find more trouble than she expected simply by asking about Rivun'Cur. Or she might just stick out for being an outsider. Either way, she would attract some level of attention, and Eli wanted to avoid that. He did not want Lord Edgun knowing they were coming, for surprise was a powerful weapon.

He turned his gaze back to the town, studying it closely. He did not much like the idea of sending Jit down there by herself. He was starting to get a bad feeling about what was to come, and Eli had long since learned to trust his gut. So far, his instincts had kept him alive. He bit his lip as he thought the problem through, scanning the town more closely. He snapped his fingers.

"You going alone is too much of a risk," Eli said to Jit and then gave a low chuckle. "Besides, I have a better idea."

"Care to share that with us?" Mae asked when he did not say anything further for several heartbeats.

Eli had begun scanning the buildings of the town, looking for what he knew must be down there. "In a town the size of Brek, there are undoubtedly taverns, what the humans call watering holes, wine dens, drinking shacks, the list goes on." Eli waved at the town with a hand. "After a long day, human soldiers enjoy a drink. It has been my experience that soldiers do not stop at just one. A good number regularly drink to excess and then some."

"You want us to grab one?" Mae surmised. "A drunk soldier and question him?"

"Exactly," Eli said. "We find a suitable tavern, one that is away from prying eyes. Then we lie in wait. When a soldier emerges to relieve himself, we seize and question him."

"And if he doesn't have any information on where they are holding Rivun'Cur?" Mae asked. "What then?"

"Oh," Eli said, brightening, "he will. Human soldiers love to talk, to spread rumors, gossip, that sort of thing. Lord Edgun has captured a High Born. Such an event will get tongues flapping. I wouldn't be surprised to learn that the entire population of the town has already heard the news. The man we take might not know why Rivun'Cur was seized, but he'll likely know where he is being held. I am certain of that."

"It makes sense to me, then," Jit said, "and it's as good a plan as any."

"If I recall correctly"—Eli turned to Jit—"you know where a tavern is located."

"I do," Jit said, "and I also know for a fact soldiers frequent the place. It's called the Iron Nail and it's situated on the edge of town, a perfect place to snatch someone without attracting attention." She pointed. "There, see it? In front of that sheep pen, the ugly brown building."

Eli studied the building for a long moment. Though distant, he could see she was indicating a squat one-story building with an arched roof. The window shutters had been thrown open, likely for some of the fine weather.

His gaze moved from the tavern through the fields. There were at least three hundred yards of open ground, a wheat field that had yet to be harvested, from the tavern to the forest beneath them and cover.

He glanced up at the cloudless sky. When night fell, and without cloud cover, the half-moon would make them stand out as they moved through the open field. That was especially true if they were dragging a prisoner away from the town. Anyone with a keen eye might spot them. It was certainly not ideal, but there was no helping that. Eli blew out a resigned breath and then suppressed a grin. It was just one more challenge to overcome, and Eli loved challenges. They tended to keep things interesting.

"Well, it seems we have some time before darkness approaches," Eli said lightly. "Let's eat something and then get some rest. I have a feeling it will prove to be a long night."

"You're hungry?" Mae asked. "We ate less than an hour ago."

Eli stood and looked over at her. "I have found a full belly helps one nap, especially"—he glanced up at the sky— "on a fine day like this one. And I can't think of anything else I'd rather do right now than have a nap."

He turned away and began moving back under the cover of the trees and out of sight of anyone below. Eli selected an old oak not too far from where they had been studying the town. The tree had a wide trunk and was easily ten feet around. Eli shrugged off his pack and set it down against the tree as a light gust of wind rustled the leaves gently overhead.

"Are you sure about this course of action?" Mae asked, joining him.

"No," Eli admitted. "I am not. But I think it is better than just walking up to the castle's gate and asking to see Rivun'Cur."

Mae gave a grunt. "I think I might like to see you try that."

"Do you have a better plan? If you do, I would love to hear it."

She shook her head. "No, I do not."

Eli sat and placed his back against the hard bark of the tree. He opened his pack and pulled out his haversack, untying the rope knot that held it closed.

Mae took a seat next to him. Eli pulled out a hunk of cheese and cut it in half with one of his daggers. He handed her one of the slices.

"This is a peaceful enough spot," Mae said, "even if we can smell the human settlement on the wind. I can only imagine how much stronger the stench is down in the town itself."

"Eventually, you become accustomed to such smells."

"I find that difficult to believe." Mae wrinkled her nose.

"Truly," Eli said. "Given a sufficient amount of time exposed to the smell, you will hardly notice it, even something as pungent as the town's reek."

Eli looked over at Mae when she failed to reply. Her gaze had fallen upon Jit. He got the feeling Mae was troubled by something, and deeply so. He shifted his gaze to the human, wondering what that was. Jit had not moved, but was still staring out at the town, as if committing it to memory.

"The Pool of Reflection," Mae said in a near whisper, and then fell silent for a heartbeat. She opened her mouth to speak. "I—"

"I already told you," Eli said, without looking over, "that is a personal experience, one best kept to yourself."

"And if it showed me something that—?"

"Whatever it showed you," Eli said, interrupting her again, "was meant only for you. I'd caution against sharing."

Mae did not immediately reply. "Why?"

"You were meant to learn from the experience, nothing more."

"And what if you are wrong?" Mae asked.

"I'm not," Eli said firmly.

"I forgot," Mae said, with a tinge of bitterness in her tone. "You are the infallible Eli."

"I am hardly that."

Their gazes met. Eli saw a haunted look there.

"Share that which was meant only for you," Eli said, "and it will not end well."

"How can you so be sure?" Mae asked, sounding torn.

"Because," Eli said, with a heavy breath, "the caretaker cautioned me against doing just that. I was young, and thought I knew better. To my everlasting regret, I did not heed his advice."

"What happened to you?" Mae asked.

"Let's just say it did not end well. I would spare you that experience, for it was painful."

Mae returned her gaze to Jit. The human was a few yards away, still gazing down at the town. She had yet to move.

"And—what if the pool showed me more than something about myself? What if I was given a vision of the future?" Mae asked. "The kind of things where the people you care about die or are hurt? What then?"

Eli looked at her sharply. Mae's gaze was still fixed on the human. He had not heard of the pool showing someone their future. The thought of it doing so was troubling, for the future was unwritten. At least, Eli had always thought so. Could she have been mistaken? Had she really seen what was to come?

"I would still keep it to yourself," Eli said. "That was the advice passed to me."

Their gazes met and he held hers for a long moment, then turned to look upon the human. Who was she? Why was she important to Rivun'Cur? He had the uneasy feeling whatever had been shown to Mae somehow involved Jit. Then there was the castle and Lord Edgun, not to mention their mission in hunting down Mik'Las. This venture to free Rivun'Cur was a diversion from their true task, and yet, somehow, Eli felt it wasn't.

"I suppose you are used to this sort of thing." Mae took a bite of her cheese as she drew his attention again.

"You mean waiting for the fun to begin?" Eli asked, before taking a bite himself. The cheese had been provided by the caretaker. It was plain, with little taste, but it was nourishing.

"How do you manage to remain so calm?"

"The waiting is always the worst part," Eli admitted.

She raised an eyebrow.

"The real trick is showing the world you are cool as can be, even when, on the inside, you are not. Master that and a true ranger you will become." Eli flashed her a grin. "Perhaps one day, if you become good at it, you might even learn to walk in my boots. Imagine that, the status it would give you. Your mother might even appoint you to the council in my stead."

"My mother? Me? The council?" Mae stared at him for a long, hard moment, as if deciding whether or not to take offense, then laughed deeply. It was the first laugh he had heard from her in days. To his surprise, Eli found he enjoyed the sound. Somehow, it made the day a little brighter. But as soon as he noticed, it was as if a cloud passed over that brightness, leaving him cold. Why did he find this feeling to be more concerning than what they might face in the hours to come?

CHAPTER TEN

"It stinks something awful," Mae whispered. She sounded personally offended. "Are all human towns so—so unsanitary?"

"Not as bad as this one," Jit hissed back to her. "But, believe me, I've seen and smelled worse." She spat. "My people would never, could never, live like this, in such filth. To do so would be a dishonoring of the gods and invite disfavor."

In the darkness, Eli glanced back at them and fought off a scowl. Jit was right behind Mae. He considered saying something, reminding them of their task, what might happen if they were discovered. Instead, he settled for a stern look and raised a finger to his lips.

Mae's lip curled slightly as their eyes met. She seemed more amused than anything else, which Eli found mildly irritating. He turned back, stepping into the alley between buildings. It was wide enough for two people to easily walk abreast of each other. They had seen the patrons of the tavern using it to relieve themselves. And it did stink, terribly. Eli could not deny that. He could not ever recall smelling a stench so foul and strong.

Trying not to think of what he was walking through, Eli worked his way forward, almost to the end of the alley and the adjoining street. Numerous raised voices came from the tavern on his right. He was about to peek out onto the street when he heard someone approaching. He hastily retreated into the shadows. Someone was whistling a tune and coming closer. Without looking back, he flashed a warning sign to Mae and Jit. Eli wrapped a hand around one of his daggers and readied himself should the need come.

The whistling, Eli thought, was quite painful to the ears. He pressed his back to the tavern's plastered wall, which was crumbling from age and outright neglect. Eli stilled and waited for the whistler to pass. He held his breath and began counting. Ten heartbeats later, a man, dressed in a simple tunic and sandals, moved by the alley entrance. Still whistling, he continued down the street, completely oblivious to the fact he was being observed. Eli let go a breath he had not realized he'd been holding.

After another thirty count, he could no longer hear the whistling. He untensed and released his hold on his dagger hilt. From inside the tavern came an increased level of drunken merriment. The wall even seemed to vibrate with it. The raised voices grew abruptly louder. A man inside bellowed in outrage, and a heartbeat later, a woman laughed coarsely. This was followed by a chorus of general laughter.

The moon was up, hanging almost directly overhead. It shone its pale light upon the land below, partially illuminating the alley. The light was not as bright as a full moon would have been, but it was enough that even a human could see some distance in the open. Once again, Eli wished for some cloud cover, but wishing for a thing to happen did not seem to work. In fact, in his experience, it rarely ever had.

Eli was about to move when the heavy crunch of boots falling in unison drew his attention. He flashed another warning sign to Mae, then once again became still. The sound of the boots neared and then a patrol squad of eight soldiers marched by, moving opposite from the man he had just seen. What Eli took to be a corporal or sergeant marched at their side.

These men were kitted out differently than those they had encountered in Taibor. They carried large, rounded shields that were almost oval in shape and were armed with narrow swords a little longer than the imperial short sword. They were also armed with javelins, a weapon similar to ones imperial legionaries used. Their armor was a studded leather that covered the stomach and chest. Eli noted their equipment was uniform and appeared well maintained. That told him the soldiers were professionals, which made them dangerous. Were the rest of Lord Edgun's men as professional? Eli had an unhappy suspicion they might be. That would make their task more difficult, but not impossible; he was a ranger after all.

More importantly, the patrol seemed alert and watchful, and there was no talking, which he thought an oddity. If anything, the soldiers seemed tense, as if on edge. Eli noticed how they watched both sides of the street as they moved down it, heads swiveling. It was almost as if they expected to be attacked.

Once the patrol had passed, he glanced back down the alleyway. Mae and Jit had retreated to the shadows and were waiting at the far end, nearly where he had left them. He signaled to Mae that the threat had passed. She nodded in reply.

Eli turned and peeked rapidly around the corner, first looking right and then left. The street was packed dirt. Candle – and firelight shone dully from the nearest windows. No one was on the street, other than the squad of soldiers that had just passed, and they were moving steadily away, disappearing into the night.

Taking a step back, Eli immediately glanced down. He had stepped in something that squished with an audible squelch. A wave of revulsion washed over him as he ran his boot over the ground in an attempt to wipe whatever it was off. After a moment of effort, he gave up, deciding his boots were hopelessly contaminated and would need a thorough cleaning later.

The building opposite the tavern was a tannery. That stunk sourly as well, adding to the general unpleasantness of the alley and town. As near as he could tell, there was no one inside. But just because there were no lights was not a guarantee it was empty.

The tannery's roof was low and, like the Iron Nail, slightly arched, the outer edges flat. Most of the buildings in the town had been constructed in this manner, likely due to the harsh winters of the north. The roof of the tannery partially hung over the alley, just a few inches above his head.

Ready? Eli flashed the sign to Mae.

Yes, she replied in fingerspeak.

Satisfied, Eli jumped and caught the edge of the tannery's roof with both hands. Deftly, he pulled himself up and onto it, then immediately lay flat. He scooted back down the length of the alley a few feet, far enough that anyone passing on the street would be unable to see him.

Now, it was time to wait. And wait he did.

Lying there and trying to ignore the stench of the alley below, he looked up at the moon, more to kill time than anything else. Eli could see pockmarks on the moon's white surface. He wondered what they were or what had caused them.

He recalled the hawk from earlier in the day and another question hit him. Could birds fly high enough to reach the moon? It was an intriguing thought. What was the moon like? It had the look of being all chalk.

Some of his people, especially those who had traveled from Tannis, thought the moon just another planet like their own, Istros. Eli had always thought that an interesting line of thinking. He'd heard it said the stars in the night's sky were like the sun that rose during the day.

Still, since no one had ever managed to travel to the moon, it was a question that seemed impossible to answer. Eli let out a light breath. He had so many questions. Whenever he seemed to solve one mystery, more presented themselves. He found that frustrating, at times to the point of distraction. No matter how much one learned, there was yet more waiting.

The tavern erupted in boisterous song, pulling his thoughts away from the moon and the mysteries of the universe. The tune was badly sung, by more than a dozen voices. It was loud, obscene, and about a milkmaid who loved soldiers, not for their looks, but for their coin. Eli had heard dozens like it.

Eli waited, doing his best to ignore the song, like the smell. Humans could be coarse, offensive, and thoroughly uncultured. There were times he could barely stand them. But they were also fascinating creatures, with many living their short lives to the fullest, like a fast-burning wick. Over the long years, he had even named several as friends.

His own people tended to become stale, stuffy, and uninteresting with age, at least in Eli's estimation. It was a wonder he enjoyed his own people's company. Or did he? Perhaps that was why he spent so much time out in the field and away from home. Maybe being an outcast, like Rivun'Cur, was not such a curse after all? When they found him, it might not be a bad idea to ask.

As the singing continued, the door to the tavern banged open, then slammed closed. Eli readied himself, straining his ears to listen. The sound of shambling footsteps came next as someone entered the alley.

"Bloody hell, I've got to go," a gruff voice groaned. "Oh sweet gods above and below, let it flow."

The sound of a bladder emptying its contents came next, followed by a heavy sigh of relief. Eli almost smiled with anticipation as he lay still and continued to wait. It seemed to go on and on. Then, it ceased.

"Now that was a bloody fine piss," the gruff voice said. "The finest of fine."

"Hello there," came Jit's voice from the far end of the alley.

"What?" the man gasped in surprise. "Bloody gods, woman. What are you doing out so late? Don't you know there's a curfew?"

"Looking for a good time, soldier?" Jit's voice had turned seductive, almost sultry. "I know I am."

That was Eli's cue. He rolled onto his side and glanced over the edge of the roof. Almost immediately below and illuminated by the moonlight was one of Lord Edgun's men. He was short and compact, though, Eli judged, muscular. He was also older for a human soldier, perhaps in his late twenties or early thirties. He wore a simple tunic. The man's pants were down around his ankles.

He was peering blearily down the alley at Jit, who was standing in the shadows. He swayed slightly as he stood there. The pale skin of his exposed legs seemed to glow under the moonlight. Though Eli could see well enough, he knew human night vision was poor. Eli, on the other hand, could see her just fine. Mae was crouched down behind Jit, at the very end of the alley, nothing more than an indistinct shadow. Mae was watching for anyone coming the other way.

"A good time?" The soldier took two shambling steps forward. With his pants around his ankles, it was almost comical. "You're a whore?"

"I'm whatever you want me to be—for a price. You do have the copper, don't you?"

"Copper?" the soldier asked, his speech slurred. "Sure, let me see you. Step out into the light, darling. I want to see what I'm going to get. I won't be buying no old hag with sagging tits and sores."

Soundlessly, Eli dropped down behind the soldier. As soon as his feet touched the ground, and before his mark could react, Eli moved. Drawing both of his daggers, he sprang forward and came up right to the soldier's back. Eli placed one of his blades to the man's throat. The soldier stiffened.

"Now that," Eli said quietly, "is no way to talk to a lady."

The man made to move. Before he could, Eli shifted his dagger close against the man's throat, the razor-sharp edge breaking the skin and drawing a trickle of blood.

"Friend," Eli breathed in the other's ear, "it would be a shame for me to have to cut you further."

The man became very still, then took a deep breath. Anger filled his voice when he spoke. "You're making a mistake by doing this...a big mistake."

"Perhaps," Eli said. "Though, were I you, I would not make the mistake of moving or testing my resolve."

"All I need do is shout for help and my comrades will come running. You will be in a world of trouble then."

Eli glanced at the man's tunic sleeve and saw rank insignia that indicated he was a sergeant. He felt a surge of triumph. They had caught a big enough fish that their prisoner should know where Rivun'Cur was being kept and why he had been seized in the first place.

"Maybe, but I have a knife to your throat." Eli shifted his other dagger around and lower, the longer blade that was curved at the middle, to press against the shaft of the man's penis. He hesitated a heartbeat before continuing, "And your little friend." Eli moved slightly, so he was glancing around the man's shoulder and down his front. "It is quite surprisingly little. I would even say underwhelming. Do you lie to the ladies or just keep things simple and pay for love?"

"Bastard," the sergeant spat and then sucked in a breath. Eli felt the man tense, clearly readying himself for action.

"Shout and I promise I will cut that little something off." Eli's tone became rock hard, deadly even. He shifted his hand slightly, jerking the edge of the curved blade against the soft flesh.

"Do it and there will be reprisals," the sergeant growled in pain and anger. "Your neighbors will suffer. Lord Edgun will see to it."

"Fortunately," Eli said, "we are not of this town."

Mae caught his attention.

It's still clear, she signaled to him from the far end of the alley.

"Secure him," Eli said in reply. Mae left her position and moved around Jit, who was watching the prisoner from her position in the shadows. Jit's expression was intense and spoke of loathing. Those inside the tavern began to sing another song.

Mae came up next to Eli. She had a gag in hand and swiftly tied it around the man's mouth, making the knot tight. He grunted as she jerked on the knot to test it. Jit stepped forward and relieved the sergeant of his dagger, which had been secured to a belt that was around his ankles. He wasn't carrying a sword.

"Remember me?" Jit said as she stood up, moonlight shining on her face. "Because I well remember you."

The man's eyes went to her. He gave a nod. Eli could now sense concern coming from him for the first time.

"That's right," Jit said, "I told you I would come for you and now I have."

"Get his pants up," Mae said impatiently to Jit. "We need him to be able to move on his own and I don't feel like carrying him."

Without ceremony, Jit pulled the pants up and tied the leather belt securely in place. Eli stepped away a couple of feet and into the light as Mae turned the man around and grabbed both of his arms, roughly pulling them back behind him. She began tying his wrists together with rope.

The sergeant's eyes widened as his drink-addled brain began working and he saw who else had captured him. He looked between Eli and Mae, clearly realizing for the first time that both were High Born. A moment later, he began to tremble and then shake in fear.

With a disgusted look thrown to the sergeant, Jit moved past them, toward the corner of the building. She looked out onto the street, first left, then right. The door to the tavern opened.

"Boys, I'll be back after I drain the dragon," a man shouted.

Eli turned to face the end of the alley. Jit retreated two steps and leaned back into the shadows, against the corner of the building, almost where he had been a short while before. At the same time, she drew her sword.

Eli glanced at Mae. There was simply no time to hide what they were doing. Things were about to get complicated. He saw that recognition in her gaze. Fortuna had taken a hand in events.

So be it, Eli thought as the door banged closed and another man came around the corner, this one burly and staggering badly from drink. He was staring at the ground as he walked. He was humming a tune from the tavern, where the singing had continued without interruption.

He passed Jit without seeing her and came to an abrupt, staggering halt as he suddenly realized he wasn't alone. He looked up and took in Eli and Mae standing there in the moonlight with the prisoner, likely the man's sergeant. He blinked several times before straightening.

"Shay...what goes on here?" His speech was slurred heavily by drink. "What are yoush doing?"

"Hello, friend," Eli said congenially and stepped forward, holding both daggers well out to his sides. "I assure you, this is most certainly, exactly what you think it is."

The man's eyes narrowed, and he moved to draw his sword. As he did, Jit came up behind him and hit him hard with the pommel of her sword in the back of the head. It was a strong blow and made a solid clunking sound that caused Eli to wince. The soldier tottered a moment, before his eyes rolled back in his head and, like a felled tree, he collapsed forward, landing heavily in the slop of the alley.

He did not move.

"That went well," Eli said to Mae. He pointed his curved dagger at Jit. "I'm glad we decided to bring her along."

"As if you had a choice," Jit said, stepping forward and crouching next to the soldier she had just brought down. She felt at his neck for a moment and looked up. "He's still breathing."

Eli thought she sounded slightly disappointed. With no little amount of effort, Jit rolled the big soldier over and began searching him.

"What are you doing?" Eli asked, curiously.

"What does it look like I am doing? Taking his purse." Jit came up with it. She smiled in triumph and waved the purse before him. It jingled heavily with coin. "When they find him, it will appear like a simple robbery. With luck he won't even remember us being here."

"I like your thinking," Eli said.

"Perhaps we should just kill him," Mae suggested. "That way he will tell no tales."

"No," Eli said firmly. "A robbery is a more plausible explanation. Kill him, and it might rouse his comrades to take their vengeance out on the townspeople. I would not have that on my conscience. Worse, it could put Lord Edgun's men on guard, possibly making our task of finding Rivun'Cur more difficult."

"I agree," Jit said.

"Well, we're wasting time talking about it," Mae said. She had a firm grip on their prisoner's arm. In her other hand was her sword. "If we don't get moving, there will be more company before long."

Eli gave a nod and stepped closer to their prisoner, who eyed them warily. He was still shaking with fear.

"Now, my friend," Eli said, "we are going to take you for a little walk. Once we are away from town, you will answer our questions. Cause any trouble, try to draw attention or run, and I promise we will end your pathetic excuse for a life in a heartbeat, no matter the consequences to the civilians in this town. If you cooperate, we might even let you go." Eli waved his wickedly curved dagger before the man's face. "Understand me?"

Eyes almost impossibly wide, he gave a nod.

"Excellent that we understand one another." Eli looked back on Jit, then on Mae. "It seems we're ready. Let's get going."

CHAPTER ELEVEN

Jit threw their prisoner face-first roughly to the ground in the clearing. Hands tied behind his back and unable to catch himself, he landed hard with an audible "umph."

Looking back up at them resentfully, the sergeant rolled onto his side. He took a moment to crack his neck before shifting into a sitting position. It was clear to Eli that the man was now completely sober. There was anger and hate in his eyes as he glared back at them. The fear was still there, but he had managed to regain a semblance of himself in the short time it took to travel from the town, across the fields, and into the cover of the forest.

They had brought their prisoner back to a small clearing Eli had selected. It was a hundred yards into the trees, with thick cover between them and the town. If it came to it, there was little chance anyone would hear screaming.

Mae had remained behind at the edge of the tree line to make certain they had not been seen and followed. She would stand watch on the town while they asked their questions, at least for a time. When she judged it safe, she would join them.

A few feet away from the sergeant and near the edge of the clearing, Eli dropped down to a crouch. He fixed his gaze upon the man, knowing it would be intimidating. Humans viewed the High Born not only with respect, but fear. In truth, humans feared that which they did not fully understand. The High Born did not suffer from such an affliction.

Illuminated fully by the moonlight, the sergeant's face was marred by multiple scars. The old wounds had made his face ugly, brutish even. His nose had been cut badly at the bridge, leaving a thick patch of twisted skin and a noticeable indent. His forearms showed the telltale marks of extensive arms training, years' worth.

Eli had no doubt the sergeant was a tough old veteran, *old* for human soldiers. Over the years, Eli had known many just like him. They were the glue, indispensable men, that held human military formations together during the worst moments.

After a few moments of scrutiny, Eli decided the sergeant was putting up a brave show as he glared at Jit. His jaw worked against the leather gag, as if he were attempting to saw his way through it.

"Miggs," Jit said to Eli.

"What?" Eli asked, not understanding what she was telling him.

"His name is Miggs and he's a bastard, one of Captain Jesset's sergeants. I encountered him in Taibor. Actually, I tried to kill him. His men arrived. I was forced to run."

Eli thought that last admission was a painful one. She was clearly a person who did not enjoy running from a fight. But Eli knew that, to survive, one did what one needed to, even if that meant legging it to fight another day.

"When Lord Edgun's men arrived in Taibor and rounded everyone up, this man pulled me away from the others," Jit continued, in a tone that leaked with anger, mixed with embarrassment and self-condemnation. "His intention was to rape me. I did not give him the chance."

Miggs stilled as he glared up at Jit. She regarded him for a long moment, then quite deliberately dropped her hand to the axe secured to her side. She gripped the axe head and lifted it up and out from her belt. His eyes warily followed her move.

"No one takes me without permission," Jit said, her eyes still upon their prisoner. She sucked in a light breath. "You may not have ordered it, but you are responsible for what happened to Taibor just the same. You murdered everyone in that town."

Jit tossed the hand axe up into the air, spinning it. The dull metal glinted in the moonlight. She deftly caught the shaft a heartbeat later, seeming to snatch the spinning axe right out of the air. At that moment, Eli knew without a doubt she was just as proficient with the axe as with the sword, perhaps more so. He could feel the anger directed at Miggs. It radiated forth as if it could be touched, felt.

Unconsciously, Eli reached down to the doll tucked into his belt. He felt a stirring of his own anger at what had been done to the little girl and the rest of Taibor. She was but one more life cut tragically short.

He had seen such things before and was no stranger to suffering and horrible deeds. Just the same, it never ceased being painful. He forced his anger back in check. Eli reached for his core, his center, something every ranger was taught to do. He allowed a sense of calm to flood his being. With it came perspective, one gained only after experiencing centuries of life, both the good times and the bad.

"We need answers from him," Eli said in Elven. "No matter how we feel about what he and his people have done, intelligence is the priority."

"I understand," Jit replied tersely in the same tongue, without turning to look. Her gaze still fixed upon the sergeant, she switched back to Common. "Miggs, I'd readily send you onto the afterlife." She hesitated, as if the next part was particularly difficult. "Fortune, however, favors you. I guess you could say this is your lucky night. We need information." She stopped again, allowing that to sink in. "Tell us what we want to know, and I will keep him"—she pointed at Eli with the axe—"and his friend from killing you for seizing one of their own."

The man's gaze shifted, and Eli read doubt, uncertainty, and worry in his eyes. Eli glanced over at Jit. Her entire being was focused on the sergeant. It was as if she were a predator who had gone too long without a meal, and Miggs was the prey. Initially, Eli had thought to conduct the questioning himself but decided to allow her the honor. Besides, her approach had the chance to work, and she had already taken the lead.

"He is your prisoner," Eli said in Elven. "Get what we need."

Jit glanced over, gave a nod, and turned back to Miggs.

"Now," Jit said to the sergeant, "I am going to remove the gag. No one will hear you this far out into the forest. That said, scream, call out—I hurt you. Lie to me and I will hurt you. It's that simple. Do we understand each other?"

Miggs did not move or make any type of reply. He was staring at Jit, hate pouring forth from his gaze.

Jit's tone became dangerous. "I asked"—she took a step closer—"if you understood."

Miggs hesitated a heartbeat, then gave a nod. Eli knew it for what it was, a show of resistance, nothing more. Their prisoner was a tough character. He had been through and seen a lot. He suspected Jit understood as well.

She bent down and hooked the edge of her axe into the leather gag. With a strong and rapid jerk, she ripped the gag violently away. The leather snapped, making a cracking sound as it broke.

"Bitch," Miggs hissed. He moved his jaw around, clearly working out the pain. A trickle of blood ran from his mouth down his chin. "You will pay for that. You both will."

Jit did not reply.

Miggs abruptly drew in a deep breath and yelled, "Help me! Help—!"

Without hesitation, Jit kicked him hard in the stomach. He gave a heavy grunt and curled into a ball as the wind was driven forcibly from his lungs. Jit took a step back and away.

"As I said, I will hurt you. Inflicting pain on others has never bothered me, especially when it comes to those who have earned it."

After struggling for several moments, Miggs managed to suck in a ragged, gasping breath. When he recovered, he stared daggers up at her. But he did not attempt to cry out again.

"You're a vile bitch," Miggs growled, "who doesn't know her place."

"My place is where I choose it to be," Jit said firmly. "You and no one else has a say in what I do or where I go. Your first mistake was assuming that not to be true."

"The men I left should have hunted you down and killed you. I knew I should have stayed and seen to it myself."

"They failed," Jit said. "They're all dead."

"You lie," Miggs breathed.

"She speaks the truth," Eli said quietly. "The men you left behind in Taibor are no more than fodder for the worms."

In disbelief, Miggs looked between them. "All?"

Eli gave a nod.

"Bitch." Miggs spat at Jit and missed. It landed next to her boot. "Some of those boys were my friends."

"They should have kept better company, then." Jit waved the axe before her. "Now, if you like, you can suffer more pain, or you can start answering my questions."

"Fuck you, bitch," Miggs said.

Jit kicked him again. As she did, he lashed out with a leg, aiming for hers, only it wasn't there. She had clearly been expecting such a move. Jit dodged the attack by jumping over his kick. When she landed, she immediately lunged forward and lashed downward, striking him viciously across the side of the head with the flat portion of the axe. It made an ugly thudding sound that caused Eli to wince.

The blow, which was powerfully delivered, knocked Miggs to the ground, hard. He lay there for a long moment, blinking, as blood ran from his temple. Stunned, he groaned, then rolled back and forth on the forest floor, clearly in great pain.

"Bloody gods, above and below," he gasped.

"Are you ready to start talking?" Jit asked. "Or would you like more? I assure you I am quite skilled at hurting people."

"Screw you," Miggs groaned, voice strained by the pain as he sat back up. Doing so was a struggle for him. He shook his head as if to clear it.

"Ah," Jit replied, as if considering. "I think I'll pass on that. I thought I made that clear during our last meeting."

Still squatting, Eli decided he was content to let Jit handle things, at least for the moment.

"Once they discover I'm gone, people will come looking," Miggs said through gritted teeth. "You will be hunted down like the dogs that you are."

Jit gave a shrug to show she did not much care.

"Let's begin again," Jit said. "I ask the questions and you answer. Lie or refuse to tell us what we want to know and there will be more pain. I am going to assume you understand."

Miggs said nothing, just glared hatefully at her.

"I will give you a guess as to my first question."

Miggs looked as if he might refuse to answer, then he glanced over at Eli, who simply stared back, giving the man nothing. A look of calculation stole over the sergeant.

"You want to know where your companion is?" Miggs asked Jit. "I might know."

"Tell me," Jit said.

"What's in it for me?"

"I can let the elves have you. I am certain they won't be so gentle."

Miggs looked to her before glancing over at Eli again.

"I would answer," Eli said in Common. "Do yourself a favor."

"If I do, I want your word you won't kill me," Miggs said to Eli. "I will tell you everything you want to know. In exchange, I want to be freed. I've heard elves don't lie. Give me your word and I will sing like a bird."

Jit looked over at Eli sharply. Eli ignored her as he stared back at Miggs. He sensed the man would tell the truth if he agreed to the deal, only Eli did not want to, not after what he had seen in Taibor. He remained silent for several heart-beats, as if considering.

"If you speak true," Eli said finally, "neither I, nor my companion, Mae'Cara, will kill you. When we are done, you will be set free." Jit gave an unhappy hiss. Her grip tightened on the axe. Ignoring her, Eli continued. "Speak an untruth and I will know it, for I am of the High Born."

That last part was not exactly true, but Miggs did not need to know that. Eli's determination of a human being truthful or not was more a character study, watching the human's mannerisms and behavior, than anything else. He had lived and worked amongst the humans for so long, he could usually tell when one deliberately lied to him, especially one under stress.

Eli turned his gaze to her and switched to Elven. "As I said, he is your prisoner."

Miggs looked between Jit and Eli. "I have your word, then? I would hear you say it."

"You have my word," Eli affirmed.

Miggs's shoulders sagged slightly as he relaxed. He shifted his sitting position to get more comfortable. Blood ran freely down the side of his head. It stained the shoulder of his tunic a dark color.

"He's been sent to the mine," Miggs said and looked over at Jit. "Your elf friend is in the mine."

Eli did not like that, for the underground was no place for one of his kind. Just the thought of being underground for an extended period of time made Eli uneasy.

"Why?" Jit asked. "Why send him there?"

"I heard he wouldn't answer Lord Edgun's questions," Miggs said. "So, he was sent to the mine to reconsider. He was to be given a taste of what his future would be like if he did not cooperate. Tomorrow morning, he will be pulled out and Lord Edgun will question him again." Miggs hesitated, then plunged on. "I understand the lord will not be as gentle as the last time. At least, that's the word that's going 'round. Edgun always gets what he wants in the end. Everyone breaks."

"What does he want with Rivun'Cur?" Jit asked.

"I don't know," Miggs said, "and I don't fucking care. Now, I've done my part. I've told you what you wanted to know. Let me go."

Jit raised the axe.

"All right. All right," Miggs said hastily. "If I had to bloody guess, it's because he thinks the elf is a spy, a spy for his people." He jutted his chin at Eli.

"Why would he be concerned about my people?" Eli asked. "By seizing a High Born, he risks the Castol's interests as a whole. I don't believe your king would be too pleased to hear of such behavior."

"Edgun doesn't care about the kingdom," Miggs scoffed. "He doesn't give a rotten fig for the king. Fearic is old, sick, and his son is a weakling with no strength. Soon enough, the old bastard will die. Prince Toban won't last a fortnight. Everyone knows that. Lord Edgun wants to be a king. He is preparing to carve out his own kingdom, right here in Brek. All you have to do is look at his castle. A blind man could see it."

"And he is concerned my people will not approve?" Eli surmised.

"Your people's borders are only a day's march away," Miggs said. "He wants to know where you elves stand on the matter. Or, more likely, if you've taken a side."

Now, Eli thought, that was interesting and explained a great deal. He had finally gotten to the heart of the matter. Did the warden know the Castol were preparing for a fight over succession? Did she even care? Was she backing a side? Did Mae know anything about this? How about Rivun'Cur?

"I am telling you the truth," Miggs insisted. "I swear it upon the gods."

Jit looked to Eli.

"He speaks true," Eli said. He read no deception in Miggs's manner.

Jit lowered the axe. "How many guards are there at the mine?"

"You would be a fool to try to go for it," Miggs said, "to free your friend."

"Just tell us," Eli said. "Let us decide what is foolish."

"There's a half company assigned as a guard. At least a hundred men. Most will be on the surface. There's a wall around the barrack and mine, with sentries. Might as well just forget it."

"Why so many?" Jit asked.

"Is that a serious question?" Miggs asked, looking between them. There was real astonishment in his gaze. "You mean you don't know?"

"Tell us," Jit said in a hard tone. She tapped the axe head against her palm. Miggs did not miss the movement.

"First, it's to keep the slaves in line. Then there's that bastard Karenna. His band have been raiding in these parts. We lost several men close to the town in the last few days. Two entire companies are out in the field hunting for him as we speak. Even so, it's why we don't usually venture out at night, and if we do, we go in force. The mine has been fortified to keep Karenna from freeing the slaves. He'd have to assault the walls of the fort, and I don't see that happening. His band is not that organized, let alone trained."

"Who is Karenna?" Jit asked.

"I can't believe you haven't heard of him. He's a bandit and thorough bastard of a man. He and his attacks are the reason Taibor was razed. If they capture one of ours, they torture him to death and then leave pieces around Brek for us to find." Miggs spat in disgust, then gave a shrug of his shoulders. "So, a message was sent in return, one he can't ignore. Lord Edgun will see him dead before this is done and over or all the villages that are supporting him will see similar treatment. The locals will eventually get the message that you don't fuck with us. And if they don't wise up, what happens to them at that point is their fault."

Eli leaned back slightly, thinking on what he had just learned. Missing pieces of the puzzle were falling into place. It now seemed Rivun'Cur had been in the wrong place at the wrong time. He had been swept up in events as Edgun's heavy hand had seen a predictable result. The people were beginning to push back. Karenna was likely more than a bandit, a local hero to the people and leader of a budding revolt that would, given time, turn into a full-fledged rebellion.

"Where is Rivun'Cur being kept?" Eli asked, deciding to return to the subject at hand, the one that mattered to him.

"In the mine," Miggs said. "All of the slaves are held there. They're never allowed to leave. Most don't ever see the surface or the sun."

"Do you know how many slaves work the mine?" Eli asked. Before Lord Edgun, the miners had been free men. Things had changed greatly since he had last been through this region. He had heard of slave mines in the empire. A person consigned to such labor measured their lifespan in months and sometimes even weeks.

"No," Miggs said. "I don't. I've never been there and don't want to go. I've heard it's far from a happy place. A lot of people have been sent to dig the copper. Lord Edgun is the power in these parts. Cross him and there are consequences. The mine is just one of the better punishments."

"He is a minor power," Eli said quietly, thinking that he definitely needed to have a conversation with Edgun. The sooner that happened the better.

"He is the only power," Miggs responded.

"Not anymore," Eli said, feeling the sudden urge to be off. He looked to the north, in the direction of the copper mine. If they moved quickly, before the sun came up, they might catch most of the guards sleeping. There might even be the opportunity to break into the mine and free Rivun'Cur before anyone knew that they were there.

"Do you have all you need?" Jit asked with more meaning than her simple question.

"I have enough to work with," Eli said, looking back, knowing what she was asking. A wave of sadness came over him. He forced the feeling aside as Jit turned on Miggs, her face hardening. She raised the axe as she stepped forward, clear menace in her intent. With his hands tied, Miggs tried to scoot away from her.

"You said you would let me live," Miggs said to Eli.

"No, I said I would not kill you." Eli hardened his heart. "I never spoke for Jit. That is not my place and you both have unfinished business."

"You swore to let me go. You promised."

"In a manner of speaking, I am letting you go. You willingly serve and support a man with a black heart. Lord Edgun crossed a line when he took Rivun'Cur. We do not take such things lightly. Besides, you have earned your fate, especially after Taibor."

"No," Miggs breathed in horror, scooting back on his butt to put distance between himself and Jit. He turned his gaze from Eli to Jit as she advanced upon him. He took a panicked breath, which was followed by a deeper one. Within a heartbeat, he seemed to calm himself, apparently realizing with utter certainty there was no escaping his fate. He became still as he watched his personal doom approach.

"I am shield-maiden to Reginheri, the greatest leader of my people. Through no fault of my own, I have traveled far from my homeland, my people, and all that I knew. I swore vengeance and blood debt to my gods, who are not known in these lands, but are kept by me. With your deliverance, Thor has directly answered my prayers." Jit raised the axe higher as she gazed down upon Miggs, eyes fierce, almost blazing.

"I am not afraid of death, bitch," Miggs said in a hard tone, meeting her gaze. "I always knew it would come for me. *When* was the question. Do it and be done. Stop wasting my time."

Jit gave a grudging nod at his bravery. "This is for Taibor and for trying to take me without permission."

The hand axe came down hard and bit deeply into the side of his throat. Blood sprayed outward and across Jit's face. Miggs collapsed heavily to the ground and thrashed about as blood spurted in short jets from the terrible wound she had inflicted. His eyes bulged as his lifeblood left his body. After several moments, the jets of blood grew weaker, as did his thrashing about, until the blood just flowed, sullenly pouring out and pooling onto the forest floor. Miggs fell still. Jit stepped back as the dead man gave a final twitch of the legs and moved no more. His eyes, impossibly wide, stared straight up at the sky.

Looking down upon the man she had just killed, Jit reached a finger up to her face. She ran it down her bloodied cheek, then touched her fingertip to her tongue.

She said something in a language Eli had never heard. He recognized only the word Thor.

"Though he died like a man, he deserved worse," Jit said quietly, switching to Elven, without looking over. "He should have suffered more."

Eli did not say anything. He waited, for he sensed she had more to say.

"I misled you somewhat," Jit said, looking over. There were tears brimming in her eyes. "I did not want to run, to seek flight. When this bastard"—she gestured with the bloody axe—"took me behind a lodge to have his way with me, I overpowered him. They must have heard us struggling, for I was about to kill him when his comrades arrived. There were so many. I should have stayed. I should have finished him off and fought for Taibor, for Rivun'Cur, and met death with honor. It is my great shame that I did not. Instead, I ran, like a little scared and unblooded girl. I ran and the village was burned that night." Jit fell silent for several heartbeats. When she spoke next, her tone had hardened. "The next morning, I began taking vengeance upon those who had been left behind to finish looting the town. That is when you found me. They thought they were hunting me, only it was the other way around. I was hunting them, meting out my revenge."

Gazing upon her, Eli sensed a great sadness within that encompassed more than just Taibor. Here before him was a tortured soul, someone who had suffered and, unlike Miggs, deserved better.

"Instead of running," Eli said, "if you would have fought at that moment, would you have died?"

Jit gave a nod. "Their numbers were more than I could handle."

"Then you did the right thing," Eli said simply.

"How can you say that?" Jit asked, anguish plain. Her voice caught as she spoke the next part. "Death would have been the honorable path."

"There was no possible way you could have saved the village or Rivun'Cur by remaining to fight. Honor aside, any such attempt would have been a sacrifice without meaning." Eli took a moment, gathering his thoughts before he continued. "I have lived many of your lifetimes and seen much in my time, including other Taibors—more than I care to recall. There are nights where I am unable to sleep. I watch the sun set and rise, all the while recalling past horrors I have witnessed and been unable to stop." Eli took a breath. "I myself have had to run, when I wanted nothing more than to stand my ground and fight. Instead, the best I could do was hand out what little justice I could, when I could. Jitanthra, I do not know your god, Thor, or of your people. But the ways of all gods are mysterious. Their will is not always apparent. Is it possible Thor meant for you to run? To live for another day? Perhaps he has a plan for you yet."

"A plan?" Jit asked, not sounding quite convinced.

"You swore to avenge yourself upon Miggs and others," Eli said. "Tonight, he was delivered into your hands. It was a start, but justice was served here in this clearing."

Seeming to consider his words, Jit glanced at the body.

"Life is a journey," Eli added, "death a destination. I have a feeling Thor means for your journey to continue, otherwise ..."

"I would be feasting in Odin's halls at this moment," Jit finished in a near whisper as she continued to stare at Miggs's body. "You have given me much to think on. Thank you for that."

Eli did not reply but turned his head as Mae stepped into the clearing. She stopped, herself staring at the body, then looked between them, before settling on Jit. Mae's expression cried of disapproval and disgust.

"Why have you killed him?" Mae asked Jit. "He was our prisoner."

"We have what we need," Eli said, before either could speak. He stood and turned to face Mae. "Were we followed?"

"No," Mae said. "There has been no call of alarm from the town. They may have not even found the man she took down and robbed."

Eli looked up at the sky. The moon had moved, but it was still almost completely overhead. They were running out of time. "They are keeping Rivun'Cur in the copper mine. We need to get there before dawn and"—he glanced at the body—"before this one is missed, or we may lose the element of surprise."

"A mine is no place for the High Born." Mae's tone was filled with sudden concern.

Without answering, but silently agreeing, Eli picked up his bow, where it rested against a tree, and his bundle of arrows. He started off in a jog, heading northward. Looking back, he saw Mae and Jit were following a few yards behind him. Using the moonlight, he increased his pace through the forest. Dawn was only a few hours off and they were in a race against time now.

CHAPTER TWELVE

L etting go one hand at a time, Eli shifted his grip from the rope to the top of the wall. He could feel the rough, hacked edges of the log against his palms. Making as little sound as possible, he pulled himself up and over the wall. His feet came down silently upon the walkway just behind, which was little more than planked boards that had been nailed together.

He crouched down under the top of the wall, doing his best to become one with the shadows.

Surprisingly, the sentries manning the walls were standing around the few torches that had been lit. It was as if they were afraid of the darkness. They were not even walking the walls, performing their rounds, or gazing outward for trouble.

Three men were less than a hundred yards away, standing next to a torch, facing one another, clearly talking amongst themselves. Their lapse in basic security and attentiveness was an unforgiveable breach.

Eli did not begrudge them for their incompetence. In truth he was grateful for their lack of sense and discipline. It had made sneaking into the fort a relatively easy affair. These men who had been posted to guard the mine were clearly not amongst Lord Edgun's finest.

With barely a sound, Mae dropped down next to him. He could hear Jit making her way up the wall, her feet scraping against the thick logs as she climbed. Jit was over in moments and sank down to a knee next to them.

Eli watched the guards in view carefully. None had moved or looked around, let alone gazed curiously their way. They had clearly heard nothing. That was good, very good.

He turned and grabbed the rope, which had been tied into a loop on the end. He lifted the loop off the top of the log, which was just one of hundreds that made up the outer wall of the fort.

The end of the log had been thoughtfully sharpened into a near point. Once they had found some rope, the point had made scaling the wall almost easy. He dropped the rope back over the other side and into the darkness.

"Why'd you do that?" Jit hissed at him. "That rope was our way out. It's a fifteen-foot drop down to the other side into that trench with spikes at the bottom."

"If I had left it," Eli replied in a whisper, "and one of the guards had found it, they would have raised the alarm. I would prefer to get in and out, without them discovering we were here, at least until we are long gone."

She gave a reluctant nod of her head, then something clearly occurred to her. She scowled at him. "Why not just bring the rope with us, then, or stow it somewhere until we need it again?"

Eli stared at her for a long moment, wishing he had thought of that himself. He mentally kicked himself, then gave a shrug. That was now water under the bridge, and it was just one more challenge to overcome. And challenges made life exciting.

"Such thinking would have been helpful a short while ago," Eli said, "you know—before I dropped the rope back over the other side."

Jit gave him a hard look as he glanced around the interior of the fort. It was dark and silent. There were no watch-fires within, only a handful of torches mounted along the walls where the sentries were located.

"Is he always this maddening?" Jit whispered to Mae.

"Most times, he's worse."

The sky had finally clouded up and was doing a solid job of hiding the moon. The air had become humid, which potentially signaled a coming rain. An hour ago, Eli would have been pleased and even welcomed it. Now, the cloud cover made things harder to see, even for him.

Still, he could make out four buildings and the far wall of the fort. One of the structures he recognized as the place where the entrance to the mine had been originally located. He reasoned it was likely still there. They had just built a structure over it. Another off to the right looked to be a storehouse. The largest building was two stories and clearly a barrack. There were no lights coming from its windows, but smoke from a solitary chimney drifted up and into the night sky. Positioned behind the barrack was what looked like an open structure of some sort, with a roof. In the darkness, he could not tell what it was used for.

"It's a wonder you took him as a mate," Jit said.

"What?" Mae asked, astonishment creeping into her tone. "He is most certainly not my mate," she hissed back in outrage. "He is my partner."

"Oh," Jit said, "is that what you elves call it? Well, such things did not ever come up in conversation with Rivun. He never spoke on elven relations."

"Elven relations?" Mae was thoroughly scandalized. "You think we are together?"

"You both talk like a married couple," Jit said, "so, yes."

Eli grinned at Jit. "I am liking you more with every passing moment. I truly am."

Like Mae, Eli had left his bow behind and outside the fort. He drew one of his daggers before Mae could continue. Mae already had her sword out. They needed to move and get out of sight.

"Come on," Eli said, then deliberately looked over at Mae. It was difficult to resist a smile. "This way, *partner.*"

Her gaze hardened as he dropped down from the walkway and to the ground three feet below. The interior of the fort was mostly dirt, with a scattering of grass and weeds. It wasn't well maintained, not like an imperial fort would have been, which reinforced his belief that the soldiers posted here were not of the finest quality. That gave him hope they might be able to get in and out without too much trouble.

Resisting the temptation to glance back at Mae, he started across the open area and toward the entrance to the mine, moving quickly and as soundlessly as possible. He sensed Jit and Mae following.

Their movement did not seem to catch the attention of the sentries, as they made it all the way to the structure built over the mine. There was no cry of alarm, which Eli thought incredible.

"Is this too easy?" Mae asked in a hushed tone as she placed her back against the wooden wall of the building next to him. "Or is it just me?"

"Don't jinx us," Eli hissed back. "Questioning good fortune tends to bring on the bad. I don't think we need Fortuna to take an interest in what we are doing here, do you?"

"Would the opposite logic work then?" Mae asked. "Do you think wishing for some trouble or more difficulty might be helpful? I could try it, if you like?"

"Like Jit, I am starting to enjoy your company more with each passing day, *partner.*"

Mae's eyes flashed dangerously at him. Eli grinned. He loved moments like this, doing dangerous things, but also poking at Mae, getting a rise out of her. He moved over to the door and gripped the handle with his free hand. He looked back on Jit, who had moved up right behind him, and met her gaze, then looked meaningfully toward Mae. She gave him a nod to proceed.

Eli steeled himself for what was to come. He lifted the handle and opened the door. The hinges squeaked slightly. Dull candlelight from inside spread out onto the ground at his feet. He stepped inside and saw a sleepy guard sitting at a table with a mug and a ledger before him, along with several wax tablets.

There was a thin candle burning on the table. A trail of smoke rose from it toward the ceiling. The man had clearly been reading by candlelight. He looked up and blinked in apparent astonishment. Eli did not give him the chance to cry out. In a smooth motion, he threw his dagger. It flew true, embedding itself deep into the man's throat.

Eyes wide in shock and pain, the man staggered to his feet in surprise, kicking his stool back and over. Gagging and drowning on his own blood, he grabbed feebly for the hilt of the dagger sticking from his throat and made to pull it out. Eli was across the small room in a flash, before the soldier could make more noise. Eli grabbed his opponent firmly by the shoulder with one hand holding him in place and the other forcing the man's shaking hands away from the dagger. He gripped the hilt and, in a heartbeat, completed his work, ripping open his victim's throat. With a final powerful jerk of the blade, Eli severed the man's spine.

Feeling some regret at having killed, Eli lowered the dead man gently to the floor as Mae moved by him, heading for a small hallway that led off the room and deeper into the building. Jit stepped inside and closed the door behind her.

Eli spared one more look down upon the man he had just killed. The feeling of regret at taking a life intensified. He forced it away and then studied their surroundings. The room seemed to be some sort of administrative office, or perhaps even a guardhouse. Crates were stacked against the left wall, as were two brooms. A rack of weapons, mostly long swords, lined the right wall. There were at least two dozen of the blades.

Eli heard a strangled gagging sound from down the hallway and moved to investigate. The passage ahead was dark and silent. A few steps brought him to a door that led to a small room on the left. He peered inside.

An oil lamp had been left burning on a table in the room. There were two cots, one along the left wall and another on the right. A man lay dead on the left cot. His throat had been slit from ear to ear. Blood slicked the floor under and around the cot. Mae was over the other one, straddling the man there, holding him down.

She had a hand covering that man's mouth and had plunged her dagger deeply into his side. She pulled it out and stabbed a second time. The man jerked, groaned, and kicked violently at her. One of his hands reached up and around Mae's back and found her braided hair. He seized on it and pulled, snapping her head back.

Before Eli could even react or move to help, gritting her teeth, Mae brought the dagger up and drove it into his neck. Working the dagger rapidly around, she sawed the throat open. Blood spurted everywhere, fairly coating her as it sprayed outward. A handful of heartbeats later, her opponent released his hold on her braid. His hand fell away to hang loosely over the side of the cot. He kicked once more, then fell still.

Letting out a relieved breath and straightening, Mae looked around and spotted him. Eli plainly read the horror in her eyes and felt terrible regret for her. Being a ranger was no easy job. It certainly wasn't for the faint of heart either.

"He woke," Mae whispered as she wiped blood from her face with the back of her arm, "while I was silencing the other." She fell quiet for a heartbeat. "I do not enjoy killing."

"No one does," Eli said plainly before turning away and stepping back out into the hallway.

Jit had appeared with the candle. She moved past him and started down the hallway. Eli followed and they soon found themselves in a larger room. No one was there. Two piles of rock sat between what looked like a heavy metal door that lay across the floor on his right and an even larger two-sided trapdoor on the left, this one wood. A large pulley system hung over the trapdoor. The metal door had a handle for opening.

"Grab a torch, would you?" Eli asked Mae, pointing to a line of torches that lay against the wall. She picked one up and held it out to Jit, who touched the flame of her candle to the business end. The torch flared to life, hissing loudly in the silence. The light in the room grew and illuminated an oversized sliding door to their left. Eli assumed that was how they got the ore out and, with the pulley system, how they hauled it up to the surface.

He stepped forward toward the metal door in the floor. A thick bar lay across it, locking into a frame to either side. The bar was hinged. Eli unlocked the bolt and, trying to make as little noise as possible, swung the bar to the side. He gripped the door's handle and pulled.

It was heavy and at first did not budge. He put more effort into it, muscles straining. The door began to move. A blast of cold, musty air shot up from underneath. Eli thought that almost ominous. Thankfully, the hinges were oiled. The door did not squeal as he had expected. It sort of groaned instead as he strained. When he got it fully open, Jit helped him lower it to the ground on the other side without additional noise.

"Steps," Mae said, holding the torch out and looking down into the darkened hole. "It looks like they lead to the underworld itself."

A chill breeze continued to blow up from the underground. The torch hissed in protest and guttered wildly, casting shifting shadows along the walls around them.

"In a manner of speaking, it does lead to the underworld," Eli said as he took the torch from her, "and we're going down there to find Rivun'Cur."

Holding the light out before him, Eli started down the stairs. He stopped and turned to Jit, who was preparing to follow.

"Remain here," Eli said to her. "Stand watch. Silence anyone who comes into this building. Come get us immediately after."

Jit looked about to argue, then clearly thought better of it. It was as if she did not enjoy being ordered around. She gave a firm nod.

"I will remain. Any who come, I will kill."

"Hopefully, we won't be too long." Eli turned away and continued down the steps. He felt uneasy as he descended into the darkness of the underground. The steps had been carved from stone and were worn smooth at the middle, from years of use and thousands of feet passing through. They were so smooth in places as to be slippery.

The torch provided plenty of light, but Eli still wished he had more. Slowly, taking it one step at a time and listening for any hint of sound ahead, he went deeper. To either side, he could see chisel marks on the walls from those who had long ago carved this passage. He made it twenty steps before the tunnel reached a small landing and turned to the left.

Despite the chill air of the underground, he was sweating and feeling terribly confined. It was as if the walls were slowly closing in on him. That made him feel jumpy, even unsettled. At least, that's what he thought was causing it.

Mae was right behind him. Their steps and breathing were unnaturally loud, magnified by the stone walls. Eli followed the tunnel another thirty feet before he was confronted by a second set of steps that led downward. These were steeper and nearly vertical. They were just as worn as the others and would require careful negotiation. A slip could have serious consequences.

Dull yellow light shone up from the bottom, which he estimated was at least sixty feet away. He could faintly hear noise below, a scraping sound. Someone was down there, possibly more than one person.

He glanced back at Mae. She was pale and, despite seeming unsettled, looked determined, fierce even. There was just something unnatural about the underground. It seemed to weigh heavily upon all High Born, as if the rocks were telling them that they did not belong. In all his years, Eli had never met another elf who had been comfortable being under the surface, in any type of subterranean environment.

He took the steps as quietly as he could, and yet maddeningly, they still made noise, which carried due to the stone all around them.

"Is it morning already?" a groggy voice from below called as they neared the bottom. "That was a quick passing of the night."

A man appeared at the bottom, just feet below Eli. He was wearing armor and had a sword belted to his side. He peered upward. Their eyes met. His seemed almost to bug out in shock. Before the man could react further, Eli jumped the rest of the way down the steep incline. Both of his feet slammed into the soldier's chest plate, hard, throwing his opponent back against the far wall with incredible force. The man's armor made a crashing sound as it connected with the stone, a heartbeat before his unprotected head cracked back against it.

Eli landed hard on his butt. He scrambled to his feet, prepared to fight, as the soldier slid to the ground. Blood streaked down the wall from where the man had slid to a slumped position. He lay there, unmoving.

From the corner of his vision, Eli saw movement. Another soldier, who had been seated on a stool before a table, scrambled to his feet. The man fumbled for his sword, hastily working to draw the weapon.

Before Eli could move, sword in hand, Mae flashed by. She stopped just before the soldier, blade point held at his throat. Weapon half drawn, he froze, his eyes upon the point of her sword, which was leveled before him. He swallowed and slowly removed his hand from the sword hilt. It slid back down into the scabbard, making a clicking sound as the blade went home.

"I surrender." His voice cracked as he held up both hands.

Eli glanced around. Two corridors led off from the room he found himself in. Several stools and a battered table were the only furniture in view. An oil lamp hung from a hook set in a thick wooden beam supporting the ceiling. The lamp provided plenty of light.

The remains of two meals lay on plates on the table, as did a half-eaten loaf of bread. There were also two wooden tankards on the table and a pitcher. A piss bucket sat in the corner to his left. There was no one else in sight. A locked iron-barred gate acted as a door to each of the two corridors that led from the room, reminding Eli of a jail. Both corridors were dark and seemingly silent. Eli suspected Rivun'Cur was down one of them.

"How many more guards are there?" Mae asked in Common.

The man did not immediately answer. He seemed fixated by Mae, frozen by not only fear but amazement, and the sword point at his throat. He was young for a soldier, likely still in his teens. As Mae spoke, he began to shake. The shaking turned to violent trembling. Mae was covered in blood from the two men she had just killed upstairs. It looked like she had bathed in it.

"I asked you a question," Mae said firmly. "Answer me."

"None," the soldier stammered. He seemed frightened almost beyond belief as he looked from Eli to Mae. He started to cry. "Don't kill me—please. You are elves. Don't kill me."

"And you are a true master of observation," Mae retorted. "Where are the prisoners kept? You know the one I want. Tell me."

The soldier, with a shaking hand, pointed toward the corridor on the left. "The last cell. He's alone. I—I did not touch him. I am from Brek. They forced me into the guard last month. I do not want to be here. I'd rather be home with my ma and pa, at the farm."

Mae studied him for a long moment, then glanced over at the locked gate. "For your sake, I hope you can open that gate."

"The key is on the hook, there on the wall there." He pointed. "Take it and your friend. Just don't kill me, please."

Seeing a large iron ring with two keys, Eli moved over to the wall and took it off the hook. Stepping over to the gate, he tried the first key. It did not work in the locking mechanism. The second, with a heavy turn, unlocked the gate. The bolt gave a solid clunk as it moved back.

"Stay here and watch him," Eli told Mae in Elven. "No matter how young he looks or what story he tells you, don't trust him. Right now, he is an enemy. I will get Rivun'Cur."

"Got it." Mae eyed her prisoner closely. "I have him covered."

Bringing the torch with him, Eli moved quickly down the corridor. Every ten feet, there were rusted iron doors to either side. They were no more than pounded sheets of metal, with no window to show what or who was inside. Each was held closed by a simple locking bar. Eli assumed the slaves were locked inside and, sure enough, heard some faint voices wondering what had caused the noise. He could not imagine surviving long under such conditions.

He reached the last door, which was thoroughly rusted over. The corridor continued on into a darkness that seemed a complete void, a black maw where existence ended. Eli shivered at the thought of having to go farther. He was relieved he did not have to.

Sheathing his dagger, he lifted the locking bar out of its place and set it aside on the floor. Eli opened the door.

It squealed and screeched loudly as it moved. The sound echoed painfully off the walls.

Darkness from within greeted him. He held the torch out and took a step inside. A stone rectangular room with a rounded ceiling stretched before him. It was twenty feet deep and five wide.

At the far end was a single sleeping pallet, with a bowl of water set next to it. A bucket for waste was off to the side. Upon the pallet sat an elf with his arms wrapped around his legs. He wore only a rough spun human tunic that was gray in color. Given how cold it was, he must be chilled beyond belief. Shaking from the cold, the elf held his arm up, shielding his eyes against the torchlight as he gazed at Eli.

"Rivun'Cur?" Eli asked as he moved into the room and approached the pallet.

Blinking against the light, Rivun looked up at him. "I expected you to arrive sooner. It certainly took you long enough."

Rivun's voice was strong and firm, which Eli found a relief. It meant he was in better shape than he had expected. As he gazed down upon the outcast, a person who was famous amongst his own people, Eli's anger fired. Rivun had been thoroughly worked over and beaten. There was a patchwork of bruises across his face and exposed arms and legs, ranging from pink to shades of deep purple, cuts too. Rivun's lower lip was split and one of his eyes had swollen shut. Crusted blood covered his tunic.

Beyond his injuries, Rivun had brown hair, was thin like most elves, and would have stood tall. Eli assumed he would have been fair-skinned and attractive, like most of their kind. However, with the treatment he had received, Eli could not be certain of that.

"If I had known I was expected," Eli said in a lighthearted manner, "I would have endeavored to come sooner."

Rivun'Cur gave an amused grunt that caused him to cough. He spat blood onto the floor, then looked back up at Eli. "I am sure I look quite a sight. I assure you, in my time I've had worse beatings."

"Can you walk or will you need assistance?"

"To get out of this hole in the ground, you bet I can walk on my own. I'll even run if I have to." Rivun held out a hand, which Eli clasped firmly then used to haul him to his feet. He held on to make sure Rivun could stand on his own. When he was certain, he released his hold.

"I cannot say I'm too impressed with the accommodations Lord Edgun has provided you." Eli made a show of glancing around the room. He turned his gaze back to Rivun. "For one of the last of the Anagradoom, I would have expected a little better. It shows a lack of respect. Some humans can be so shortsighted."

"This room is rather lacking." Rivun coughed again and spat up a gob of blood.

"We will have to speak to him about that," Eli said, his voice turning deadly, "perhaps even lodge a complaint."

"I do believe I would enjoy that." Rivun eyed him for a long moment. "You are Eli'Far, aren't you?"

"It seems my fame precedes me," Eli said, injecting a pleased note into his tone, though he was surprised that Rivun had heard about him at all.

"I would not call it fame exactly. Garus was a friend. Occasionally he made time to visit when he traveled south. Over more than one campfire, he bitched about you more than anything else. He said you were a regular pain in his backside, but showed potential." Rivun nodded toward Eli's sheath, with the curved dagger. "Besides, that's his old dagger, the one I gave him when he first became a ranger."

Eli glanced down at the blade, even more surprised. "Garus passed it on to me when he stepped down from the Ranger Corps."

"I asked him to do that—when he had seen, or really had enough, of the wider world. It is fitting he gave it to you." Rivun started moving toward the door slowly. He limped as he walked. "Who else came with you?"

"Jit and Mae," Eli said as he followed.

Rivun stopped and turned to face him. "It pleases me greatly to learn Jit made it and that you found her. I have become fond of that human girl."

"She is interesting," Eli said.

"That is an understatement." Rivun moved to turn away, then stopped. "Wait—did you say Mae? You brought Mae'Cara here? The warden's daughter?"

"The warden sent us after the criminal Mik'Las," Eli said, suddenly on guard and alarmed by Rivun's concern. "We learned about what happened from Jit and decided to free you before continuing on with our mission."

Rivun gave an understanding nod, but Eli read serious concern in his manner as he glanced toward the door with a worried expression. "I don't think the warden will be too pleased to learn you placed her daughter in such a dangerous position. Lord Edgun is not what he seems. He has great ambitions."

"She is a ranger," Eli countered. "Danger comes with the job."

"That may be so, but she's also Si'Cara's daughter, her only daughter, and I am certain you know the warden has a temper that exceeds that of her brother, Kol'Cara. She will be pissed when she learns what is going on here."

That gave Eli pause. He recovered quickly. "There's danger and then there's danger."

"Oh really?" Rivun asked wryly.

"What's life without a little excitement now and again?" Eli forced a grin, then turned and moved by Rivun toward the door. He was feeling the pressure to move things along. The sooner they were out of the fort and away, the better. "Come on, let's go. We can worry about Lord Edgun after we get you out of here."

CHAPTER THIRTEEN

With Rivun following a few steps behind, Eli led the way back down the corridor to the guard room. He found Mae standing by the stairs, gazing upward. Her head cocked slightly to the side, as if she were listening for something. A ghost of a frown crossed her face.

The guard was sitting upon a stool, his hands bound behind him. He was staring at the ground and weeping softly, shoulders shaking. It was a pitiful sound. His head snapped up as they entered the room. Tears ran freely down his cheeks as he gazed upon Eli fearfully, then Rivun. He gave a shiver at the sight of the freed prisoner.

Eli glanced over at the man he had knocked into the wall to see if he had awoken. He had not stirred and was in the exact position Eli had left him.

"He's dead," Mae said simply, catching his look. Her gaze moved beyond him, to Rivun'Cur. Eli read not only fascination, but intense curiosity in her gaze. Mae's face tightened and her lips drew into a line as the realization of what had been done to him registered.

"Trust me," Rivun said to her, "I feel much better than I look. You must be Mae'Cara. I knew your mother well, girl, and once considered her a close friend."

"And you are Rivun'Cur, of the Anagradoom," Mae said, "a living legend and willing outcast who follows the God of Shadows."

"Guilty as charged," Rivun said, "though I am not too certain about being a living legend and, now that I think on it, actually following that deity. Think of the arrangement more as a marriage of convenience, with both sides getting something that they desire, but not everything."

Eli glanced over at Rivun, wondering what he meant by that. He decided the subject required more exploration, but at a later time. He turned his gaze back to the dead man.

"I killed him?" Eli asked as he gazed at the body. He had driven the man hard into the stone wall and he had not been wearing a helmet. "I thought I had just knocked him out."

"I checked. You cracked his skull and—" She turned away to look back up the stairs.

"What's wrong?" Eli asked.

"I thought I heard something above, a ringing of some sort, like a bell. It was faint but it is gone now."

"Sounds get distorted down here." Rivun gestured at the man Eli had killed. "I would not feel too sorry about him. He was a real bastard of a jailer. No kindness in that one. He enjoyed his work too much. When he wasn't bothering with me, I heard him abusing and tormenting the slaves. If you had not killed him, I would have done it before long." Rivun turned his gaze on the boy and let out a disgusted breath. "Though he did not lay a finger on me, he was not so friendly either." Rivun glanced back down the corridor where he had been held. "I was becoming resolved to do things the hard way."

"Are you trying to tell me you did not need a rescue?" Eli looked over at Rivun, feeling some uncertainty. Here was one of the storied Anagradoom, a small group of mystical warriors who had long ago willingly exiled themselves from their own people, something that was unheard of amongst the High Born.

That had happened well before Eli had been born. It was said they had been granted occult powers, but what those were, no one knew. Their chosen god, besides that of the High Father, was not quite good nor evil, but somewhere in between.

The powers had supposedly once helped them guard a magical relic of some kind. What that relic had been, Eli did not know.

Such things during the Time of Sorrows were not much talked about. Eli understood that period to be a painful one to his people. They had lost nearly everything. Even his father spoke little on the subject, and what he did say was given not only sparsely, but grudgingly. What Eli had managed to learn he had pieced together on his own over many years of careful listening, and he was still unsure of what was fact or embellishment.

"It looked to me like you were going nowhere," Eli said to Rivun, "at least until I unlocked your cell."

Rivun gave a slight shrug of his shoulders as his gaze moved away from the weeping and fearful boy soldier. It fell upon the table and the food. He moved over, limping badly, and picked up a mug, dumped out the contents on the dusty stone floor, then grabbed the pitcher with a hand that shook from exhaustion or the cold, perhaps a mixture of both.

He peered inside and sniffed before frowning slightly. He poured himself what looked like red wine. Under the lamplight, it was more a dull burgundy than anything else.

Eli knew it was likely terrible stuff, heavily watered-down, with a strong aftertaste of vinegar. Regular soldiers could not afford to purchase good-quality wine, so they typically settled for the horse piss that no one in their right mind wanted, then did their best to guzzle it down at an enthusiastic pace. Eli had never understood that. He would rather choose plain water and risk sickness over drinking poor-quality wine.

Placing the pitcher back down on the table with a heavy clunk, Rivun took a deep drink, tipping the mug back and draining it completely in one go. Letting out a satisfied sigh, he set the empty mug back down on the table next to the pitcher. He grabbed the half-eaten loaf of bread, tore a piece off, and took a healthy bite, chewing ravenously.

"They fed me nothing. You know"—Rivun paused between chews, becoming thoughtful—"hunger is truly the best cook." He glanced with his good eye at the loaf of bread in his hand. "Otherwise, I would never touch this stuff. It is half stale. My mind says it is terrible, but my tongue and stomach tell me otherwise. Imagine that."

"If you like, we can wait for you to finish your meal." Eli gestured toward the stairs with the torch. "I am sure your jailers would be pleased to have you back under lock and key. And if we don't start moving, that will become a reality."

"You think so?" Seeming amused, Rivun glanced at the prisoner.

"What are you saying?" the prisoner asked. He had begun rocking back and forth on the stool. "I didn't mean any of it. Really. I just wanna go home. Let me go. I don't understand what you are saying."

Rivun switched from Elven to Common. "I said you were awful hosts, who do not properly cater to your guests' needs. Seriously, no food, no water. What kind of inn is this?" He looked to Eli, focusing on him with his good eye. "Such an outrage. Honestly, I am quite offended. I should really demand to speak to the proprietor of this establishment."

"Indeed," Eli said dryly in Elven, then made a show of sniffing at the air. "They could have at least drawn you a bath. Perhaps when we leave this place you might consider taking some time to clean up a bit, say a dip or two in the river?" Eli lowered his voice conspiratorially. "Trust me, Mae is easily offended by foul smells and you don't want to get on her bad side."

"The only one that offends me is you, Eli," Mae said.

Eli gave an amused grunt.

"Inn?" The guard seemed confused, looking rapidly between Eli and Mae. "What's he talking about? Has he gone mad? You are going to kill me, aren't you?"

Ignoring their prisoner, Mae continued to speak in Elven. She tilted her head to the side as she looked meaningfully at Eli. "We need to get moving, before someone decides to check in above and discovers Jit, along with the bodies."

"You need not worry. That woman can look after herself," Rivun said. "She is one of the best killers I have ever had the pleasure of knowing."

"No matter how good Jit is, Mae's right," Eli said. "I will help you up the stairs—that is, if you need it. We've wasted enough time here."

"I am not going," Rivun said.

"What?" Eli allowed some irritation and exasperation to leak into his tone. "What did you say?"

"I am not going," Rivun repeated himself.

"What do you mean you are not going?" Eli asked in disbelief.

"Well, I will go, but not right now," Rivun said casually as he chewed. It was as if he did not have a care in the world. "Would you like me to clarify my position?"

"I would love for you to make yourself plain," Eli said.

Rivun stopped chewing as he winced from pain, then, after a heartbeat, resumed, this time more slowly. He leveled a look at Eli. "I am not leaving until we free the slaves—all of them."

Eli gave Rivun a long, hard look. "We came for you, not them. As it is, we are on borrowed time. The sun will be up shortly and there is bound to be a change of guard. When that happens, we will be in real trouble. We do not have time for this, and even if we did, once the prisoners are out on the surface, the guards are bound to notice. That might prove a little inconvenient in effecting an escape."

"Why would you care about human slaves?" Mae asked, sounding confused. "Look what the humans did to you. From what I have seen, they are little better than animals."

Eli almost winced.

"Your words do the daughter of Si'Cara little justice and credit. Mae'Cara, you have a lot to learn about the wider world and, dare I say, life in general."

Mae flushed at the rebuke as Rivun took a hobbling step toward Eli.

He gestured about them, waving the half-eaten loaf of bread about. "You know what it is like down here. Would you willingly leave others to such a fate, even if they are only human?"

Eli glanced back toward the two corridors. One gate was still locked. Eli did not want to be down here one more heartbeat than he needed to be. His skin was fairly crawling at the thought of further delay.

"No," Eli said after a moment's hesitation. "I would not willingly do so. Still, I cannot help but point out we do not have time to assist them. Perhaps we can come back another day."

"No," Rivun said, refusing to be put off. "If necessary, I will free them myself. I would give them a fighting chance.

It is the least they deserve. Anything is better than the fate they have been consigned to."

"Someone's coming," Mae hissed, drawing their attention from the stairs. "Ah, it is Jit."

"Hurry up," Jit hollered down from somewhere above. "The alarm has been sounded. I looked outside. I think the fort is under attack. The guards are going crazy and running for the walls. Most don't even have their armor on, but they're armed."

Eli closed his eyes, took a deep, calming breath, and then opened them again. He let the breath out as thoughts went to Miggs and what he had told them about the rebels. Though it was likely only a harassment raid, he intensely felt the frustration of the moment. It was as Mae had said; things had been too easy. Fortuna had finally stepped in and taken a hand in events.

The entire guard would be up in arms now and mustered by the time they got topside. He turned back to Rivun and stared at him for several heartbeats. For his part, Rivun seemed wholly unconcerned.

"At this moment, I cannot think of anything I would want more than having the garrison woken. Oh wait, they are already up and arming themselves." He paused, glaring hard at Rivun to show his disapproval. "How can we possibly make things worse, draw more attention to ourselves? Say, Rivun, can you think of a way? Oh wait, I can. Let us free the slaves."

"I can see why Garus took a shine to you and wanted you as his trainee." Rivun grinned broadly at Eli, then winced as his swollen lower lip split and a dribble of blood bubbled up from a cut that had recently scabbed over. "We free the slaves. This will work to our advantage."

Ignoring his split lower lip, Rivun took another casual bite of his bread. He still appeared relaxed and thoroughly unconcerned by their predicament, which Eli was beginning to find distracting, maybe even a little maddening.

"I'm not seeing how this can work," Eli said. "The idea was to sneak back out with you and you alone." Eli pointed at Rivun with the torch to emphasize his point. It hissed and guttered as he moved it through the air. "Now that is clearly not possible. They are going to be manning the walls. That means fighting our way out." He jerked a thumb toward the ceiling. "You might not know it, but there is a very large garrison up there."

"If I recall, there are also some weapons upstairs," Rivun said. "At least there were when they first brought me down here. Listen, it is really very simple. We free the slaves and let them fight for their freedom. Then, we slip away in the confusion." He turned to the guard and switched to Common. "How many slaves are kept down here?"

"What? Why do you want to know that?" The soldier's voice trembled as he spoke.

"Just answer my question."

"I don't know for sure. Over a hundred, maybe," he said, his gaze flicking nervously from Rivun to Eli and then back again. "Why?"

"It is not a bad plan," Mae said from the stairs, speaking in Elven. "Freeing the slaves will create quite a distraction, maybe enough of one that we can slip away unnoticed."

Eli felt the situation spinning out of control. No, he had already lost control. Seeing no alternative, he went to the stairs and looked up them. Jit stood at the top, looking down. The candle in her hand illuminated the top of the stairs in a dim yellow light. He glanced back toward Rivun. Eli realized he had been backed into a corner. He physically suppressed his anger, forcing it back down as his frustration intensified to new levels.

"Oh, all right," Eli said to Rivun. "You win. We will free the slaves."

"I knew you would see it my way." Rivun beamed.

"We found Rivun. He is okay," Eli called up to Jit. "Don't let anyone inside. We're going to free the slaves, then we will be up."

"Right," Jit called back, relief flooding her voice. "Hurry. They are bound to check on the mine when someone thinks on it."

"Time to get to work, then." Mae brushed by Eli, moving toward the corridor he'd gone down to free Rivun.

Eli was still holding the ring with the keys and the torch. He looked at Rivun, who was leaning against the table and gazing back at him calmly as he ate the last of the bread. That irritated Eli immensely, for he was the one who was supposed to do the irritating, not others, especially not an outcast.

Eli moved over to the unopened gate and unlocked it. The bolt clunked heavily. He looked back toward Rivun, brightening at the thought of what they were going to attempt.

"You know," Eli said, "whatever happens, it should prove terribly exciting."

"That is how I view things," Rivun said. "We free the slaves and let events take their natural course."

"Start climbing the stairs," Eli said to Rivun as he swung the gate open. "We will catch up."

Rivun gave a nod and started to turn away. "You know, I am not as hobbled as you might think. I can help."

"The limp and beating you took say otherwise," Eli said. "Enough stalling. Now get moving."

Limping badly as he went, Rivun started for the stairs.

"Mae," Eli hollered. "Only open the first door. Let the slaves free themselves, understand? We want to be upstairs before they begin to start working their way up."

"Already way ahead of you," she called back. He heard the grinding of a door from the other corridor as it swung open.

Eli hastily went down the corridor to the first door. He shifted the locking bar aside and swung the door wide. It screeched as it moved.

A man wearing a ragged tunic came to his feet just on the other side. Behind him, many others were huddled together, likely for warmth. The light from the torch only illuminated the first few people, but there were a lot of them packed into the room, which was far larger than the one in which he had found Rivun. They had been locked in complete darkness.

The stench of the room—filth, unwashed bodies, and waste—was awful. It washed over him, as if the smell itself sought escape. He breathed through his mouth to avoid smelling it, and even then, he found he could taste it.

The man before him was unkempt and dirty, with wild brown hair. Ugly sores covered his face, arms, and legs. His tunic was threadbare, ripped, and badly stained. Eli fought the desire to take a step back, for he was likely overrun with vermin. The man instead shied back from the light, as if it were causing him physical pain.

"I am here to set you free," Eli said, switching to the common tongue.

"Free us?" someone said from the mass of huddled humanity behind him. The voice was female, and he could hear the flaring of hope within her tone. "Really?"

"Our prayers have been answered," someone else said. "Thank Kator the Gray."

Someone coughed, and a heartbeat later, a young child began to cry. Under the light, Eli could not see the child. However, his heart, like a leaden weight thrown into a pond, sank. Lord Edgun had sent children to the mine—children.

What kind of a monster did that?

He thought of the doll tucked into his belt and the little girl who had had her life cut short in Taibor. Eli glanced back down the corridor toward the guard room. Rivun'Cur was no longer in sight. The bastard of an Anagradoom had known there were children imprisoned down here. Eli was sure of it. His gaze shifted back to the people before him, and with it, his resolve hardened.

No matter that they were human, their coming fight for freedom had just become his fight. There would be no cutting and running during the confusion, no slipping away. Eli would stand with them until it was all over. Fate had truly intervened.

"Are you willing to fight for your freedom?" Eli asked the man.

"With my bare hands," the man replied firmly, standing up straight. There was steel within that tone. It was as if he were physically shedding the bonds of slavery before Eli's eyes. He held out his dirty hands before him and balled them into fists. "I will fight with my bare hands, nails, and teeth if I have to. If I must, I will claw my way to freedom."

"Good," Eli said. "You may need to. What is your name?"

"Utreek." He lowered his arm and squinted at Eli. "You're an elf. The guards told us they had one of your people. We didn't believe the bastards." He took a step forward and glanced out into the corridor, looking toward the guard room and then down the other way. The torchlight fell off after several feet. "Is that why you came?"

"Yes, that is correct. Utreek, I am Eli. We do not have much time. The fort is under attack and the garrison is distracted. Can you open the doors and free the others?"

"I can," he said firmly.

Eli handed him the torch. "There are some weapons up top. I will see you and the rest up there. Go free your comrades. You will need to fight for your freedom, understand? We will stand with you."

"We?" Utreek asked.

"Me and my companions. Hurry, we do not have much time. As I said, the fort is under attack."

"Thank you for this." Utreek moved past Eli and into the corridor. "Thank you for this chance for—for our freedom. We shall be forever in your debt."

"Just free the others. That will be enough."

"I will. You have my word of honor on that."

"Honor?" Eli spared another glance toward the rest of the people in the room. Several men had come to their feet and were moving toward the doorway. They looked to be nothing more than half-starved scarecrows, but there was a fierceness to them that spoke of desperate determination. "It is difficult to imagine one keeping their honor under such circumstances."

"No matter how bad things get, there is always honor," Utreek said, firmly. "That is what sets us apart from the beasts, the animals."

"Even the ones that enslave you?"

"Not them," Utreek said. "Such men have no honor."

Eli gave a nod and left Utreek to his task. He hastily jogged back to the guard room. There he found Mae already heading toward the stairs. He followed after her.

"Don't leave me," the guard begged from behind. "They'll kill me."

"What about him?" Mae asked, stopping with a foot on the first step. Eli halted as well.

Rivun was already halfway up, hobbling painfully, one step at a time, while placing a hand on the wall for support. He glanced back toward the guard.

"If we leave him," Mae added, "they might kill him."

"Might?" Eli glanced back at the guard. He had stood up and was coming toward them. Two of the slaves emerged, ragged and thin men with hard, intense eyes. They focused on the guard, their hatred becoming apparent.

"And where do you think you're going, Josk?" one of the freed slaves asked as he grabbed the guard roughly by the arm. "You've some explaining to do, son."

"They made me join, Felton," Josk said, his tone panicked. "They made me."

"Is that so?" Felton asked, his tone dripping with disbelief.

"Honest," Josk said. "You have to believe me. I didn't want to. They made me do it all, everything, then stuck me down here."

"That's not what I heard," the other man said, with a dangerous note in his tone. "You turned your pa in, boy, for working with Karenna. All he did was slip Karenna and his band some food from the harvest, nothing that would ever be noticed, and you went and told Lord Edgun."

Felton physically shook Josk. "What was the reward? A few coppers? Maybe a silver? Lord Edgun's men murdered your ma and pa. How can you sleep at night? How can you manage to even live with yourself? And now you are one of our jailers? You are a traitor."

Josk began blubbering incoherently. The other slave spotted the sword that Josk had worn. Mae had propped it up in the corner of the room. He went for it and picked it up. He looked down at the weapon in his hand, as if it were something he had desperately longed to hold. He tested the blade's weight, then turned his cold, hard gaze to Josk.

"He lied," Mae hissed in shocked outrage. "He lied to us. He turned on his own people, his family."

"Yes," Eli said in barely a whisper. He felt another surge of terrible regret, mixed with sadness. His mind flashed to the crying child who had been locked in this tomb. His heart hardened and so too did his tone. "This is no longer our concern. They will decide what to do with him."

"Don't let them have me," Josk pleaded as he struggled against the hold of his captor. Felton punched Josk hard in the face. There was a nasty crunch as the nose broke. He fell back and to the ground, blood covering his face, as more of the freed slaves emerged into the guardroom. Disgust plain, the man who had retrieved the sword advanced on Josk.

"So, Josk," the sword-carrying man said, "betraying your own family, your people—was it worth it?"

Without another look, Mae began climbing the stairs, taking them two at a time. Eli followed. Behind them, their former prisoner began to scream. The sound of it echoed painfully against the walls.

Chapter Fourteen

Eli found Jit by the door. She had it cracked open and was peering outward into the darkness. The candle had been left on the table where Eli had killed the first guard. Undisturbed, the body lay slumped on the floor, surrounded by a halo of drying blood. There was so much blood, Eli could taste the iron in the air.

Indistinct shouting that sounded like orders being given could be heard from outside in the fort. A bell rang frantically, a garish sound that grated on the ears.

"What do you see?" Eli asked as he and Mae moved up behind her. They had left Rivun to work his way slowly up the stairs. Eli had offered to help but had been flatly refused.

"The garrison's out and on the walls," Jit said, without turning. She blew out a long breath. "From what I can see, they are massing at the south wall. So, whatever is happening seems to be focused there."

"The fort's gate is on the east side, right?" Mae asked.

"Yes," Jit answered. "I can't see it from this position."

"Let me see." Eli switched places with Jit. Without opening the door too wide, he peered out into the darkness. The sky had begun to lighten. There was a hint of a blue tinge overhead, where before it had only been darkness. The sky was studded with clouds. The moon was nowhere in view.

He judged they had maybe an hour and a half before daybreak. Since the door was facing the south wall, he had a good view of what was going on there, but not much from the other sides.

Mail chinking with every footfall, two men jogged by, just yards away from the door. Each carried a pair of javelins. One had a helmet on. The other was without and barefoot. Neither had shields. Their relative state of undress told Eli that whatever was happening was serious enough for the garrison to be ordered to the walls without taking the time to properly arm themselves.

Though neither looked his way, Eli closed the door until the two men had passed, then cracked it again and studied everything in view. Fires and torches had been lit along the south wall. Dozens of men had assembled there, representing a good portion of the garrison's strength, which Miggs had told them was around a hundred men. He hoped that was an accurate assessment, for if there were more, things would quickly become difficult.

Most of the defenders had been positioned strategically along the wall, several feet separating each man. They stood, facing outward, their attention focused beyond the south wall. Some were still dressing, putting on armor and boots they had thought to bring with them.

For the most part, the defenders carried shields and spears. Several were armed with bows. What looked to be an officer or perhaps a sergeant was moving behind the men along the fighting platform built behind the wall, his stride confident, bold, and exuding command authority.

After several moments of watching, Eli decided he was a sergeant. His armor did not appear to be as fine as an officer's would have been. He was shouting something that could not be heard over the sound of the bell.

The sergeant stopped next to a man. He said something, patted the soldier on the shoulder in a comforting manner, then continued on along the platform and resumed his shouting. Eli assumed whatever the man was doing was for encouragement, lending his men some of his strength for what was to come.

Two men came into view, moving from the east side of the fort toward the southern wall. Both were fully dressed and wore armor that was more ornate. They walked at a determined pace, but not a rushed one. These were the officers then. They made their way to the wall and climbed up and onto the platform, found an open spot along the wall, and gazed outward.

After a moment, one of the two said something to the other and began gesturing about the fort. The other officer gave a crisp salute and moved off, presumably to carry out his orders.

"Remain here," Eli said to Jit and Mae.

"Where are you going?" Mae asked.

"Out to get a look at the gate, and the rest of the fort," Eli said. "I will be back shortly."

He opened the door a little wider and stuck his head out. He looked quickly left and then right, making sure the coast was clear. Satisfied, he stepped outside and closed the door carefully behind him.

Knowing it was easier to spot someone moving rapidly in the darkness, he slowly made his way to the right, first eyeballing the west wall. He counted only twelve defenders, who seemed more interested in watching what was going on along the south wall than anything else.

Eli wanted a look at the north wall, around the corner of the building. The problem was that there were three men standing less than twenty yards away, talking amongst themselves. They did not have the look or bearing of soldiers and were unarmed.

With the three standing there, he could not risk exposing himself to look around the side of the building. They did not appear to be in a hurry to go anywhere either. Instead, he turned around and made his way to the other side of the building, to see the east wall and the gate. He took a moment to commit it to memory.

Eli peeked quickly around the corner. He could not get a good view of the north wall. There was a large mound of dirt and rock blocking his vision. He retreated slowly back to the door. Eli opened it and slipped inside.

"What did you see?" Mae asked.

"Looks like about two dozen men holding the gate and east wall. Four or five are on the ground behind the gate. They have boards and are actively reinforcing the gate against a possible battering ram attack. The rest are up on the wall. The west wall has twelve defenders. I could not see what was going on to the north."

A horn sounded from outside the fort. It blew a long, low note, followed by two shorter blasts. When the horn fell silent, a massed cheer followed. It rose to a mighty crescendo before falling like a wave crashing onto the beach. Then the cheer came again, louder, more vociferous. It sounded like thousands of banshees screaming wildly.

In the darkness and with the fort's wall in the way, Eli knew the sound could easily be deceptive. Still, he found it impressive, to the point of being unnerving. The sound of it alone sent shivers through him. There was most definitely a significant force out beyond the fort. Whether or not they were capable of storming the walls against a trained and determined enemy was an entirely different matter.

"They are working themselves up to make their assault," Jit said.

As if to emphasize her point, the cheer came again, seemingly louder.

"Then we need to get out of here," Mae said, "and soon. I do not much like the idea of being caught while the fort is overrun."

"We're not going anywhere," Eli told her plainly. "I have made my decision. This is now our fight. We will make certain the slaves are freed. That means we remain until the fort falls."

Mae's expression hardened in disapproval, but she did not object. She had been partnered with him to learn the ways of the ranger, to get hands-on experience.

This was her apprenticeship, the final step before becoming a full-fledged ranger. And when it came to decisions like this one, Eli's word was final. That did not mean she had to like it, and Eli knew she did not. Later, should they survive, he knew he was likely to get an earful. But, in the end, standing and fighting was the right thing to do, even if it came at the cost of their lives.

"That was a heck of a climb," Rivun said, almost breathless, as he hobbled out from the hallway and into the room.

Jit turned and rushed over. She embraced him warmly.

"Easy," Rivun said, "easy there. I have had a rough time of it. Squeeze me harder and I might break."

"I thought I had lost you." Her voice was thick with emotion.

"Never," Rivun said, hugging her fondly back. "It will take more than Lord Edgun and his thugs to kill me."

Still embracing him, Jit leaned back to get a better look at his face. She reached a hand up to his bruised and

ELI

battered right cheek, touching it gently. It was a tender gesture, and yet, he winced at the contact.

"It is not as bad as it looks," he said after a moment. "They wanted to know why we had come north. They thought I was a spy. When I gave them nothing, things got hard."

"I am sorry I could not save you from this," Jit said in a near whisper. "I wanted to, but there were too many."

Another massed cheer sounded, this one just as loud as the others, if not more enthusiastic.

"You came just the same," Rivun said. "That is all that matters. Besides, I would not have you throw your life needlessly away to save a wretch like me."

"You are no wretch, and I should never have left you. I should have died first."

"Do not rush to Odin's hall, for it is not yet your time." Rivun paused a heartbeat as he gazed back into her eyes. He lifted a hand to her cheek and cupped it. "This world would be lessened were your flame to be extinguished before your time. I would keenly feel your loss."

Jit swallowed. "It was hard to run, to leave you. I did not want to go, especially after all we have been through."

"I know. But there are times when one must run to fight another day." His voice hardened and he looked beyond her at Eli. "And today is that day. Today we fight back."

"As Thor and Odin are my witnesses, the enemy will hear my blade sing," Jit said, "as will they yours."

"I am certain that song will be well sung too," Rivun said.

Utreek came up behind them, and with that, Rivun separated himself from Jit's embrace. The man had a sword in hand, likely taken from the soldier Eli had killed down below in the guard room. Others were close behind him, and Eli could hear even more coming up the short hallway that led to the entrance to the mine.

"You were the prisoner?" Utreek said as more of a statement than a question. His gaze roved over Rivun's injuries.

"Yes, I was Lord Edgun's guest, as were you"—he glanced behind Utreek at the others—"and yours. I could not leave without seeing you freed. In fact, I refused to do so. No one should be forced to live under such conditions."

Utreek studied Rivun for a long moment, then laid a hand upon the elf's shoulder and gripped it. It caused Rivun to grimace in pain.

"After today," Utreek said, "I name you a friend. I am Utreek VasKeel, of the Asteredies. I would have your name."

"I am Rivun'Cur of the Anagradoom, and though we just met, I name you also a friend. I look forward to fighting at your side and spilling the blood of your enemies, Utreek VasKeel."

"Very good." Utreek sounded pleased. "After we slaughter all of Lord Edgun's men, we shall drink to our new friendship, yes?"

"Hopefully more than one drink. After what I've been through, I could use it."

"Ha! I think we will get along just fine." Utreek turned his gaze to the door and Eli. "How does it look outside?"

Yet another cheer rose up onto the air. Eli waited for it to subside before he answered.

"There is a force of some kind out there, beyond the walls. As near as I can tell, the defenders are mostly massed around the south wall. An assault seems imminent there. The gate to the fort has about two dozen defenders and they don't seem so concerned about an attack, though they are reinforcing the gate. There is a lesser number on the west wall. I have no idea how many are holding the north."

"It is Karenna," Utreek said firmly and without hesitation. He turned slightly to the side to look back on his men. "Karenna has come to free us."

"Are you certain?" Eli asked.

"Aye," Utreek said. "There's no one else out there who would dare challenge Lord Edgun. Karenna has come for those that have been imprisoned here, myself included. The attack against the south wall will be a feint. Mark my words, the real assault will go against the gate. Karenna is skilled at making war. The gate will be the key to taking the fort."

"Sounds like we need to take the gate from this side and open it for them," Rivun said, mustering what enthusiasm and energy he could. He hobbled over to the rack of weapons and selected a sword. "When we strike, we will have the element of surprise, and with some good fortune, we will quickly overrun the defenders."

"Perhaps you should sit this one out," Eli said, leaving the door and stepping nearer. "You are in no condition to fight."

With his back to them, Rivun stood up straight, squaring his shoulders. For some reason he could not name, Eli's next step faltered. Something was on the air, he could feel it, a building power of some sort that made his skin tingle.

Gasping, Rivun seemed to give a shudder. A bitterly cold wind blew through the room. Only it was a phantom wind, for it ruffled neither hair nor clothing.

All the same, Eli was chilled by it, to the point where it made his bones ache. The gust reminded him in an uncomfortable way of being in a Gray Field, the bone-sapping cold that stole life from one's limbs. He shivered at the memory. Then the wind and sensation that came with it, in an instant, was gone.

Had it been real?

Utreek blinked, looking around, clearly wondering what had just happened. So too did the others with him, including Mae. No, Eli realized, it had been all too real. Something had just happened, something profound.

Rivun issued a soft groan and staggered back a step.

"Are you all right?" Eli asked, concerned. He took another step forward toward him, prepared to support him, should he need it.

"I am fine." Rivun's tone was stronger, harder, and firm. Sword in hand, he turned to face them. "I assure you I am perfectly fine, just right as rain."

"Good gods, above and below," Utreek gasped, stepping back, shock plain. "What is this magic? How did you manage to do that?"

There was not a mark on Rivun's face. His bruises had vanished, as if they had never been. The swelling around his eye had gone too, vanished entirely. Moments ago, the eye had been thoroughly swollen shut. It was as if he had never been beaten and worked over by Lord Edgun's men. Though he looked terribly pale, as incredible as it seemed, Rivun had somehow healed himself.

Rivun cracked his neck and swung the sword around as if in practice, testing its weight. Then he grinned broadly, showing his needle-sharp teeth, and stretched out his arms.

"Oh, that is much better," Rivun said, "much better, indeed."

All eyes were on Rivun'Cur, even Mae's. Her mouth had fallen open. Eli glanced over at Jit. Of everyone, she showed no surprise at what had happened.

"How did you do that?" Utreek asked again, his voice low. He shifted uncomfortably, changing his stance. "Is this elf magic?"

"It is—something I picked up a while back," Rivun said. "My friend, only a select few amongst my kind are able to pull it off, and then the cost is a terrible one."

"I see, but I do not understand," Utreek said, though he sounded troubled. "Such are the mysterious ways of the High Born, then."

"I would like to learn that trick," Eli said in Elven.

"Would you now?" Rivun asked, shifting his gaze from Utreek.

Eli gave a nod. "Will you teach it to me?"

"No." Rivun's expression hardened slightly, especially around the eyes. "You do not want that, not ever. It is more a curse than gift."

A tremendous shout from outside rent the air. The shout was muffled by the walls of the building, but it was impressive no less and seemed to go on and on without letup. Eli's gaze went to the door, knowing the attack had finally begun.

Rivun looked to Utreek and then gestured to the weapons rack. "I believe the time for talking is over. The time for action has begun."

Utreek hesitated a moment, eyes narrowing, then, almost reluctantly, he tore his gaze from Rivun and glanced behind him. Ten men had come out from the hallway, nearly filling up the room, and more were waiting behind them. Half-starved, filthy, and dressed raggedly, they did not look much like fighters. Eli had long since learned that looks could be deceiving. Utreek glanced back at Rivun, hesitating. It was almost as if he were afraid to come closer to the elf.

"The south wall is under attack," Mae called from the door. "It is being stormed. The defenders are fighting back men coming up ladders."

That broke the moment. Drawing her sword, Jit pushed past the men in her way to reach the door.

"Grab yourselves a weapon, boys," Utreek called, and with that, there was a rush for the weapons. "Arm yourselves. We've got some fighting to do."

Eli made his way through and back to the door. Jit was there and had taken Mae's place. She was now looking out the door again. The sound of the fighting on the wall was intense. There was screaming, shouting, the harsh clash of sword on sword. Eli could tell the fighting was brutal and unforgiving.

Mae's gaze was on Jit. Mae seemed tense. Eli leaned close to Mae and lowered his voice so only the two of them could hear. "This will be your first battle."

She nodded.

Eli could sense her nervousness and anxiety, as well as her desperate resolve to see things through. Mae was determined to prove herself, to carve her own destiny. That was one of the reasons he liked her and had agreed to take her on. She reminded him of himself.

"It will be chaotic and confusing," Eli said to help calm her. "You have been trained for this sort of thing. Keep your head, stay cool, remember your training, and stay near me."

"I will." Her eyes searched his face for several heartbeats. With both hands, she grabbed the front of his tunic and pulled him close. Before he could react, she kissed him full on. At first, Eli resisted, then gave into the kiss, losing himself against her soft lips and probing tongue. A moment later, she broke contact and pushed him forcibly, almost roughly away.

Their eyes locked for a heartbeat, then Mae's expression became hard, angry. She drew her sword and looked away. Eli was left staring at her, not quite sure what had happened.

Somewhat confused, he scowled slightly. She was covered in dried blood, but to his eyes, the beauty of her fiery spirit shone through. He had the strong urge to pull her close and hold her tight, to do his best to keep her safe. Only, he knew he could not do that.

"How do we want to do this?" Utreek said from behind, having come up. With him was Rivun.

"At this point, a detailed plan is sort of out of the question," Rivun said, glancing around at Utreek's men. "I am afraid we will just have to improvise as we go."

Eli shook himself, more to clear his head than anything. He glanced back at Rivun, still amazed that he had somehow managed to heal himself. There was not even a hint he had ever been beaten to within an inch of his life. Rivun looked as hale as could be, and Eli found that simply incredible.

Rivun caught his look, his gaze flicking to Mae speculatively, before shooting Eli a knowing wink. Eli felt his cheeks heat.

"He's right," Eli said, returning his focus to the job at hand. "We do things the old-fashioned way. We keep it simple—storm the gate, kill all the defenders, and open it for Karenna."

"Then we hold it," Utreek said firmly, raising his voice so the men behind him could hear. "We take and hold the gate, boys. You got that?"

There was a chorus of firm ayes.

"I don't have a sword," someone called from behind.

Eli glanced around and saw that one man had taken up a broom for a weapon and another a leg from a stool. There were now more than twenty men crammed into the small room, with additional men and women waiting in the hallway beyond.

"Don't you worry about that," Utreek said. "There will be plenty of swords soon enough. When one becomes available, grab it. Until then, use whatever you can. We must take the gate. We fail and it means death for us all." Utreek hesitated for a moment and his voice rose an octave. "We will take that gate. Understand? What are we going to do?"

"Take the gate!" came a steady chorus.

"I see no sense in waiting." Eli drew both of his daggers. He spun them rapidly in his hands. "Jit, let's go."

Sword in hand, Jit opened the door and stepped out into the darkness. Drawing her own blade, Mae followed. Then he was moving forward and out into the night.

The time to fight had come.

CHAPTER FIFTEEN

With a heavy grunt, Eli blocked the overhand sword strike with his larger dagger. The two blades met in a ringing clang that shot a small shower of sparks into the night.

Ignoring the pain in his hand caused by the impact of the two blades, he used his opponent's momentum to guide the sword strike away and to the left. At the same time, Eli spun around to the right and stabbed with his other dagger into the side of the soldier's neck.

The blade went in deep. It tore a wide gash as Eli continued his movement, as graceful as the finest of dancers. A wash of hot blood sluiced across his hand and arm as he moved beyond the man, yanking his dagger out as he went.

Even before his opponent collapsed, Eli was spinning around to face the next threat, a charging soldier screaming a war cry and already in the act of slashing his sword at Eli's midriff.

His opponent was quick, but Eli was faster and threw himself to the left, contorting his body to avoid the edge of the blade. It swished harmlessly by. Eli landed on his shoulder. Taking the impact in stride, he rolled away and came back to a crouch.

As he recovered from the monstrous swing, the soldier cursed at striking nothing. He was just beginning to turn to continue the attack when Eli threw his dagger, tossing it hard and true. The blade ripped right through the man's tunic and buried itself up to the hilt in his stomach.

The soldier gave a heavy grunt from the impact and staggered to a stop. Eyes impossibly wide, he looked down at the hilt of the blade protruding from his stomach. He took a stunned step backward and dropped his sword to the dirt. Blood began to freely run down his crotch and legs, staining his pants a dark color. Hands shaking, he grabbed feebly at the hilt, groaned once, and then collapsed to his knees as his legs gave out.

"How?" he asked Eli, then slumped over and onto his side.

A primal scream of rage to Eli's immediate right drew his attention. Jit was engaged with an older soldier. She was screaming as she fought, speaking in a language he did not know.

The man she battled had a dark, bushy mustache and scarred, gaunt face. Her sword was a blur as she fought him, furiously trading blow for blow and forcing him steadily backward. It was all he could do to fend her off, and from the look in his eyes, he seemed surprised by it. Just beyond Jit, Mae took down a man, sinking her blade deep into his side.

Eli glanced around, looking for his next target. As Jit finished off her opponent with a backhanded slice, he saw no one close by to fight. His gaze was then drawn to Rivun, who had climbed up onto the platform.

The Anagradoom's sword was a scythe of death. Rivun took down two men in rapid succession and threw a third from the wall, who screamed as he fell.

With no immediate threat around, Eli paused for several heartbeats and marveled at Rivun's sheer skill with a blade. He had never seen anything equal, as Rivun began working to clear the wall over the gate of defenders. The display was not only fearsome, but beautiful, and it struck him to the core.

A shout rose on the air behind him. With Utreek at their head, the freed slaves rushed forward and joined the fight, storming toward the wall. Behind them, more ragged, dirty, and desperate men spilled out of the mine in a steady stream. They screamed their pent-up rage at the world as they came.

Freed slaves thundered around and by him. A handful of the defenders standing on the wall's fighting platform braced themselves to receive the attack. The rest turned and ran, fleeing along toward the north and south walls of the fort.

Shouts of alarm were now going up across the fort. It was clear the defenders realized they were being attacked from within. Eli knew the difficult part lay ahead, when the defenders organized themselves and counterattacked, for surely they must. They had no choice. It was either that or defeat and likely death.

In the darkness, something hissed by Eli's head. A fraction of a heartbeat later, one of Utreek's men, who was running for the wall's platform, was thrown forward and to the ground. An arrow had sprouted from his side.

Following the track of the missile, Eli spotted three archers. They had come down from the south wall and had advanced a few yards toward the gate before dropping to a knee. Two additional men with bows were climbing down from the platform with the clear intent of joining the others.

Beyond the archers, the officer Eli had seen earlier was snapping orders, pointing at the gate. A man who had been standing at the officer's side went dashing off for the west wall.

Though the south wall was under heavy assault from Karenna's warriors, the sergeant had begun hastily pulling what looked like every other man and sending them down from the platform. He was actively organizing these men into a line of battle facing the east gate.

Each man had a shield and was armed with a sword, though some had no armor at all. Eli knew it was only a matter of time until this line was thrown forward and into the attack.

Eli snapped his gaze to the west. The runner had reached his destination. The west wall was not under active assault from outside the fort. In unison, nearly every man climbed down off the platform and began jogging to join the line forming before the south wall.

He shifted his gaze north. He did not have a good view of the wall or how many defenders were even there. But those he could see appeared to be staring in their direction, almost as if they were uncertain as to what to do.

Another arrow hissed by, harmlessly impacting the dirt a few yards beyond him. Sticking up out of the ground, the missile quivered with unspent force.

In just a span of heartbeats, the time it had taken to glance around and study what was going on throughout the fort, the action had moved completely by him. The freed slaves were fighting those few who had remained behind to resist on the wall. Rivun too.

"Utreek," Eli called, spotting the man as he viciously cut down one of the last remaining defenders on the platform over the gate. Utreek had chopped the man down from behind as he tried to flee. Hearing his name, he looked around and spotted Eli. "We're going to be attacked," Eli called back. He pointed to the forming line of battle. "Get your people ready for it."

"Got it," Utreek said. "We will deal with it when it comes."

Eli heard the twang of a bow close at hand. Mae had found a bow and was shooting back at the enemy. One of the archers fell back, an arrow lodged in his chest. Screaming in agony, he rolled back and forth on the ground. It was just one more noise layered into the din of the growing fight.

"Good shot," Eli called to her, as he retrieved his dagger, pulling it from the man's stomach. His wounded opponent gave an agonized groan. Knowing the wound was mortal, and seeing that he was barely conscious, Eli efficiently slit the man's throat, more to grant him an easy release from this life than anything else. The human soldier gagged briefly and then expired.

Mae did not look around but had kept her gaze focused. She loosed a second arrow. It flew true, hammering dead on into another archer's chest. He slumped forward and did not move. The third archer drew a bead on Mae and loosed, even as she calmly nocked her next missile. Eli stopped breathing as he watched the arrow speed toward her. Then it flashed by, mere inches over her head. Eli felt a wave of intense relief wash over him. Mae did not even pay it any mind as she aimed and fired her next arrow.

On the other side of the east wall, a horn sounded, drawing Eli's attention. A tremendous shout followed. It seemed to rend the very air.

"Karenna is attacking the gate," one of the freed slaves standing on the wall's fighting platform shouted. He was pointing out beyond the wall, fairly hopping with excitement. A moment later, an arrow struck him squarely in the back. He stiffened, then toppled over the wall and fell out of sight, all without uttering another sound.

Eli looked to the gate. The defenders before it were down. Those enemy that had remained were now dead. The freed slaves were seemingly everywhere. Some were standing about, clearly not quite sure what to do or where to go. Others were up on the platform, moving both north and south, clearing the walls as they went.

Most of the newly freed men were unarmed, but Eli was pleased to see several had taken the opportunity to arm themselves by retrieving swords and shields from the fallen enemy. The rest held planks, stool legs, rocks, and even shovels.

Mae's bow twanged again. Eli did not look to see, but instead glanced rapidly at the organizing battle line and knew he had to take action. The gate must be opened to let Karenna's fighters inside, and they did not have much time.

"Open the gate," Eli shouted, running forward. "Open the gate! Let them in."

Several planks had been wedged against the gate. It was a halfhearted effort to reinforce against a potential battering ram attack. The locking bar was firmly in place too. It was a huge beam of wood, really an entire tree trunk that had been shorn of its branches and then smoothed and sanded. It looked heavy, and Eli knew without a doubt it would take serious effort and several people to remove it.

Eli sheathed his daggers and grabbed at one of the reinforcing planks that had been wedged against the gate and ground. He threw it aside. A man joined him and pulled another down. The shouting outside the gate grew nearer.

"Hurry," Utreek shouted from just above. He was leaning over the other side of the wall. "Get those ladders up, boys. Come on. Come on. We're working at getting the gate open. It won't be long now. Come on. Use the ladders until the gate's open."

Heavy thuds landing overhead against the top of the gate and wall told Eli the first of the assault ladders had been thrown up. More followed.

"Climb, damn you," Utreek shouted. "Climb faster."

Eli pulled another reinforcing plank down, just as an arrow hammered into the gate less than a foot to his right. Eli looked around and saw Mae release an arrow. Thirty yards away, the last of the archers, the man who had just shot at him, went down.

From the north side of the fort came a massed shout and the pounding of many feet. Eli turned to see a group of the fort's defenders rushing toward the east gate, charging and sprinting for all they were worth. There were more than a dozen men and they screamed wildly as they came. In an effort to retake the gate, whoever had been in command there had likely pulled everyone from the north wall.

"Kill them all," Utreek roared to his men. "Kill them all."

From the fighting platform along the wall, Utreek was pointing his sword at the onrushing attackers. Dozens of freed slaves responded, bracing themselves and moving forward to meet the attackers rushing headlong for them. A man right before Eli picked up a discarded shield and spear. He grunted as he threw the spear. It was an excellent toss and flew true, snatching a soldier backward and to the ground as the heavy weapon easily pierced his chest.

Eli drew his daggers and prepared himself for what was coming. A heartbeat later the attackers crashed into the freed slaves. Almost immediately, Eli was confronted by a soldier bearing a shield and armed with a sword.

The man bashed his shield forward and stabbed with his sword at Eli, who reflexively danced back and away. The soldier made to follow, but a freed slave, armed with a plank, swung and connected solidly with the soldier's shield. It made a thunking sound.

Distracted, the soldier instead turned his blade and stabbed at the man with the board. The tip of the sword dug deep into the slave's shoulder. Crying out and dropping the plank, he fell back to the ground. Eli took that moment to attack. He lunged forward, batting at the shield and forcing it aside, even as he jabbed at the man's sword arm.

Eli's razor-sharp dagger ripped open the forearm, exposing the muscle and tendons. His opponent gave a tortured scream that was part squeal and released the blade, even as he attempted to back up and away from his tormentor. Before Eli could move or make a second attack, two more freed slaves descended upon the soldier. One was armed with a large rock, the other a stave.

The man with the rock hammered it down upon the back of the man's helmet. The blow was delivered with savage force, and it staggered the injured soldier. Stunned by the blow, he stopped screaming over his wounded forearm. The other slave struck at the soldier's left knee. The stave connected with a solid slapping sound, and with that, the soldier went down. Eli stepped back as the two freed slaves fell upon the soldier, mercilessly beating at him with rock and board.

About to turn to look for a new opponent, Eli was abruptly knocked to the side as a shield bashed violently against his back. He recovered and turned to see Jit closely engaged with a soldier. The man had inadvertently hit Eli while trying to ward off her furious and unrelenting assault.

Hurting from the blow and feeling a little battered, Eli shook the discomfort off. All around, there was screaming, crying, shouting, grunts, the clash of sword on sword. The sound of it all assaulted the ears and senses. Bodies littered the ground, more freed slaves than soldiers. Fights like this were always confusing melees. The trick to surviving was keeping your head and remaining situationally aware, which was exceptionally difficult at the best of times.

From the corner of his peripheral vision, a sword swung down at him. Eli dodged and reflexively stabbed out at this new attacker. His blade connected, scraping against armor, and Eli realized he was facing one of the officers.

The man had a hard face. His teeth were bared in a determined grimace as he pressed the attack forward. Eli blocked a powerfully delivered strike aimed at his head. The force of the blow sent his smaller dagger flying away and set his hand aching painfully.

With only his main dagger left, Eli dodged and blocked. His opponent was well trained and skilled. Eli found himself completely on the defensive, giving ground, one grudging step at a time, and praying he did not trip on a body.

Then Mae was there, lashing out with her sword from behind Eli's opponent. Her blade came down into the back of the officer's leg, slicing through muscle and tendon. He cried out in agony as the blow drove him to a knee.

Taking advantage of the opportunity and without hesitation, Eli lunged forward. Shoving the officer's shield aside, he plunged his dagger down into the man's collar, forcing it deep. Eli gave the dagger a savage twist and felt a hot stream of blood spray across his face.

The officer went rigid before almost immediately relaxing. He gave a last sigh as he died. In death, his face softened. A heartbeat later, he fell backward and off Eli's blade, where he slumped to the ground and lay still.

"That's one you owe me." Mae flashed him a triumphant grin.

Eli was about to respond, when a sword seemed to come out of nowhere, aimed squarely at Mae's back. She did not see the charging man.

Desperate, Eli lunged forward and with an arm knocked Mae roughly aside while catching the end of the sword blade with his dagger, a mere inch from where she had been a fraction of a heartbeat before.

So fast had he moved, the attacking soldier's eyes widened in shock as their gazes locked together. Eli felt a rush of heated anger that this man, this human soldier, had almost ended Mae's life.

Before the soldier could react, Eli pressed forward, stepping closer and sliding his dagger down the length of the other's blade while forcing it away and back. The two blades grated against each other with a painful screeching sound that clawed at the ears.

The soldier tried to take a step back and away from Eli. He stumbled on a body. Before he could recover, Eli twisted his blade around and sliced into his opponent's fingers holding the sword, opening two of them to the bone. The soldier gave a tortured scream.

Still gripping the sword, he tried to back away. Eli stayed with him. Grabbing the man's forearm with his free hand, Eli held the man's sword away from him while he stabbed with his other into the chest. His blade found purchase, sliding between two ribs and digging deep. From the angle, Eli knew he had plunged his dagger right into his opponent's heart. Without uttering a further sound, the soldier sagged, went limp, and fell away to collapse in a heap at Eli's feet.

As rapidly as it had come on, the swirling fight moved beyond them. The freed slaves had swarmed the attackers and were now forcing them backward. Armed with whatever was at hand, they fought madly, some even clawing at the soldiers with their bare hands.

Though they were overwhelming the soldiers, the newly freed men were taking horrific casualties. The fight around the gate had been an intense one. The evidence of that was all around. Dead and wounded slaves lay so thick upon the ground around Eli and Mae, it was difficult to move without stepping upon a body, let alone a splayed limb.

Breathing heavily, Eli looked around for Mae. So fast had everything happened that she was still on the ground where he had knocked her. She was looking up at him, eyes wide with the realization she had almost been killed.

Seeing that she was okay, Eli let out a relieved breath. Attempting to make light of the moment, he spun his bloody dagger and forced a grin.

"I make this look good."

Her face tightened with consternation, and she pulled herself to her feet. Mae dusted herself off and then looked up at him, her eyes flashing with anger and what he took to be hurt.

"You seem to think you make everything look good," Mae said.

"I guess we're now even," Eli said with a shrug as his gaze went to the top of the wall. Warriors had made it up the ladder and were coming over the top. They were hopping down onto the fighting platform in ones and twos. He suddenly remembered the gate, which was still barred. Sheathing his remaining dagger, he turned and ran to the locking bar.

"Help me," Eli yelled at those around him as he struggled to lift the beam. "Help me open the gate!"

A freed slave joined him. Then Rivun was there too, straining to lift the beam from its holders. The last Eli had seen him, Rivun had been overhead and on the platform. Jit and Mae joined the effort.

The wooden beam was incredibly heavy and at first stubbornly resisted their efforts. Grunting, they lifted it between them and out of its holders.

"Advance!" someone shouted above the din of the fighting that had spread throughout much of the fort. The voice was deep, practiced in its tone, and accustomed to command. It came from the direction of the southern wall. Knowing the line of soldiers there had started forward, Eli did his best to ignore it as he struggled with the rest to move the bar. At this point, all that mattered was opening the gate, for if they failed, everything would be lost.

"At them," Utreek shouted from behind Eli. "Get at them, boys."

There was a massed shout that came from Utreek's men, the pounding of many feet, then a loud crash of contact, followed by a calamitous tumult.

Eli ignored it all as they worked to move the frightfully heavy beam aside from the gate. Finally, after much straining, they set the beam down, off to the side and out of the way. Breathing heavily from the effort, Eli looked up and around. Two other men were already in the process of opening the gate.

Having dealt with the attackers from the north wall, the freed slaves, with Utreek at their head, had rushed forward and engaged the line of soldiers bearing down on the gate from the south wall. Many of the slaves were still unarmed, save for whatever makeshift weapons they could lay their hands on. The soldiers, on the other hand, almost to a man, carried shields and swords and were organized into a coherent line. They also appeared well-trained and were fighting as if their lives depended upon it, which they did.

Eli estimated there were at least forty soldiers. The fighting was brutal and as violent as Eli had ever seen. Locking shields, the line ground steadily forward against the unarmored slaves, who battered, clawed, and hacked back at the enemy, that was, if they were lucky enough to have a sword.

One of the freed slaves carried an axe, the type used for splitting firewood. With a powerful overhanded swing, he slammed it down onto a soldier's shield. The soldier holding the shield staggered under the impact. The axe stuck fast, and the man pulled, attempting to free it. Instead, he yanked the soldier, who had a firm grip on the shield, forward and out of the line. The soldier stabbed with his sword and the axe wielder went down. A moment later, exposed and unprotected by the line, the soldier was cut brutally down.

Behind Eli, there was a deep groaning as the heavy gate opened. At first it was a crack, then it became wide enough to admit a single man. A moment later, it was fully opened. Hard, grim-faced men began to stream through, first a few, then more, until it seemed a veritable flood was pouring into the fort.

Eli stepped back as the warriors flowed by and around them. Some wore armor, but most did not. All carried a sword and shield. Mae joined him, as did Rivun. Eli had no idea where Jit had gone.

A huge man pointed a sword at the line of soldiers still attempting to fight their way to the gate. He shouted something indistinguishable over the noise of the fight and, swinging his sword above his head, led the way forward.

The newcomers followed and, with a deafening roar, charged. In moments, the reinforcements, all looking for blood, crashed into the battle line. At first, it looked like the line would hold, then the pressure mounted as more and more warriors joined the fight. Together, with Utreek's men, they swamped the soldiers. In mere moments, the line broke in two and then lost all cohesion.

Bloodied and looking weary, Utreek made his way back to them as more warriors continued to pour into the fort. His grin was broad, delighted even. There was still the sound of fighting throughout the fort, but Eli knew the battle for control was essentially over. They had won. It was only a matter of time now until the last of the soldiers either were cut down or surrendered.

"Well fought." Utreek clapped his hands together. "Well fought, my new friends."

"It was a good fight," Rivun said. "I found it very spirited."

"Yes, it was," Utreek agreed.

The flood of warriors streaming into the fort fell off, until no more came. Along the south wall, the defenders had finally been overcome. Uncontested, additional warriors were climbing up the ladders and coming into the fort from that quarter.

Eli suddenly felt tired and weary. He stifled a yawn as he glanced over at Mae. Their eyes met and he could sense the same in her. For Mae, he knew it would be worse. First battles always were.

"You did good," he said, laying a hand upon her shoulder. "More importantly, you survived. That is what matters. With each fight we learn and do better."

She gave a nod as several heavily armed and armored warriors moved through the gate. Swords drawn, their gazes were watchful, suspicious even. They looked dangerous and mean, and they spread out before the gate entrance. Those nearest, freed slaves who had been wounded but were still on their feet, moved back and away from them.

Through the gate strode a warrior wearing plate mail. Utreek stiffened, the exhaustion slipping from him. Staring, as if in a dream, he took a hesitant step forward, then stopped. It was as if the man could not believe his eyes.

Neither could Eli, for the warrior's armor was incredibly ornate, graceful to the point of being impractical. The chest plate was etched with an eagle and an owl sitting upon a branch. Both animals were looking at the other, as if staring one another down. The armor was highly polished and maintained, almost to an impossible degree. Even in the last shades of the darkness and rapidly bluing sky, the armor seemed radiant.

Eli blinked to make certain he was not seeing things. The armor the warrior bore was clearly his people's work. And it was ancient, likely beyond ancient, having been made long before the High Born had come to this world. Only the oldest of elven families owned such armor, which was rumored to be enchanted.

Making such works had become a lost art. Those suits of armor that had survived the ages and trials of his people were usually reserved for the head of the family and only ever used when the need was great. Even as powerful as his family was, Eli's father did not own such armor.

Were the rebels being led by an elf and, more importantly, an elder? Had the warden taken a direct hand? It now seemed likely that she had.

He glanced over at Rivun, who met his gaze. He read a shock there too. It was clear to Eli that he was thinking the very same thoughts.

What was going on here?

CHAPTER SIXTEEN

Gaze moving about the interior of the fort, particularly studying the carnage spread out before the gate, the warrior came to a halt. The warrior's helmet had a face shield, an emotionless face made of silver, and in the darkness, little could be seen of the eyes as they came to rest on Utreek. The warrior seemed to freeze, becoming very still, then slowly reached up and removed the helmet.

Eli was shocked to see it was a female, a human female. Her hair was fiery red and had been tied into a single, tight braid. He judged her to be in her mid-twenties but could not be sure, for there was a certain grimness that seemed to lend her years. She was attractive, with a heavily freckled face. Her left cheek was marred by a thin scar. Her eyes were locked wholly on Utreek. Almost absently, she tucked her helmet under an arm.

"Utreek, I feared I had lost you." Her voice was thick with emotion. She took a hesitant step forward before coming to a halt once again, suddenly unsure. As if her speech had broken the moment of shock on his part, Utreek rushed to her. The guards did not move to stop him and the two embraced warmly.

"Karenna, woman, I knew you would come for me," Utreek said. "I never lost faith, not once."

"It is good Lord Edgun's people did not know who they had caught," Karenna said, still in his tight embrace. He kissed her and she returned the kiss. "Otherwise..."

"I would be waiting for you in the afterlife." With tears, Utreek gave her another kiss. He cupped the side of her face with his palm and stared at her for a long moment. "I dreamed so long of this. I can scarcely believe you are really here."

"I too, my love," Karenna replied.

"It is a good thing Edgun is an unimaginative man. He would never—could never believe our leader would be a woman... and my wife."

The armed and armored warriors that had accompanied Karenna seemed to realize that Eli, Mae, and Rivun were not human. One stepped forward menacingly and lowered his sword toward the elves. The others followed suit and moved forward to surround them.

Wiping his tears from his face, Utreek scowled at the guards and broke away from Karenna. He interposed himself before the warriors.

"What are you doing?" Utreek demanded hotly. "These are friends. Without them, we would not have escaped from the mine and opened the gate. The assault on the fort would have proven more costly."

The guards hesitated, as if unsure how to proceed. One of them, who Eli took to be the leader, an older, grizzled man, glanced over at Karenna in question.

"What are your orders, Karenna?" the warrior asked in a gruff voice.

Karenna's expression hardened as she looked beyond Utreek and upon the elves. Where a moment before she had been overwhelmed by emotion at the reunion with her husband, a studied mask, one cold as winter ice, had fallen into place. Eli suspected it was the one she regularly showed the world.

"Stand down." Karenna raised a commanding hand, and with that, the guards stepped back and relaxed, lowering their weapons. They were, however, still watchful, eyeing the elves with suspicion.

Utreek gestured at Rivun and looked back at Karenna. "After today, they are all my honored friends."

"I see." Karenna was silent for a long moment as she eyed them.

"You will accept them as friends," Utreek insisted. "You must."

Karenna's eyes flashed with a flicker of anger before it passed. "I thank you for freeing my husband and our people. I daresay it is as Utreek said. Without your efforts, the assault would have been more costly. The tribes owe you a debt. My apologies. You have indeed proven yourselves to be friends."

Eli found Karenna's gaze piercing and filled with intelligence. She moved like one born to command and spoke Common with an accent—an imperial accent that was, if he was not mistaken, noble in nature. He had the suspicion she was educated and could read and write.

What was an imperial noble doing leading an uprising amongst the Castol? And a woman at that?

"Lord Edgun has a debt to pay," Eli said, "and we will help you make sure it gets paid. That is, if you wish our help."

Karenna shifted her gaze to him, and her eyes narrowed. Eli figured trust was something with her that was earned over time. She took a step nearer to them. Her guards shifted uncomfortably in response. Eli got the impression that each would, without hesitation, lay down his life for her.

"What is your name, elf?" she asked plainly. Her tone was firm and hard, her gaze boring into his own.

Most humans felt unnerved around elves. Clearly, Karenna was the exception.

"You may call me Eli."

"And why did you choose to fight here this day?" Karenna asked. "Why bother to free our people?"

"That would be my fault," Rivun said. "They came to free me, for I was being held prisoner."

"After what I saw in Taibor," Eli added, "I swore a reckoning upon Lord Edgun. That was before we knew he had captured one of our own." Eli gestured at Rivun and recalled how he had been boxed into freeing the slaves. "Then, it really became my business."

Karenna's gaze flicked to Rivun for a moment before returning to Eli. "Edgun has much to answer for. Tell me, Eli, do your people stand with us? Will the warden come to our aid?"

"The warden?" Eli asked, surprised by the turn.

"Will the great Si'Cara support our cause? Or is it just you who offer to fight at our side for the coming struggle? I would know where I stand with the elves, for after we remove Edgun from his castle and this life, we will surely need help to find a separate peace with our king. Your warden could assist with making that a reality, for we do not rebel against our king."

"Some of the noble lords of the Castol will take issue with us killing one of their own," Utreek said. "Most, like Lord Edgun, view themselves as untouchable. They will seek retribution."

"I speak only for those here," Eli said. "I do not speak for the warden."

"Are you certain?" Karenna asked.

"On speaking for the warden?" Eli asked, glancing at Mae and then Rivun before returning his gaze to Karenna. "I am bold, but not that bold." Karenna did not reply, and Eli sensed there was more meaning to her line of questioning. "Why do you ask?"

"We've had word the elves are working with Lord Edgun, supporting him in his efforts," Karenna said.

That surprised Eli. "I know nothing of such things."

"Two were seen in his company as recently as two days ago, at the castle. They stood in Edgun's very court. That was before this one"—she waved an armored hand at Rivun—"was taken in Taibor."

"You know about that, eh?" Rivun asked.

"I know most everything in these parts," Karenna said firmly.

Mae snapped her fingers and glanced over at Eli. "The soldiers he met up with must have been Edgun's men."

"I would say, with what we just learned, that is likely an accurate assumption." Eli still did not see why Mik'Las was working with Edgun. It made no sense, for he could see no advantage to such a union. Then again, Mik'Las's reasoning in most things eluded him.

"Of whom do you speak?" Karenna asked plainly, looking between them.

"We are after a criminal," Eli said slowly, "one of our own. His name is Mik'Las. The warden charged us with bringing him back dead or alive. We tracked him to a point where he met up with a group of soldiers. That was not far from here. I now suspect he has been dealing with Lord Edgun for reasons that are unknown to us."

"And yet," Karenna said, "my report says he was not alone, that he was accompanied by another elf, a female. Can you explain that?"

"He took someone with him." Eli found the next part difficult to say, especially to a human, who had no real knowledge or understanding of how elven society worked. "We believe it was against her will. When he took her, he murdered her brother in the process of making his escape."

Rivun looked over, his gaze intensely curious. Eli knew without a doubt that when they were alone there would be questions. Elves rarely murdered one another.

"I see." Karenna gave an unhappy nod. "He was accompanied by an elven female. Though from the reports I received, she was there willingly. I was told it was as if the two were lovers."

Eli did not much like the sound of that, for if true, it would complicate matters.

Karenna's gaze roved over Eli, studying him more closely. There was something in her look that flickered with what Eli almost took to be recognition, which was odd because he had never met her before today.

"By your dress, you are an elven ranger, yes?"

Eli gave a nod. He glanced around the fort. Much of the fighting had died down. Toward the north, he saw several of the last remaining defenders jumping down from the walls and over the other side, clearly fleeing for their lives.

"I have never met a ranger before," Karenna admitted. "I am pleased you have decided to join our cause. I accept your offer of help, ranger. Before this is all said and done, we will need every blade, and yours is most welcome. If it is within our means, we will help you apprehend this fugitive."

Eli gave a respectful nod in return. "May I introduce Rivun and Mae?" Eli gestured at each in turn. "We have a human companion about, somewhere. Her name is Jit."

"Well met." Karenna nodded to them in greeting. "After much suffering at Lord Edgun's hands, and at long last, the forest tribes and villages have come together. This is the first time we fight unified as friends and allies. Together, we will rid the plague that is Lord Edgun from these parts. Then, after, we will see if we can come to an accommodation with the king."

"Perhaps," Rivun said, with a glance over at Mae, "the warden might be persuaded to help with that. We may even be able to assist there."

Eli glanced sharply over at the Anagradoom. What influence did the outcast have with the warden?

"You think so?" Karenna asked, her mask cracking a little.

"Over a long life, I have learned it does not hurt to ask," Rivun said. "The worst the warden can say is no."

"Then we shall ask," Karenna said. "I will remain hopeful that Si'Cara will support us in such an effort."

A shout went up from inside the fort. It was one of triumph and exultation. It came from hundreds of voices. Eli glanced around again. The fighting had ended. Karenna's warriors filled the fort. Slaves, mostly women and children, were now emerging from the mine. Scattered around the fort, several of the defenders had been captured. Bodies lay all over, particularly around the gate where they'd stood, as did wounded, who whimpered, begged, or cried out for help.

A few yards off, a group of three soldiers had surrendered. Surrounded and held at sword point, they were disarmed and forced to kneel before their captors.

A large warrior with a burly beard, the one who had led his men into battle earlier, stalked up. He was wearing black studded leather armor. He carried a small, rounded shield that had a large chunk missing. His sword was sheathed at his side, and he was covered in blood and gore. His beard was matted with it, and his arm bled freely from a superficial wound.

"Utreek," he said, spotting the other man, "I never thought I would be fighting with you, not once, not ever. We are allies now, friends even, though the thought of that galls me. The gods in their ways are truly strange and mysterious."

"And I always thought I would one day gut you, Beekus, to end your miserable days." There was no heat in Utreek's tone. He seemed almost regretful that they were now allies. "No matter how disagreeable a bastard, you were always a worthy enemy."

"Perhaps when this is all done, we will have the chance to settle who is the better warrior, eh?" Beekus turned and touched a hand to his forehead. It seemed like a mark of respect. "Karenna, the fort has fallen and is ours. What are your orders?"

Karenna was silent for several heartbeats. She glanced around, studying everything in view, then turned her gaze back upon the burly warrior. A large group had gathered around, clearly intent upon hearing what was said.

"Beekus," she said. "The Aventry have acquitted themselves as the warriors I always knew them to be. Your people have fought exceptionally well. I am pleased."

Beekus said nothing. He simply waited. His men, however, gave a hearty cheer.

Karenna did not speak until the cheer died down. "Escort the women and children, and those who were held here, out of the fort and to the rally point. I want them moved to safety before it is too late. Tend to and move the wounded as you are able, then prepare your defense. You have command of the fort now. Do whatever you feel is required to hold it." She paused, eyeing the large warrior coldly. "We will proceed as discussed."

"And what of the prisoners we've taken?" Beekus asked. "Do you desire them as slaves?"

"Slaves?" Karenna glanced over at her husband. A look of disgust slid across her face, momentarily cracking the mask. "No. We will keep no slaves, not ever again. Execute them. All who serve and support Lord Edgun have earned death. We are finished taking prisoners. That is our decree."

"It will be done, Karenna." Looking satisfied, Beekus turned away and pushed through the crowd of his warriors. He began shouting orders in a tongue Eli did not know. The man's fighters broke up and moved to action.

"I am surprised you used his men for this assault," Utreek said, when Beekus was out of hearing. "The Aventry are our blood enemy."

"Were our blood enemy," Karenna corrected. "In war, sometimes distasteful choices must be made. No matter our past history, and the wrongs placed upon our doorstep, I have put it all aside for the good of the tribes and the forest peoples. We have common cause. Beekus and his people are now our allies, at least in this fight, maybe longer if things work out."

"And when matters are concluded?" Utreek asked. "What then?"

"One can only hope we have started something here that will prove lasting and end the blood feuds." Karenna paused, running her gaze around the fort, seeming to study Beekus's warriors. "Like the others, they are all my children now."

Mae tilted her head to the side as she watched Karenna. Eli could almost read her thoughts. They matched his own. Who was this woman who boldly wore a relic from another age and commanded as if born to her station? More importantly, she was being treated like a holy warrior and representative of a god. He glanced at the etching on her chest armor, studying the eagle and owl. It was familiar. He had seen something like it before, long ago, but was not quite sure where or in what context.

Utreek looked around. He scowled, clearly thinking upon his wife's words. "And where are our men, our warriors? But for your guards, I do not see them."

"The Asteredies, Vendeleks, and Keirsa are waiting a few miles away at the rally point." Karenna glanced over as women and children began moving by, shepherded through the gate by Beekus's warriors. Like Utreek and the rest of the slaves, they looked ragged, thin, and emaciated. They moved slowly, but all as they passed fell silent, turned their gazes reverently upon Karenna, and touched their foreheads in a show of respect.

A scream sounded a few yards off. One of the defenders had been executed as he knelt before his captors. Another scream rang out moments later. This was followed rapidly by several more. Karenna did little more than glance over dispassionately.

"The Keirsa have joined us too?" Utreek seemed even more surprised by that than Beekus becoming an ally.

"Yes," Karenna said. "In the coming days, additional tribes will join our cause. I have high hopes the Walcots and Dasde will be next amongst the flock. I know the Killsmeads are marching even now to our standard."

"I still do not understand using only the Aventry." Utreek was silent for a long moment. "Surely all of our strength would have been better served in taking the fort. Unless you mean to weaken Beekus's people?"

"Much has changed in the months since you were captured," Karenna said. "Our strength has grown. We have real power now and I intend to use it to settle matters once and for all, as was shown."

In the distance, a horn blew a long and mournful note. Karenna's gaze snapped to the west, in the direction the horn had blown. The mask cracked once again and her expression filled with great satisfaction, and with it, she almost smiled.

"Lord Edgun has grown foolish," Karenna said, sounding triumphant. "He has always been arrogant. And it is the arrogant who make the worst mistakes."

Eli, wondering what was going on, exchanged a look with Rivun.

"What do you mean?" Utreek asked, giving voice to the question.

"Lord Edgun has put three of his finest and most experienced companies into the field to hunt us, over six hundred of his best soldiers. They do not know our true strength. How could they? I have hidden it well." She paused, and when she spoke, her eyes blazed. "Those companies are now three miles distant and closing on our position. They believe we planned to attack at dawn and mean to stop us, to catch us in the act. When they arrive, they will discover Beekus and his warriors in possession of the fort. They will also find my banner flying from the fort's walls. But I will not be here."

"You are going to ambush them?" Utreek said in a startled whisper, understanding becoming plain. "Attacking the fort was just a distraction."

"No," Karenna said. "Not a distraction, an opportunity to draw them in and free our people held here before it became too late. That is why I only used the Aventry for this attack. I could not risk our enemy discovering our true numbers. Besides, their tribe was all that was needed. Now,

Beekus and his warriors will hold the fort against Lord Edgun's men, who will surely surround it in quick order, for they will want to prevent a breakout. With any luck, Lord Edgun will send more men, believing he has me trapped."

"And you will move in behind them with most of our strength?" Utreek said, sounding impressed.

"And that is when I will destroy them." Karenna sucked in a breath and returned the helmet to her head, tying the strap tight. "Whether that be here or elsewhere I will see to their destruction. And now we must go, before the enemy arrives." She looked at the elves, only her eyes visible through the face shield. "Come, all of you. I am afraid our camp is a bit of a hike. There we have food and drink. From the looks of things, you could use it, along with some rest." She turned her gaze upon Utreek. "Especially you, my love."

"I owe this one a drink," Utreek said, gesturing at Rivun. "Hopefully, there will be spirits."

Karenna did not respond, but turned away and started off, her bodyguard moving before her and clearing a bubble of space around their charge as she moved toward the gate.

Utreek shot Rivun a look. "Later we will have that drink. On that, you have my word."

"I recall that being more than one drink," Rivun said, perking up.

With that, Utreek turned and hurried after his wife, joining the other freed slaves as they streamed out through the gate.

Rivun looked around. Eli followed his gaze and spotted Jit. She had dropped down from the fighting platform and was making her way over to them. She held her bloodied sword in one hand and a severed head in the other by the hair. She dropped the head at Rivun's feet.

"Can you believe this bastard thought to take my head?" Jit asked, sounding shocked by the prospect.

"Are you trying to say he lost his in the attempt?" Rivun asked with a trace of a grin.

"You know me only too well."

"You know," Rivun said, eyeing the severed head, "I once had a pet cat. She used to bring me her kills too, trophies of her prowess as a hunter."

"Are you comparing me to a pet?" Jit's tone became dangerous.

"Come on, we're leaving," Rivun said, suddenly sounding exceptionally weary. He gestured at those streaming out of the fort and started forward. Jit fell in at his side. He looked over at her. "They apparently have a camp where we will find food, and drink."

"All someone ever has to do is offer you food and you follow along like a blind fool," Jit said, sounding exasperated. "You think too much with your stomach."

Rivun gave a chuckle. "At my age, one has to take pleasures where they can be found."

"Your stomach keeps getting us into trouble," Jit said. "You know that, right?"

Amused, Eli watched them walk off, then glanced over at Mae. "Sounds like things are about to get interesting."

She did not immediately reply. It was almost as if she had not heard him. There was something strange in Mae's gaze. She stared at Karenna's back as the rebel leader and Utreek moved through the gate and out of view.

Eli did not like her look, for it was haunted. Then again, he was tired and so too was she. They had been up all night and then fought for their lives. Fights were always stressful, and this had been her first battle, too. He decided he might be reading into things too much. He studied her for several silent moments.

Mae was covered in dried blood and gore. He recalled her unexpected kiss before the fight and found himself moved, something he had not expected. Eli felt the pull of desire tug at him strongly. At the same time, from a logical perspective, he fought the impulse. Becoming romantically involved was not something he desired in his near future. Besides, they were clearly not suited for one another and personality-wise were opposites. Her mother was also the warden. That was more than enough reason to steer clear.

Her gaze shifted to him, eyes searching his face.

"What?" She scowled. "Why are you looking at me like that?"

"There is something I need to do," Eli said. "You may not like it."

"And what is that?" Mae asked suspiciously, her brows drawing together.

He reached out and drew her close, and then kissed her full on. She did not resist but seemed to melt into him and kissed him back.

CHAPTER SEVENTEEN

With his arms wrapped comfortably around his knees, Eli sat on the ground, staring into the low-burning flames of the campfire. His thoughts were turbulent and troubled as he reached over and threw another log onto the fire. He rubbed at his eyes, which were dry. Though he had managed a few hours of sleep, he was still tired and in need of more.

It was late afternoon and the sky above had fully clouded over, giving the day a grayish cast. The air was warm and had turned quite humid, presaging a coming rain.

A short while before, thunder had rumbled menacingly off in the distance, sounding like a cavalry charge. Looking up at the sky, Eli wondered when, if ever, the weather would break. He had always enjoyed the aftermath of a good rain and was looking forward to the cool air that would inevitably follow. Water also meant life, and if you knew how to listen to the voice of the forest, you could hear the trees rejoicing.

An excited cry of a child drew Eli's attention back to the mundane world. Around him sprawled the rebel camp. It could not really be called a proper camp. It was more akin to a gathering than anything else.

Karenna's people had taken over a small valley about ten miles from Brek, and five miles from the mine. There was a small stream-fed lake at its center. The valley had once been farmed. Since it was mostly open land, that much was clear. All that remained of the farmhouse and barn were overgrown ruins and a handful of charred timbers over a lichen-covered stone foundation, a testament to what had once been.

Amidst the tall grass, dozens of trees and brush had already sprung up. Within the next few years, the forest would fully return, taking back the valley as if by force.

Such was the way of things. Elven eyes had taught him that nothing was ever permanent. That was the sad truth. Change was the true master of the world, an inexorable power that could be slowed but never stopped.

There were hundreds of campfires and thousands of people all around, men, women, and children, entire families mixed in amongst the groups of warriors. They came from the tribes and villages that inhabited the region.

There was a jovial, uplifted air to the gathering. Eli was reminded of a country festival. Tents of all kinds, both large and small, had been pitched seemingly everywhere.

With great enthusiasm, children ran wildly about, playing. Their laughter and cries hung on the air. They ran around the campfires and tents, chasing one another or playing a myriad of games. One group was playing king of the hill on a small mound. All the while, the adults gathered in groups around fires, talking, sharpening their weapons, cleaning armor and kit, feasting, and drinking, as if at a grand picnic.

The smell of cooking was strong. Though he had just eaten a few hours before, Eli found himself hungry to the point of being ravenous. He considered pulling out his haversack for some of their traveling rations, then discarded the idea. A hot meal sounded far better, and he knew if he made the effort, he would easily find someone willing to share.

To his immediate right, mumbling something inarticulate, Mae shifted in her sleep. She rolled over onto her side and pulled her blanket tighter about herself, sighed softly, and then settled back down to sleep. Her face was peaceful and relaxed. Unexpectedly, Eli found himself enjoying looking at her while she slept. There was something about it that warmed his heart.

After several moments, his gaze moved on. Rivun slept a few feet away on the opposite side of the fire. So deep was his slumber, he barely moved, save for the telltale rise and fall of his chest.

Jit's sleeping pallet was empty. She was up and about and had told Eli she was going to find some food. That had been more than an hour ago. e sHe suspected she was wandering the camp, exploring. Eli had felt the urge to do so himself but was tired and had instead settled for just relaxing by the fire for a time.

Before they had left the area around the mine, he, Mae, and Jit had managed to retrieve their things, along with their bows. Once at the camp, Utreek had seen that food was delivered. They had eaten a meal of salt pork, bathed in the lake, and washed away the sweat, gore, and grime of battle.

Eli found his gaze traveling back to Mae. Feeling more than a little troubled, he eyed her for a long moment. He was not quite sure what they had, but it was growing. He could feel it as if it were a tangible bond between them, and that worried him more than going into battle ever had.

Without a doubt, a serious fight was coming. Their lives would once again be put at risk. Eli felt a strong desire—no, a powerful need to shelter Mae from harm. To be sure, it was an irrational impulse. He knew that, but he felt it just the same.

Mae was a ranger, an elite guardian, the first line of defense for their people. Just as his was, her life would be filled with danger and risk. Eli had accepted that for himself, but he was not quite so certain he could do the same for her.

Did he even have the right to try?

Other rangers had become emotionally involved with their partners. When it was discovered, the end result was always the same. They were broken up and reassigned new partners. They were barred from working together. It was either that or they hung up their bows and stepped down from the Ranger Corps.

There was no thought to giving up the Corps. Eli loved what he did, and if he allowed their relationship to grow, they could not remain partnered. It simply would not be allowed. There were no exceptions. The thought of being separated from Mae pained him. That in and of itself was a surprise too, one he found he did not much enjoy.

Then, there was Mae's mother to consider. Eli had no idea how she would respond when she learned of her daughter's feelings, let alone Eli's. Heck, he did not know how he felt about it himself. He certainly was not ready to settle down and begin a family. Studying Mae, he knew she would feel the same.

But one thing he did know, Mae had unexpectedly grown on him. And now, as odd as it seemed, he could imagine no one else filling her place in his life. Without meaning to, he had become attached to her. She had filled a hole, something he had not been aware was missing from his life.

How had that happened? Eli was truly mystified. It was yet another mystery of life to ponder, one that required some serious thought.

The scuff of a step broke him from his thoughts. He looked up to find Jit had returned. Standing on the other side of the fire, she held two wooden bowls that steamed in the afternoon sunlight. A thick hunk of dark brown bread stuck out of each bowl.

"I found some stew." Jit raised one of the bowls higher. "I thought you might like some. There's an open place over there where we might eat." With a jerk of her head, she indicated a felled tree a few feet away.

Stomach growling with hunger, Eli pulled himself to his feet and followed Jit as she led him away from the fire and the two sleeping elves. She handed him the bowl. Eli took the bread out, which was hard-crusted but clearly fresh. The other half was sodden and dark with brown stew.

He took a bite, chewed, and swallowed. "It's good." He dipped the bread back into the stew to sop up some more. The stew had sliced carrots, potatoes, and peas, along with small chunks of venison. It was salty, the venison likely having been salted to preserve it. "Quite good actually. Thank you for this."

"I had to wait until the woman making it had finished cooking," Jit explained.

"Thank you for that also," Eli said between a mouthful of bread. "I have had undercooked meat before, and it never seems to go down well. Besides, this is better than the rations we have been carrying."

Jit looked amused by the statement.

"You know, the woman's village is over thirty miles away," Jit said, after swallowing a bite. "There are people from all over the region coming to this camp, with more arriving all the time." Jit took another bite of her bread and chewed thoughtfully for several moments. "Many of the villages not only sent their warriors but have sent food too. Incredible, isn't it?"

"Yes," Eli said, glancing around, "quite amazing. In all my years, I have never seen the like."

"Edgun's been harsh," Jit said. "Had he taken a softer approach to rule, things might have been different. The people might have accepted him."

"That is all water under the bridge now. Lord Edgun has cast the die. This is the result."

Eli sat down upon the tree that had been chopped down. The trunk had been shorn of its limbs, and it was only a matter of time until it was broken up for firewood. Jit took a seat next to him. Eli sopped the bread some more and took another bite. As he chewed, he continued to look around, marveling at all that was before them.

People were everywhere, not just women and children, but warriors too. There was no organization to the camp, no defenses. People had simply settled down wherever there had been room. He knew there had to be sentries out, but still, it was nothing like an imperial legionary encampment or any other camp he had ever spent time in. And he found it all terribly fascinating.

"It's like a big family gathering," Eli said after a moment's thought, "an extended family at that."

"My people typically don't take their children to war." Her tone had become distant, almost wistful as she watched a group of young children playing a game of tag. "Only men who reached age were accepted and..."

She fell quiet.

"Shield-maidens like you?" Eli prompted.

"Yes," Jit said quietly.

"Someone brought you along, then," Eli probed. "Is that it?"

"Like he had a choice," Jit snorted. "I told my man I was coming and that was the end of it. Besides, it wasn't like it was my first time out. I've gone on raids and expeditions before. We are a strong people, and the women are free to do as they choose." Jit took another bite and chewed slowly as she spoke. "My man died soon after our boat slid up onto the beach." She became quiet for several heartbeats. "I mourn his loss still."

"I am sorry. It must be painful."

"He died well," Jit said.

In Eli's experience no one ever died well. They just died, some before their time and others through old age. Either way, the result was the same: Their spirits traveled onto the next life, leaving behind only the shell of their body.

"He's in Odin's hall, feasting away," Jit continued, "likely drunk as can be and having a great time boasting and telling tall tales for others' enjoyment. For a warrior, there is no happier place to end up."

"I do not know Odin," Eli said.

"Few in these lands do," Jit said with a sigh, falling silent as she chewed on the bread.

"Did you intend to come here?" Eli asked.

"Do you mean to the Kingdom of the Castol or crossing of the ocean?"

"The ocean," Eli said. "The Eastern Ocean. That is where you landed, right?"

"We don't call it that," Jit said. "But in answer to your question, no. We were headed elsewhere, an island actually, and had no intention of landing on imperial shores. A storm blew us far, far off course. I doubt any of my people have ever made it to these lands, for they are very rich. If we had, you would have seen more of us and known the fear of our coming."

Eli looked over at that and read only seriousness in her expression. "Knowing how well you fight, I can only imagine."

"Our land is a harsh one and there are far better fighters than me, and a lot of us too," Jit said. "Trust me on that."

There was no doubt in his mind she believed what she said.

"How did you find Rivun?" Eli asked.

"It was the other way around. He sort of found me," Jit said as a gaggle of young boys ran by.

The group slowed as they passed and eyed Eli with interest before picking up the pace again and dashing off. Many others had stopped by throughout the day to stare and ogle the elves, but that had grown old. Only the children came by now.

"I like this valley," Jit said, running her gaze around the steep ridges that hemmed it in. "With all the families here, it is a happy place."

Eli agreed. He glanced down at his bowl of stew. "I am surprised you did not bring any food for Rivun."

Jit looked over at the sleeping Anagradoom a few yards away. Eli read concern in her gaze. "He needs his sleep more than he needs food right now. Rivun is recovering his strength. When he wakes in a short while, he will eat like a mother bear after hibernation, then likely sleep some more."

"You have seen him heal before," Eli said as a statement and not a question.

Jit looked away for a moment, as if to consider her answer, then gave a curt nod.

"I have."

"You don't like it, do you?"

Jit shook her head. "Each time he heals, the effort takes a measure of what he calls his lifeforce. He's told me, over the years, he has used up much of what the gods gave him." She hesitated a fraction of a heartbeat. "Healing is a gift he now wishes he'd never received, for it comes with a terrible price."

Eli turned slightly to look over at Rivun. Was it true? Was that the bargain he had made with the God of Shadows? Had the rest of the Anagradoom done the same? Under the light of the afternoon sun, Rivun looked a little ashen to Eli's eyes. He glanced back upon Jit and read the naked worry there, the fear of losing one she loved.

"He does not have much time left," Eli said, his heart suddenly feeling heavy, "does he?"

Once again, Jit did not immediately answer. She turned her gaze to the ground at her feet and set her unfinished stew by her side.

"I don't believe so."

Eli felt a fountain of sadness well up within. "That is unfortunate."

"The first time I saw him do it, heal himself," Jit said, "was to save me, just after we first met. He had been left for dead and was really in rough shape, worse than how we found him down in the mine. He had been stabbed multiple times and was near death. After—after the healing and saving me, he slept for two days straight." Her voice turned to a whisper. "I thought he would not wake up. I fear one day he will use up all he has left and then leave this world for good."

Eli sucked in a breath and let it out. He glanced again over at Rivun, then returned to work on his stew, with less interest than before. After a time, Jit dipped her bread back into her stew and ate almost mechanically, her gaze distant and staring out at the camp, but really not seeing.

Together, they worked at the stew in silence, neither saying another word. Eli knew the conversation between them was at an end.

The sound of soft crying and sniffing carried over the sounds of celebration. It was something he had not heard in the valley, not until now. Having finished the last of the stew, he placed the bowl down on the log next to him.

A small redheaded girl off to the left, around four or five years of age, was sitting by a fire. She was painfully thin, and her clothes were threadbare. Though she had been cleaned up and her hair brushed and braided, Eli knew from her dress and pale skin she was one of the freed slaves who had been locked in the mine. With an arm around her shoulders, a woman sat with her, holding the little girl, comforting her as she sobbed.

At times, there was so much sadness in the world that Eli felt his heart would break into a million pieces. His hand inadvertently went to the ragdoll tucked into his belt. He glanced down at the doll. It was really a sad thing.

He now knew why he had been driven to take it with him. Eli stood.

"Where are you going?" Jit asked curiously, breaking the silence.

"To see if I can ease a measure of sadness and to give some comfort."

Jit's gaze went to the girl. Grabbing her bowl and then Eli's, she stood. "I think I will clean these down at the lake and then return them to the kind woman who shared her meal with us."

"Thank her for me."

"I will," Jit said and strode off.

Turning away, Eli walked over to the fire where the little girl and woman sat. The woman looked up as he approached. Her gaze was wary and guarded.

"What's wrong?" Eli asked the woman. "Why is she crying?"

"She misses her parents," the woman spoke with a coarse accent, "and everything else that's been done to her. Bloody blackhearted Edgun."

"Her parents—did they...?" Eli suddenly found he could not finish. He felt like he'd been punched in the gut.

"No," the woman said. "She was taken as a hostage, along with others, from her village. By taking their children, that bastard Edgun thought it'd keep the people of her village in line."

Eli felt a wave of relief. He glanced around, then returned his gaze to the little girl. "They are not here, are they?"

The woman shook her head. "I know them both and will make sure she gets back to her kin. I won't leave her alone, if yer worried about that."

Eli knelt before the little girl. She had stopped crying. She gave a snuffle as she looked up at him with eyes that were puffy and red, but unafraid.

"What is your name, little one?" Eli asked.

"Sophi," she said in a small voice.

"That is as pretty a name as I've heard." Eli smiled reassuringly and pulled the doll from his belt. He glanced down at it and thought of the girl who had once owned the ragged thing and loved it. "I have something for you."

Her eyes fell upon the doll and lit up. Eli looked to her and then back down at the doll. He found himself choked up. With not a little effort, he cleared his throat and handed it over. The girl took it and held the doll tight against her chest.

"The doll's name is Inna," Eli said. "Do you think you can take care of her for me? Keep Inna from being scared?"

"Inna," she said, trying out the name.

"She belonged to another little girl, just like you. Her name was Destina and she does not need it anymore. I—I think she would like you to have Inna, to take care of. Do you think you can do that for me? Can you be brave for Inna and look after her?"

Sophi gave a serious nod. Though he felt like weeping, Eli forced a smile. He reached out a hand and gave her a pat on the top of the head, then stood.

"Thank you," the woman said, and Eli saw tears brimming her eyes. "Thank you for that."

"I wish I could do more."

"Don't we all," the woman said.

Eli turned away, prepared to move back to his own fire. He found Karenna standing a few yards from him. She wore her armor but for the helmet and was watching. With her was Utreek. They had seen the entire encounter with Sophi. Two of her guard stood a few feet from her. Eli eyed the redheaded leader of the rebellion for a long moment.

He had the feeling she had come to find him.

"I guess it is time we talked," Eli said to himself and made his way over to her. The guards watched him warily as he approached but did not move to bar him from her. That confirmed his suspicion.

She wanted something. That much was plain.

CHAPTER EIGHTEEN

"That was a kind gesture," Karenna said, her gaze going back briefly to the little girl before returning to Eli.

"Agreed." Utreek held a wineskin. "It was."

"Some days I feel I have witnessed too much suffering," Eli said, glancing back at the little girl, who was alternating between kissing the ragdoll and hugging it protectively. "Were I able, I would render more kindness."

"Suffering and loss is a part of life," Karenna said. "There are also many blessings. We must each treasure what we have been given to help us through these bad times."

"You sound like a philosopher," Eli said.

"Hardly," Karenna said, running her gaze across the camp. "My eyes have been opened, is all. I have been given the opportunity to reach beyond my own immediate needs, to serve others, like little Sophi there. I offer hope, a brighter future, where before there was none."

"Nobly spoken," Eli said.

She looked back at him, and Eli found her expression a strange one. Once again, he had the uncomfortable feeling she had not been surprised to find him in the fort.

Utreek held up the wineskin and shook it. "I came to find Rivun. I owe him a drink."

"He seems pretty tired." Eli glanced back on his campfire, where Rivun and Mae still slept.

"He wanted a drink," Utreek said. "I am a man of my word."

"That you are." Karenna looked over at her husband and her lip curled slightly in a smile. "We will be moving shortly after sunset. Make sure you are able to walk."

"I will be able to walk and hold a sword, wife." Utreek gave an amused grunt and left them, moving toward the sleeping elf.

Eli wondered idly if Utreek would be able to wake Rivun.

"Would you care to walk with me?" Karenna asked.

"I would be honored," Eli said.

"Good," Karenna said. "It is not every day I have the opportunity to converse with an elven ranger."

Karenna started off and Eli fell in at her side as they began walking through the valley and camp. As if to contradict herself, she did not speak again for some time. Eli did not feel the need to break the silence either. When she was ready to say whatever was on her mind, he knew she would.

They snaked their way around tents, campfires, and through groups of people who stepped aside. Wherever they went, people grew silent, stood, and touched their hands to their foreheads in a mark of respect. Even the children stopped playing to watch her, in what Eli could only describe as awe.

"These are not my people," Karenna said after a time. "I only married one of them."

"From your accent, I'd say you were imperial and of noble birth."

"Very good, elf." She drew to a stop and turned to face him. "In another lifetime, I was the daughter of an imperial legate. He commanded a legion on the border, the Sixth."

"I know the Sixth," Eli said. "We are allies of the empire."

"My father's name was Lucius Ren Varreenus."

"I never had the honor of meeting Legate Varreenus, but I have heard the name."

Years before, Varreenus had been assassinated. Or was it that he had been killed in a skirmish? Eli could not recall which. At the time, his death had created tensions between the empire and the kingdom. The incident had almost led to war.

"I was his only child," Karenna continued. "Though I was not the boy he desired, he loved me all the same. I was lucky in some ways, for I never wanted, and he indulged me. My father was a good man. I learned what most girls in my position do not."

"How to fight?" Eli surmised.

"That and how to lead, to command," Karenna said. "It was great fun, until it wasn't. Little did we know how important his training would later prove to be."

"What happened?"

"My father and I, along with a small escort, were traveling between outposts on an inspection tour of the border, making certain the auxiliaries were doing their jobs. I was fifteen."

She stopped speaking for a long moment as a group of children ran past. They slowed and touched their hands to their foreheads, then sped off, disappearing around a large tent.

"We were set upon and attacked as we traveled between outposts. He was killed and I was captured." Her gaze became harder as she turned back to him. "My captors brought me north, over the border, and sold me as a slave— me, an imperial noblewoman."

"Utreek bought you?" Eli guessed.

"No," Karenna said. "Another man, Sestentus, did. He was a cruel master and showed me for the first time how low one can sink in this life." Her tone became a whisper. "He used my body for his pleasure and regularly beat me when I displeased him. I learned despair, but I never lost faith, and nightly I prayed for a reckoning."

She fell silent as they passed a group of people eating around a fire. All stood, touched their hands to their heads, and watched silently, until Karenna, Eli, and the escort had passed.

"Utreek saw me one day at market. Like a lovesick puppy, he became instantly smitten. He's a good man and I am fortunate. Perhaps it was the gods taking a hand in events, or just a lonely heart and youthful lust. Whatever the cause, he, with a band of his own people, raided Sestentus's village that night. He and Sestentus fought in one-on-one combat."

"Sestentus obviously lost," Eli said, when she fell silent.

"He lost not only me, but his life," Karenna said. "However, Utreek was seriously wounded. He and his band took me away and I helped him recover, to heal. An affection grew between us, and ultimately, Utreek came to love me and I him. He gave me a choice, return home to the empire or remain with him as his wife. He desired me for his own, but only if I came willingly."

"Why tell me this?" Eli asked.

"Because you need to understand. Though I love them, these people are not my people. Just as you are, I will always forever be an outsider to them."

"I do not understand," Eli said. "They honor you with great respect. They have accepted you."

"Yes, they have accepted me," Karenna said. "But still, I will forever be an outsider in their eyes. Worse, because of what I have done, they will hold me above them. They will revere me, defer to me. For the moment, I tolerate the behavior, for it suits my needs."

"You are their leader. It is expected."

"A temporary one," Karenna said, glancing around. "I have earned their respect, their hearts, fired their imagination for a future free of oppression. They love me for what I have done, for the hope I have given them. But I am not one of them—and I never will be."

Karenna and Eli moved around a tent and came upon a large group of warriors eating around a fire. They made to stand.

"Please, friends, stay seated," Karenna said to them. But they still stood respectfully until she had passed. She did not speak for another ten steps. "I will see that they are free of Edgun's oppression and tyranny, but I am not the one destined to lead them as a people. That is a job for another."

"How can you be so certain, so sure?"

"My time as leader is almost at an end," Karenna said, sounding suddenly weary. She stopped and closed her eyes. "I can sense that time fast approaching, and to be honest, I long for release."

"Release?"

"I never wanted this," Karenna said, opening her eyes. She looked back at her guard, who had dropped back. She lowered her voice so only Eli could hear and took a step closer. "Soon, I will be finished with this task that has been set before me—I will be free, free to live, to make a life. Though it will break his heart, Utreek will go with me because he loves me, and together, we will leave all this behind, for such was promised."

Eli stopped, staring at her for a long moment, his gaze going to her elven-made armor.

"You are a paladin."

"No, not a paladin," Karenna said as she resumed walking again.

"Then what are you?" Eli had the uncomfortable feeling he was speaking with one who had been blessed by the gods. There was something strange about her. Or was she simply crazy? Someone who had grand delusions? Eli had encountered such people before, individuals who thought they had been touched by the divine. Sometimes they led others to their own destruction.

"A holy warrior, yes, but no, not a paladin. I am not quite that pure of heart. More importantly, I desire no such an honor. Though I am faithful, I do not seek a lifetime of service. I have a smaller part to play in what is to come."

"And what is that?" Eli hurried to catch up and once again fell in at her side. "You knew I was coming, didn't you?"

Karenna glanced over at him. "I was expecting two rangers, but not you specifically."

"I do not understand."

She pointed at one of his daggers. "I was shown that, to know you, to recognize friend from foe."

Eli glanced down at the dagger. Rivun had owned it and passed it along to Garus, who had in turn given it to him. He looked back up at her and touched his dagger with a finger. "Your god showed you this? He showed you the future?"

Eli felt uncomfortable at the notion that what was to come had been foreseen, set in stone. What bothered Eli was not that she had been shown the future, but the possibility that there was no free will, that freedom was only an illusion ... that everything that was to come had been written. A small subset of his people believed in such notions. But not Eli. He had always rebelled against that, preferring to believe he made his own choices in life.

"I was blessed with a vision of a number of possible outcomes. Those each came with a price, and a choice to be made. I chose the hardest, most difficult path to walk, for if successful"—she held out her hands—"these people will benefit greatly."

Eli looked around at the people camped in the valley. "Will you tell me the choice you made?"

"I have suffered greatly." Karenna let go a heavy breath. "So too have these people. But in the end, I will suffer some more, and then I will have what I crave most, peace and a chance for a good life. That is, if we are successful here." She stopped again and looked over at him. "You and I, we have a common friend."

"Oh?" Eli asked. "Who?"

"The caretaker." Karenna started walking again.

Eli missed a step as he made to follow. He was about to respond when Karenna continued.

"The caretaker is more than he seems. You understand that, right?"

"I thought so too," Eli said, surprised she knew the caretaker. "But I don't fully understand what he represents."

"When I was lost," Karenna said, "adrift, and unsure whether to stay with Utreek or return to my people, he helped me find my way, my balance. For that I named him a friend."

"I found him to be helpful too, and also a friend. His valley is a peaceful place."

"I do not know of the valley you speak of," Karenna said, "only of his cave to the west of Brek."

"His cave?" Eli felt his brows knit together. "What cave?"

"The caretaker resides in many places," Karenna said, "and cares for many Gray Fields. He is more a guide than anything else."

"Many places?" Eli was surprised by that statement.

"You did not know?"

Eli shook his head.

"Oh yes," Karenna said, "and on many worlds, too, though in different forms. As I said, he is more than he seems."

Eli found himself rocked. He knew the caretaker was something different, an oracle of some kind, but…was there more to him? This new information had him reevaluating everything he knew about the caretaker, the valley, and—the Gray Field. And how could he be in several places at once?

"Years ago," Karenna said, interrupting his thoughts, "I swore vengeance upon the man who had killed my father and enslaved me. Soon, I shall finally have my opportunity to mete out a long overdue justice."

"Edgun," Eli guessed, finding himself even more surprised. "He was the one who killed your father and enslaved you?"

"Yes," Karenna said. "He is a mercenary, nothing more. Edgun found favor with the king and was rewarded with the town of Brek and surrounding region as his personal domain. I will kill him for what he has done, not only to me, but to many others. With the caretaker's help, I promised his soul in repayment for all the evil he has done in this life."

"And your god answered?"

"He has given me a purpose, a chance to see the deed done. It will be this blade"—she came to a stop and patted the hilt of her sword—"and this one alone that must lay him low."

"Why you and not someone else?" Eli gestured about him at the camp. "I am sure there are others here who are just as deserving. I promised to kill him for what he did to Taibor, and a little girl named Destina."

"Edgun has committed many wrongs, and terrible evil, but it must be my blade that ends him." Karenna's eyes fairly blazed. "This sword will finish him and his evil, once and for all. I will end the cycle."

Eli glanced down at the blade sheathed at her side. She had not answered his question. "Why? Why you?"

"Edgun follows Valoor," Karenna explained.

Eli had never had much contact with followers of Valoor. The religion was widely practiced far to the south and across the Narrow Sea.

"From death," Karenna continued, "his god brings back the true believers, the most loyal of servants, and rewards them, especially those most ardent and faithful, with a new life."

"You are talking reincarnation," Eli said. He had never believed in the concept. "If you kill him, won't he just be reborn to commit more evil deeds?"

"Edgun is Valoor's agent here in the north. He is a missionary of sorts and, like a cancer, works to spread that evil faith." She patted the hilt of her sword again, almost fondly. "When I kill him, it ends. This weapon is called a Mourning Blade. It is special and will break the loop of rebirth, death, and rebirth, at least for Edgun. He will cross over the great divide and find himself caught between life and death. There he will be imprisoned for all eternity. With Edgun's end, Valoor's efforts in these parts will be hindered and see a setback. More importantly, it will open the way for what must come."

Eli eyed the sword for a long moment. The hilt looked ornate and well-made. He could see nothing that seemed to make it different from other swords other than its quality. Then again, many magical items he had encountered over the years looked quite ordinary. He looked back up at her and wondered for a moment if this woman was delusional. Then again, the ways of the gods were mysterious, and she was very different from most humans he had known.

He glanced around the valley and all those who had gathered here. She had united the people in this region, who had historically feuded. She had given them common purpose and a focus. He looked back at her. Perhaps it was as she said.

"I am Champion for my god; so too is Edgun for his," Karenna said. "From the moment I picked up this blade and donned the armor, we, Edgun and I, became destined to meet on the field of battle. There, things will be settled once and for all."

Eli blinked. He had heard of such Champions before. But those had been tales of things that had happened on Tannis, the world from which his people had come. Karus, the human emperor, had been one. Yet nothing like that had occurred before on Istros, at least to his knowledge. If true, it needed to be reported back to the warden, for it meant momentous things were afoot.

"What is happening here is a contest between gods?" Eli asked. "Do I have that right? That is what you are telling me, yes?"

"What happens between me and Edgun sets the stage for what is to come. Eli, in the years ahead, you will have your own part to play, one that is—"

A warrior rushed up, interrupting her. He had a horn tied to his belt, along with a sword. He wore black leather armor. The warrior was red-faced and out of breath. She turned to face him and raised an eyebrow in question.

"Karenna," the warrior gasped. "I apologize for the interruption."

"Speak," she said. "Give me the news you bear. How bad is it?"

"Lord Edgun's army is a mile away to the south and closing on the valley."

Karenna blinked, then took a step back, clearly stunned. At first, she appeared confused, at a loss for what to do, then her expression hardened as she regained an ironclad control of her emotions and her composure. It all happened in a mere two or three heartbeats. Eli almost missed it.

"How?" Karenna demanded. "How did we not spot them sooner? What about the scouts? They were positioned miles out in all directions."

"We don't know," the man said, "but the enemy host is almost upon us. Lord Edgun has been spotted too, marching at the army's head. He brings all of his men, thousands."

Karenna was silent for a long moment, her gaze going to the southern ridgeline, almost as if she could peer through the trees and ridges that hemmed the valley in. Her eyes blinked rapidly. She was clearly thinking furiously.

"They have not taken my bait at the mine." Karenna sounded disappointed as she thought aloud. "Worse, Beekus's men are at the mine and of no use to us. How could Edgun know we are here?"

"I don't know," the man said, struggling to catch his breath. "A group of warriors from the village of Kessix, coming into the camp, spotted their approach."

"Mik'Las." Eli snapped his fingers. He knew he should have foreseen this possibility, but after the fight, he had not thought of it. He now regretted that lapse.

Karenna's gaze went to him. It was hard and cold.

"Mik'Las was once a ranger, or at least he trained as one. He is skilled at forest craft. He is responsible for discovering your presence here and has led Lord Edgun to you. I am sure of it. He also likely killed your scouts watching the route the enemy is taking to reach this valley. He is proving his worth to Edgun."

She gave a nod, then turned to one of her guards. There was steel in her tone when she spoke. "I want the chieftains and headmen to assemble their warriors on the north side of the valley, along the top of the ridge. Under no circumstances is anyone to make a stand in the valley itself, except for our skirmishers. They will fight a rearguard action. Our main body will form up there, along the heights, with all our strength. Find Utreek. My Elite are to form up on the east ridge and out of sight. They are to prepare for a movement to flank the enemy." She pointed where she wanted them. "Also see that the word is spread. Get the women and children as far from here as their legs will carry them. None are to remain and everything that was brought into the valley, tents, personal possessions, are to remain. Those can be replaced; the lives of our people cannot. Understand?"

"It will be done, Karenna." He touched his hand to his head and dashed off.

She turned to Eli and regarded him for a long moment.

"So much for my trap, then. It seems Edgun, in his boldness, has come to us, to settle things here and now." She fell silent for a long moment, her gaze once again traveling to the south. "Do you know the name of this valley?"

Eli shook his head. "I do not."

"This place is the Valley of Tears," Karenna said. "It is an apt name, don't you think?"

Eli did not reply.

"Many will surely die here in the next few hours. Much grief will come of this day." Karenna paused to suck in a breath. "A goddess was once said to reside here. When all the gods left the world of the living for Olimbus, her people, her worshippers, wept tears of grief that they could not go with her."

"What goddess was that?" Eli asked.

"Fortuna."

Eli did not like the sound of that. Fortuna was a mischievous and fickle goddess, sometimes helping, other times doing the opposite, actively working to a counter-purpose.

"Edgun, by coming to me, has made a fateful mistake."

"And what is that mistake?" Eli asked.

"He has come out from behind the walls of his castle and is now vulnerable." Karenna met his gaze. In her eyes, Eli saw a gnawing hunger for revenge. "When it comes time, *I* must be the one to fight Edgun. Help make that happen."

"How?" Eli asked.

"When the moment strikes, you will know what to do."

Her jaw gave a tic, then she looked back upon the messenger and pointed down at the horn he wore at his side.

"Sound the alarm, rouse the camp to arms." With that, she spared Eli one last look, turned away, and strode off, leaving him to stare at her retreating back.

The man with the horn brought it to his lips and began to blow.

Taaa'Hooo, Taaa'Hoo, Taaa'Hoooooo.

CHAPTER NINETEEN

Eli dropped to a knee, placing his bow down upon the bald-faced rock next to him as he turned his gaze down into the valley. A light gust of wind blew around him, rustling the leaves on the nearest trees. It brought a modicum of relief from the hot and humid air.

Mae, Rivun, and Jit were with him. They were all watching the enemy army from a large rock outcropping along the northern ridgeline. But for a handful of Karenna's people with bows below, the center of the valley had been thoroughly abandoned. These few fought a mini battle with the enemy's skirmishers as they were giving ground and retreating steadily northward.

Eli watched an enemy skirmisher take an arrow to the chest and collapse to his knees. He grabbed with both hands at the shaft of the arrow protruding from his chest and attempted to pull it free. His effort caused him to give a convulsive jerk. A heartbeat later, he fell backward to the ground and moved no more.

One of Karenna's warriors was struck next. He staggered and fell to the ground, an arrow lodged in the back of his right thigh. The missile had punched clean through the leg. With the enemy just yards from him, he hastily scrambled back to his feet and struggled to follow his fellows, only to be hit again, this time square in the back. He toppled face-first into a campfire that had been abandoned. Lying with his face in the flames, he did not move.

Eli expelled an unhappy breath at the killing and moved his gaze beyond the running fight. Farther down the valley, a column of march, two men abreast, snaked down from the southern ridgeline to the valley's base. The tail end of the column had yet to emerge from the trees, giving the impression it was endless.

Lord Edgun's soldiers were clearly disciplined, for none of the enemy broke ranks as they began moving by the first of the abandoned tents and campfires, where food still cooked over an open flame. A less disciplined force might have had men fall out of formation to loot. That told Eli the coming fight would be a difficult one.

Somewhat concealed by a thin line of trees and brush to their front and just below the outcropping of rock, hundreds upon hundreds of Karenna's warriors waited. The massing of her warriors spread out to the left and right, disappearing off into the trees, concealing thousands more from his sight. They carried all manner of weapons, axes, swords, and spears. Eli even saw a pitchfork. Some wore various types of armor, but most wore only a tunic for protection against the elements. Almost all of them carried a shield of some type.

No attempt had been made to conceal their presence, and he knew the enemy would be able to see this force waiting. Along the east side of the valley, about a quarter of a mile distant, another force of Karenna's warriors was moving through the trees. Small groups of them appeared every few moments as they moved through gaps in the trees, and then they were gone, hidden by the foliage. Could the enemy see them too? From the angle and the thickness of the trees on that side of the valley, Eli doubted it.

Karenna was nowhere to be seen. In fact, now that Eli thought on it, he had not seen her since their talk below, more than an hour ago.

Where had she gone?

On the southern end of the valley, a second column of infantry emerged from the tree line. Eli watched as this fresh column began moving alongside the first, working their way down the ridge toward the lake below. Eli estimated that between the two columns, there were at least twelve hundred men. It was an impressive show of force.

Off somewhere in the distance, thunder rumbled once again, this time a long, drawn-out grumble of discontent, as if the Great Mother was unhappy with what was about to happen.

Eli glanced skyward, just as the sun broke from behind a cloud and shone down upon the lake. The water glittered brilliantly with reflected light of the late afternoon sun. Eli lifted a hand to block the sudden brightness.

The clouds scudding by overhead were scattered, puffy, and dark. There was a disturbed look to them. Off to the left side of the valley, the edge of a huge thundercloud was in view, threatening, angry, and reaching high into the sky.

The coming fight would be bad enough without a driving rain to add to the misery. Eli hoped the inclement weather held off, but then he thought on the name of the valley and the goddess who had reputedly resided and been worshipped here.

It would rain. There was no question about that.

A small group on horseback appeared on the far ridge. With them rode a man bearing a large square standard. The standard featured what Eli took to be a boar, but at this distance, he could not be certain. For all he knew it could be a cow or more likely a bull. Yes, he decided, after studying it for a moment. It was a bull. Next to the standard-bearer rode a man in full plate mail. The armor had a dullish gray cast.

"That's Edgun." Rivun pointed at the armored man, who had his helmet off. It was held under the crook of one arm, while the other held the reins of his horse. Eli supposed the other riders were either escorts or trusted aides.

He could not see much of Edgun's features, other than he had dark hair and, sitting upon his warhorse, seemed rather a squat fellow. Spooked by something, his horse skittered sidewise. Edgun tightened his hold upon the reins and the horse steadied in reply.

The tail end of the first column finally emerged from the trees. Several heartbeats later and following, a third column of infantry appeared. This new line of soldiers, with an officer marching at their head, followed the other two down into the heart of the valley. The officer saluted Edgun with his sword as he made his way by. Edgun raised a hand in reply.

Drummers were with this column as well, hammering out a marching beat.

"I see Mik'Las." Mae pointed beyond the riders.

The criminal had emerged from the forest and was walking up to Lord Edgun. At his side was another elf, a female, who wore a flowing white dress. She had long black hair that had been tied into a single braid, which was draped over her right shoulder and down her chest. She had a hand on the braid and seemed to be playing with it, running her fingers up and down the tightly bound hair as if in habit.

"And with him is Sariss'Sa," Mae added. "We are so close."

"Yes," Eli agreed. "So close and yet so far. There is an army between us and them."

"Why did he have to take a tree shepherd?" Rivun asked. "Of all things to do, why an Atreena?"

"We do not know," Eli said. "It could be because he fancied her, or there might be some other reason. Mik'Las has always been an obtuse person, someone at the best of times who is, on the surface, inscrutable."

"He is truly a fool, then," Rivun said with heat. "Si'Cara will not rest until Sariss'Sa is returned."

"What is an Atreena?" Jit asked. "Who is she?"

"An Atreena is a person who is able to communicate with the forest far beyond the average elf," Rivun explained to her.

"Like how you occasionally meditate?" Jit asked. "I think you called it speaking to the trees?"

"Yes," Rivun said, "only her communication is on a deeper, more fundamental level. It is a rare gift amongst the High Born, one that is treasured beyond estimation. Given sufficient time, an Atreena can coax, shape, and bend nature to her will in ways you cannot possibly imagine. She wields a unique magic."

"And he took her?" Jit asked.

"Yes," Mae confirmed. "He murdered Sariss'Sa's brother and took her in the dead of night."

Eli noticed Mik'Las seemed to have spotted them. After a moment, the criminal raised a hand and waved as if in greeting. Eli could almost imagine Mik'Las smiling. Eli longed to wipe the smile from his face.

The Atreena at his side followed Mik'Las's gaze. Her hand released her braided hair and fell to her side. Eli got the impression she was nervous and had not expected to find elves here. Then she said something to him. Mik'Las replied and continued to wave at them.

"He is rather bold," Rivun said.

"Mik'Las has always been full of himself." Eli let go a breath. "Since we were children, he and I never really got along."

"Why?" Rivun asked. "What rubbed you wrong about him?"

"I do not like bullies, never have."

Rivun then looked back over at Eli. "Your history with him—is that why the warden chose you for this mission?"

"Most likely," Eli said. "That and she knows I will do whatever I need to do to get the job done. I always do, no matter how distasteful the task."

"Garus did mention you were persistent," Rivun said, "like a dog that does not let go of a bone."

"What else did he say about me?"

"Beyond you being a general pain in his ass?" Rivun asked.

"Eli, a pain in the ass?" Mae scoffed. "I find that shocking."

"Is it possible this Atreena went with him willingly?" Jit asked before Eli could respond. She gestured across the valley. Both Mik'Las and the Atreena were still looking their way. "She does not appear to be with him against her will. Do you believe they are in love? Could that explain his actions?"

"It does not matter if they were romantically involved," Rivun said, hardness coming into his tone. "Murder is one thing, messing with an Atreena is something altogether different. There will be no forgiveness for such a transgression."

"As if there is forgiveness for murder," Eli said.

"Atreenas are so rare," Mae explained to Jit, "their marriages are carefully arranged with those lines known for consistently producing the gift in the hopes of creating more such gifted individuals."

Rivun shifted uncomfortably and glanced over at Mae. "Regardless of the reason, Mik'Las's life is forfeit," Eli said in a firm tone, while shooting Mae a warning look. She had come close to revealing too much to an outsider, a human. "He will know this and that will make him unpredictable, desperate even. He is dangerous. We must be on guard when we face him."

A fourth column of soldiers emerged from the tree line, and as they did, Lord Edgun's men gave a hearty cheer. The sound of it thundered across the valley, like a wave crashing upon the beach.

"There is going to be one serious fight here." Rivun gestured with a hand at the enemy. "Those soldiers strike me as not only disciplined, but well-drilled too. They may even be veterans. Karenna's warriors will have a tough time of it."

"Yes," Eli said, "I agree. We are going to have to figure out how to get to Mik'Las and secure the Atreena."

"That will likely be tricky," Rivun said, "especially in the middle of a battle. We may not be able to reach him and the Atreena until everything is settled."

"That may prove true," Eli said. "However, we also need to help Karenna confront Lord Edgun. If he survives, this rebellion may be for naught."

Rivun looked over at him. "Are you certain she referred to herself as her god's Champion? She used those very words?"

Eli gave a nod. "She did."

Rivun looked out onto the valley again. He was silent for several heartbeats. "I had thought by coming to Istros, closing the Gate behind us, and giving it into the keeping of the First Ones, we were done with that sort of thing." He looked back over at Eli with a troubled expression.

Eli wondered what he meant by the First Ones.

"Do you believe her?" Rivun pressed. "Did you feel she was speaking truth?"

"As in she was a representative for her god?"

Rivun gave a nod. "That is exactly what I mean."

Eli thought for a moment, replaying his talk with Karenna in his mind. "I do believe her."

Rivun rubbed his jaw and turned away, gazing back out onto the enemy marching into the valley. His shoulders sagged slightly as if in defeat. "It seems the Last War has finally come to Istros. I fear difficult times lay ahead for us all, especially our people."

Eli felt a pang of worry. He vividly recalled what the caretaker had told him. By coming to Istros, his people had found a sanctuary from the unending war, a terrible struggle started by the gods. For nearly two thousand years, there had been no hint of the Last War coming to Istros, not even a stirring of possibility.

Was the time fast approaching when this world would be plunged into that terrible struggle for dominance which had almost ended his people? Eli prayed it was not so. But at the same time, he could not help but feel a little chilled by the prospect.

With the World Gate closed, sealed, and lost, his people thought themselves secure from such things. It would be a rude shock to all to discover they were anything but safe.

In fact, Eli was certain the news of even the possibility of the Last War coming to Istros would shake their society to its very foundations. Worse, many, especially the elders, would prefer to ignore reality rather than face it. They would turn their backs upon the threat in the hope it would go away. The caretaker had told him Si'Cara knew it was coming. What steps had the warden taken to prepare for it?

He glanced over at Mae and their gazes met. He saw she was having similar thoughts. Another shout from one of the enemy columns was followed up by a massed shout from the others that devolved into a steady chant. That drew his attention.

Eli could not tell what they were chanting, but it was quite loud. When it died down, Karenna's warriors, lined up on the slope before them, gave a reply that roared outward and seemed to go on and on. They screamed their rage, hate, and bile down at the men who supported their oppressor, Lord Edgun. It battered at the ears and rose from the throats of thousands, thundering across the valley.

The time for fighting was fast approaching. Both sides were working themselves up to it. Eli eyed the men moving covertly through the trees on the left side of the valley. Those appeared to have not given up a cheer with the others. That told him Karenna was doing her best to keep that force concealed as it moved to flank the enemy army.

"I think," Eli said to Rivun and pointed, "we make our way over there and go in after that force gets committed."

"I agree," Rivun said. "We can move along the entire length of the valley, perhaps even get behind the enemy's battle line." He gestured to the warriors to their front. "If I don't miss my mark, these men below us will get committed first, and those on the left, the east ridgeline, will be sent in after, as a flanking movement to try to turn the enemy's line. With luck it might even give us an opportunity to get to Mik'Las."

"That seems to be what Karenna has planned," Eli said. "Fix the enemy's attention to the front, and then smack them on the flank, rolling up the line." Eli looked over at Mae and Jit. "Any ideas or thoughts on what we're about to do?"

"No," Mae said. Her hand holding her bow was tight, knuckles white. She was nervous. So too was he, and not for himself. He worried for her safety.

"Jit?" Eli asked.

Jit had been staring hard at the enemy, her gaze fixed upon Lord Edgun. She shook herself and looked over. "I am fine with it. You and Rivun talk too much and overthink things. Let's get going before I grow old."

Eli shared an amused look with Rivun.

"All right then, come on." Rivun started off, climbing down off the ledge, which was only a four-foot drop to the slope below. He turned and looked back on Jit. "Do you need a hand down, old woman?"

Jit spared him a disgusted look and jumped down next to him. "Call me an old woman again and you will regret it, elf."

"Would you prefer 'old hag'?" Rivun asked.

Jit punched him lightly on the arm. "Next time you're captured, I'm leaving you to rot."

Eli picked up his bow and dropped down to the ground below. Mae followed. Some of the warriors to their front glanced around curiously at the elves. Eli ignored them, and with Rivun leading the way, they moved along behind the line of warriors massed thickly along the northern ridge. After a few yards, Rivun picked up the pace to a light jog, weaving his way around trees and low-lying brush, all the while continuing by Karenna's assembled warriors. Eli noticed that many of the human warriors were mere boys in their teens.

Losing sight of the valley below, they entered an area thick with brush and pine trees. As they continued to move behind the warriors, it became clear to Eli that Karenna wielded a very large force, more than had been apparent in the camp. He estimated that she had managed to bring together at least six thousand fighters, perhaps even more.

He glanced down into the valley as they came to a gap in the trees. Lord Edgun commanded perhaps five thousand men. The first two columns had made it down into the base of the valley. They were beginning to organize themselves into one long line of battle, four ranks deep. Behind the developing line, three block-like formations were coming together. These were clearly a reserve, perhaps another four hundred men each. The third column was feeding men into the main battle line and had yet to completely emerge from the trees along the top of the southern ridge.

"Quite a sight," Mae said, next to him.

"Yes," Eli agreed.

Could the enthusiasm of Karenna's warriors overcome the organization and training of Lord Edgun's soldiers? Eli did not have the answer to that question. Time, he knew, would soon tell him.

Then, the view of the valley was lost again as they plunged back into the trees. Rivun led them onward. It took them almost a half an hour to make their way to the east side of the valley, to the midway point, where Karenna had hidden the second force of her warriors.

These men had moved into position and taken a knee on a steep slope. They were thoroughly hidden from the enemy behind the trees and dense brush. He had no idea how many there were, for you could not see far with all the vegetation. They were as silent as a graveyard at night.

A cheer came from the valley. This was followed by more drumming, beating out an ominous beat.

Doon ... doon ... doon ...
Doon ... doon ... doon ...
Doon ... doon ... doon ...

Over and over the beat went. Eli supposed it was designed to intimidate. Instead, he found the incessant drumming grating on the ears and more annoying than anything else.

Rivun took a knee next to a tree that provided a partial view of the middle of the valley. Eli sank down next to him as thunder rumbled again in the distance, for a moment overriding the drumming. He wiped sweat from his forehead and looked around. Jit and Mae chose a spot ten yards away that afforded them a view.

Before them, six hundred yards distant and right after the lake, Lord Edgun's men were fully formed up in one long, continuous line of battle that intersected the middle of the valley. Four ranks deep, the enemy were facing the north ridge. The three block-like reserve formations waited behind the main battle line.

With standards flying and skirmishers out to the front, the enemy army looked impressive, overwhelming, and unbeatable. Still mounted upon his warhorse, Lord Edgun himself had moved to just behind the center of his line. He was conversing casually with an officer who was unmounted. Mik'Las stood five yards behind the man. The Atreena was nowhere to be seen. Eli found that somewhat troubling. He scanned all that was in view, searching, but could not see her. What had he done with her? Where had she gone?

Karenna's skirmishers had broken off their fight and had retreated, conceding the entirety of the valley to the enemy. They had left a line of scattered bodies, a testament to the quality of the enemy's skirmishers.

With legs that did not seem to work, a wounded man was attempting to drag himself away from the enemy skirmishers. It was a futile effort, for one casually walked up to him and stabbed him in the back with a sword.

Eli caught Rivun glancing over at Jit. His gaze seemed troubled. A moment later, he let out a low breath that sounded deeply unhappy.

"You love her," Eli said quietly to the Anagradoom, "don't you?"

"And if I do?" Rivun asked, looking back with a hard expression. "What of it?"

"You have sacrificed much for the Anagradoom," Eli said.

"More than you can possibly know," Rivun said. "I gave up everything, family, a wife, my children. I turned my back on all that I cherished so that our people could have a chance at a better future, one safe from the Last War. The price I—all of the Anagradoom—paid, was too much. I lost everything that was dear to me."

"The Anagradoom are honored and were blessed by the gods."

"Honored? Blessed?" Rivun snorted. "Those words are meaningless. For our great deed, we were cast out, exiled forever. Blessed? Cursed is more like it." Rivun looked away. Some of the heat left him. "What you witnessed at the mine, the healing—you may think that a blessing, but it is far from one. All you need know is that I can never do it again. If I try… I… I am finished. The price for healing is my lifeforce, which over the years has been greatly diminished."

"How much time do you have left?" Eli asked.

Rivun briefly looked over at Jit again. "Enough to grow old with her, to enjoy my final years with someone I have become fond of and care for deeply."

Eli gave a nod. He had expected the answer. He reached over and placed a hand upon Rivun's shoulder. "Make certain you survive today, so you can spend those years in blissful happiness."

"You do not find it repulsive?" Rivun seemed surprised.

"You and her?" Eli asked, glancing over at Jit. His gaze traveled to Mae. He felt a stab of worry for her and forcibly suppressed it.

"Yeah?" Rivun said. "She is human, and I am High Born. Do you have a problem with that?"

"I think," Eli said, looking back at him, "you have sacrificed enough for your people. Who am I to question what brings you joy in your final years?"

Rivun studied Eli for a long moment, as if to divine whether he spoke the truth or was just being kind.

"Thank you," Rivun said. "I appreciate your understanding."

"You are going to have your hands full with her," Eli said. "You realize that, right?"

"Knowing Jitanthra, it will be an exciting time. That is for certain."

Eli gave a chuckle. "Actually, I am rather envious of the excitement she will create for you."

"I'd be more worried about yourself than me."

"Me? Why?"

"That is the warden's daughter over there," Rivun said with a nod in Mae's direction. "There is no escaping that one, for she has got Si'Cara's fiery spirit. I just hope you can survive her attention and her mother, or should I say your future mother-in-law. Congratulations, by the way."

Eli resisted a grimace. "Mother-in-law? I had not thought that far ahead."

"Maybe it is time you started doing so," Rivun said.

A massive roar rose from Karenna's warriors massed along the north ridge. This was followed by the pounding of thousands of feet. The warriors gathered at the north end of the valley thundered down through the trees, brush, and long grass, screaming and shouting wildly as they charged Lord Edgun's line.

Eli watched as the tide of rage poured down into the valley toward the enemy. The hundreds of kneeling warriors before Eli and Rivun remained still, waiting, listening, and for those who could see some of the action, watching. They were silent and grim. Eli could sense the tension on the air. He was reminded of a nocked bow, the arrow waiting to be released at the enemy.

Almost in unison, below in the valley, the enemy's shields came up and locked together. Eli knew the soldiers were bracing themselves, preparing for the shocking and violent moment of contact. The enemy's skirmishers turned and ran for the safety of their own lines. A few stopped to fire a hastily aimed arrow, then legged it. Within moments, shields parted and allowed them through and into the safety of the line.

"The reserves," Mae called over to them, pointing. "They are in motion."

Eli saw that Edgun was indeed repositioning the blocks of men that waited behind the main battle line. All three formations were maneuvering to face the force that had yet to be committed, those concealed on this side of the valley. As he watched, they began reforming into a second line, forming an L-shaped defense.

Eli felt his heart sink a little. Edgun was aware of the men Karenna had hidden here on the east side of the valley. Any hope of surprise had been lost. The coming battle had just become more difficult for the rebels.

There was a tremendous crash as Karenna's charging warriors reached the enemy's battle line. The first rank of the enemy buckled under the onslaught and intense pressure from the momentum of the charge, seeming to bend in some places, almost to the point of breaking.

Eli held his breath. If the line broke, it would prove catastrophic to Lord Edgun's army. And for a moment, the enemy's line appeared like it might break, shattering into pieces.

Then with effort born of a grim determination and intensive training, those men of the second rank helped the first rank remain steady. They lent their strength to the shield wall. Within two dozen heartbeats, the enemy's line stabilized and held firm, before pushing back at the massed warriors. Eli could only imagine what the fighting was like down there, the brutality, warriors caught before the shield wall, pressed from the front and from behind by their own comrades being crushed to death, stabbed, hammered, and battered by the enemy's shields.

A horn blew from somewhere amongst the trees to their front, and with it, the men before them stood. They gave an enthusiastic cheer. The horn blew again, and as if hunting dogs released after game, they charged forward, thundering down the steep slope toward the enemy's flanking line, making their own desperate charge.

Eli stood and nocked an arrow. His eyes returned to Mik'Las, who was standing behind Lord Edgun's horse. The criminal, as if he could sense Eli, was looking their way.

"Let's go," he said grimly. "It is time to join the battle."

Eli began moving down the ridge, following the charging warriors. Mae, Jit, and Rivun went with him.

CHAPTER TWENTY

The roar of the fighting was a barrage of unrelenting noise, fully battering at the senses. It had been several decades since Eli had been in a true battle, where two armies fought for dominance and control. He had forgotten how chaotic and confusing it could be.

Mere yards to his front, thousands were doing their best to slaughter their fellow man. To make things worse, it had begun to lightly rain. Standing upon a small boulder that was rapidly becoming slick from water, Eli nocked an arrow, scanning the fighting to his front.

Thunder grumbled off in the distance.

"There." Rivun pointed his sword. "See him, right there on the left and behind the line?"

Following where Rivun indicated, Eli's bow snapped up. He found the target, an enemy officer, likely a captain from the quality of his armor. The man was pacing behind the line, shouting orders and encouragements to his men in the first rank, who were engaged with Karenna's warriors.

Aiming, Eli tracked the officer for a heartbeat, then released. His bow twanged in a satisfying manner. The arrow flew true, hammering into the man, just a hair above his chest armor. So powerful was the missile driven home that it knocked the officer backward. He disappeared behind the crush of the line.

To his right, Mae's bow released. Her arrow struck a sergeant through the neck. The man had been rushing toward where the officer had gone down, likely to render aid. There was a spray of blood, and then he too disappeared behind the battle line.

Scanning the fighting to his front and seeing no additional targets, Eli hopped down from the rock. For the past quarter hour, they had been moving along the flanking line, taking down anyone they spotted who was providing a semblance of leadership.

So far, their work had had no real noticeable effect on the fighting. However, it had become clear that word of what they were doing had spread. Many of the enemy officers had become wise. They were crouching down behind cover of the battle line, only occasionally poking their heads up to assess the fighting to their front. That was making the job of finding and eliminating the enemy's leadership more difficult.

Eli scanned the fighting before him. Despite Karenna's warriors having the numerical advantage, the enemy's lines remained stubbornly intact. Lord Edgun's army was doing an admirable job at holding back the wild and unorganized mass of Karenna's warriors. Not only that, but they were beginning to inflict heavy losses upon the rebels.

An increasing number of warriors were becoming injured or outright killed. Leaving trails and splotches of blood upon the ground, a steady stream of wounded were walking, limping, and dragging themselves back and away from the savage fighting. That was, if they were not crushed first by the press of the line.

"Against a determined shield wall," Rivun said, as if he could read Eli's thoughts, "enthusiasm just isn't enough."

Eli could only agree. He lowered his bow and glanced around, scanning the warriors both to his left and then right. He turned and looked at the ridges to the east and south, searching.

"What?" Mae asked, looking over. "What's wrong? What are you looking for?"

"Where's Karenna?" Eli waved at the fight before them. "She should be out leading her people, setting the example."

"I don't see her either," Rivun said, "not anywhere on the field."

"Neither do I," Mae said.

Eli scanned the battlefield carefully. Where had she gone? Why wasn't she here? Even her presence on the battlefield would be motivational. It did not make any sense. He could not imagine her running, so where was she?

Eli's gaze fell upon Lord Edgun's standard and next to it, astride his horse, was Edgun himself. The man was slowly, almost casually riding about the battlefield. He still had his helmet off. His hair was short and cropped. His expression was a severe one. From his manner, he appeared accustomed to command in the field.

Unfortunately, the man had not ventured near enough for a good shot. He was close to two hundred yards off. To be accurate, and for a near sure shot, Eli needed him to be closer.

Still, he decided to try anyway. He nocked another arrow and drew back the string. Feeling the strain in his arms and the resistance of the bow, he aimed carefully, then released. The bow made a pinging sound.

The arrow flew high up into the air and seemed to hang for a long moment, suspended in midair. Then it began to arc, falling rapidly toward the ground. At first, Eli thought it would miss completely, but it didn't. Surprisingly, the missile connected with the rump of Edgun's horse and burrowed deep.

The animal jumped, then gave a violent buck. Caught by surprise, Edgun rocked unsteadily on the horse's back. He clutched violently at the reins, inadvertently yanking upon them, which proved to be a mistake. The horse reared back on its hind legs, and the squat lord of the Castol promptly fell off and to the ground. A moment later, the horse turned and bolted, bucking as it charged away from the fighting.

"Not bad," Rivun commented as the standard-bearer and several of the escorts dismounted and rushed over to where Edgun had fallen.

"What do you mean?" Eli asked, outraged. "Not bad? That was over two hundred yards, maybe even two hundred and ten. And it's raining."

"It would have been better had you hit him," Rivun said. "That might have just ended the battle. Next time, try not to miss."

"How do you know I wasn't aiming for the horse?" Eli asked. "Dismounting him keeps him from riding off."

Rivun gave him a disbelieving look. "As if."

"Garus said I was a regular pain in the ass," Eli replied to Rivun. "Perhaps I was just trying to emphasize his point, in a literal fashion. At least I recall you telling me he said that." Eli waved before them. "Well, there is the proof."

"You are a regular pain in the ass," Rivun said. "I will give you that one."

With a group of men clustered around him, Lord Edgun was helped back to a standing position. He looked rather irate and shoved one of the men attending him forcefully back and away.

"You know," Rivun said, eyeing the lord, "I bet that fall hurt, especially wearing all that armor."

"I hope it did," Eli said. "He looks like he is a little peeved."

"Get down," shouted Mae urgently. "Down."

Eli and Rivun dropped. A heartbeat later, an arrow buried its nose in the ground a few yards behind them. Mae's bow twanged in reply.

"Got him," she said with satisfaction. "He's down. He was aiming at both of you. I do not believe he will trouble us again, especially since the arrow took him in the eye."

"So," Rivun said from the ground, "it was a bull's-eye, then?"

"That was a good one," Eli said as he picked himself up from the ground. The rain had stopped and a shaft of sunlight poked through a cloud, illuminating the southern ridge. He glanced over at Mae. "Thank you for that."

Unfortunately, the ground had been churned up by the fighting and was muddy. The mud was mixed with blood. Eli wiped his hands clean against his tunic and pulled another arrow from his bundle.

"Do you see Mik'Las?" Mae asked as Rivun stood and brushed himself off. "I lost him once the fighting started."

"No," Eli said, "but if they don't break Edgun's lines soon, it will not matter."

"It's not looking good," Rivun agreed. "The enemy are being quite stubborn. I do not believe Karenna's warriors will be able to break their line."

"The bastards are well-trained," Jit said from a few feet away. She had her sword drawn and was calmly watching the fighting. "Unless something changes, this battle is lost."

Eli felt an intense burst of frustration. Short of joining the actual fighting himself, he could not see what they could do to alter the outcome. And even then, the four of them would be of little help.

A whistle sounded to their front. It was high-pitched and cut through the noise of the fighting. This was followed by a massed grunt and then the enemy shield wall began to push their way forward, just one painful half-step. The sound of the fighting abruptly intensified as Karenna's warriors to their front resisted. The half-step alone was an impressive, unified effort, and the enemy managed to shove back the mass of warriors pressing against the shield wall.

There was a hesitation, then another whistle blast and a second great shove. Searching, Eli could not spot the officer or sergeant with the whistle. He had seen the imperial legions do this before, but not the Castol. Lord Edgun surely knew the business of war, for only a well-trained and disciplined force could do what they were doing now.

The whistle sounded a third time, and the soldiers to their front gave yet another massive shove, manhandling the mass of warriors, forcing them back. For their part, Karenna's fighters roared in rage, frustration, and hate. They did their best to push back at the enemy but there was nothing organized about how they fought. There was no cohesion. It was every warrior for himself to get at the enemy, and yet, it still was a titanic contest between the two armies.

Thunder rumbled again, momentarily drowning out the sound of the fighting.

"They're going to lose," Mae said, "aren't they?"

"It looks that way," Eli said, with a heavy heart. He wracked his brain, trying to think of what they could do to help, to change the dynamic. Karenna had said when the time came, he would know what to do.

Eli came up dry, with nothing.

He looked over at Rivun, who met his gaze grimly. It was clear he could think of nothing either, for he gave a shrug of his shoulders.

"When they break," Rivun said, after a few moments of silence, "we will need to make a run for it, seek the safety of the forest."

"It does not look like they are close to that," Eli said, "not yet anyway."

"This fight will carry on for some time before the inevitable happens," Rivun said. "I believe we both know that."

"So," Mae said, "it has already been decided."

"I'm not so sure. Look." Jit pointed to the top of the southern ridge, where the enemy had marched down into the valley earlier. There was excitement in her tone. "It's Karenna."

The sun was still shining through the gap in the clouds. It seemed the golden rays rained down solely upon a lone warrior, one clad in elven armor. The sunlight appeared to set the figure afire in reflected light. So bright was she that it was hard to look upon her.

"Karenna!" a wounded man ahead of them shouted, pointing. He had a nasty cut on his right thigh that was bleeding profusely and had been limping away from the fighting. He had stopped. "It's Karenna!"

"Karenna," someone else shouted. Word spread, seeming to electrify those below and around them. An enthusiastic, wild cheer went up from the rebel army. It thundered around the valley and after several long moments coalesced into her name, becoming a chant.

"KARENNNA, KARENNNA, KARENNNA."

She drew her sword. It too caught the sunlight, seeming to explode into magical fire. Eli thought it an impressive display, but that was all it was, a grand show. He could not see how one person would make a difference in the battle, other than inspire her men, who were already giving it their all and then some.

"KARENNNA, KARENNNA, KARENNNA."

Karenna pointed her sword down toward the battle and almost directly at Lord Edgun. Her people roared their approval, becoming even more enthusiastic, if that was possible. Behind Karenna, a man stepped from the trees. It was Utreek, and he had his sword drawn. Then another appeared and suddenly there were dozens of warriors on the ridge, then hundreds. Each carried a shield. They began to form themselves into a line of battle three ranks deep.

"She took a force around, behind the enemy," Rivun said. "Now, that I heartily approve of. They are going to come right down that ridge and into Edgun's unprotected flank."

Utreek shouted out something to his formation, which was drowned out by the sound of the fighting. Almost in unison, they drew their swords. Utreek moved to the formation's right side and just to the front. He shouted something indistinguishable and waved his hand forward. The meaning was clear. The order had been given to advance.

In step, this organized force began to move. It was a slow, steady, and measured march that took them down the slope and into the valley. They were advancing directly upon the enemy's rear, where there was no force to meet them. All of Edgun's reserves had been committed to the fight.

Eli looked around and spotted Edgun, who was clearly giving orders and gesturing about to emphasize what he wanted done. Eli considered taking another shot, then thought better of it and decided to save the arrow. He would need it later. Edgun was still too far for an accurate shot.

Officers and messengers ran from him to different parts of the field, and within moments, the rear ranks of Edgun's army began to peel off. Edgun was redeploying part of his army to form a blocking force.

With officers and sergeants leading them, these men hustled toward the rear of the army and began to organize into a new line. They were being positioned to confront this new threat, which, despite their slow advance, was steadily closing to contact.

Led by Utreek, this new force, what Eli took to be the Elite Karenna had mentioned during their talk, continued their measured advance, steadily eating up the ground. They were not rushing. Utreek was clearly saving their strength for the actual fighting to come, which was wise. Running while wearing armor and carrying a heavy shield and sword was exhausting. Fighting for an extended period while so encumbered was even more taxing.

Across the field, the intensity of the battle increased. Motivated by her presence, the warriors pressing against the shield wall gave it even more of an effort to break the enemy's line.

"By taking a force around and behind the enemy," Rivun said, pointing,

"Karenna has thinned much of the line."

"They have a chance now," Jit said, "if they can break the enemy's line at some point."

"I think we need to see what we can do to help Utreek and his boys. Come on," Eli called and jogged to the left, moving along the edge of the fighting raging along the flanks of Edgun's army. Behind him, Mae, Jit, and Rivun followed.

In short order, Eli came to the end of the line and moved a few yards farther out into the open space before making his way toward the newly forming line, coming to within forty yards of the enemy. Without hesitation, Eli chose and nocked a steel-tipped arrow, found a target, a sergeant, and loosed.

The sergeant never saw the missile coming. He was shouting at his men, badgering them to fall into line as rapidly as possible. The arrow took him hard in the side, steel tip punching right through his mail shirt. He stiffened in surprise, looked down at the arrow, and then crumpled to the ground, where he rolled in agony while attempting to draw the arrow free.

Mae loosed next and a man who had just stepped into position on the end of the line, a common soldier, took the hit. The force of the missile's impact threw him physically into the next man. Both went down in a tumble.

The nearest officer was too far away for a good shot. The blocking force Edgun was organizing had just two ranks and was still in the process of becoming set, as more and more men fell into it, extending the length of this new line.

Eli saw Karenna's warriors were only fifty yards to contact. No, Eli corrected himself, these were her soldiers. They were organized, clearly trained, and were moving together as a cohesive unit, meaning they would fight together and not as individuals, like the rest of her army. Karenna walked boldly at Utreek's side.

"Continue to fire into the end of the formation," Eli told Mae. "We need to keep the enemy unsettled. We do that and we make it easier for Utreek to break this scratch line."

Eli loosed another arrow. This one struck a man in the side of the head. He instantly dropped. Those around him took an unsteady step back and out of the line. Mae felled another enemy soldier. Then Eli was releasing arrows as fast as he could, his hands becoming a blur.

The distance closed to twenty yards, then ten.

"Eli," Rivun called, pointing with his sword. "Slinger."

There was an audible crack, and then something hissed close by. Having nocked an arrow, Eli dropped to a knee and turned, following where Rivun had pointed. Twenty yards away, an enemy soldier had a sling. He had just casted and was pulling another bullet out from his pouch at his side. Eli aimed and loosed. A heartbeat later, the arrow hammered home into his target's chest, and he fell backward to the ground, where he thrashed about in the mud.

Lightning flashed across the sky. Thunder rumbled in reply. The rain started to fall again, this time heavier.

"I'm out," Eli said, wiping water from his eyes as he slung his bow onto his back.

Mae's bow twanged.

"Me too," she called.

To their front was a heavy crash as Utreek's formation slammed home against the enemy's scratch blocking line. Behind the enemy line, about two hundred yards away, Eli spotted Lord Edgun. There were additional soldiers, reinforcements, jogging from the rear ranks of the main battle line. Given enough time, Eli understood the enemy position would solidify and turn firm. That could not be allowed to happen.

Eli's gaze went to Edgun. The man was limping, but he was clearly in control and command of the situation, a calming influence for his men. Edgun was giving orders, directing his men fighting. An officer moved with him. The struggle to their front was intense, hard, brutal, shield and sword against shield and sword, hammering, stabbing, and battering away at each other.

The effort for both sides was more one of willpower and strength than anything else. At first, Karenna's formation made no progress. They seemed to have struck an unmovable wall. The enemy's resistance was stiff, and they did not budge. But then, the rebel formation, under Utreek's direction, began forcing their way forward in pulses, one painful half-step at a time. With each push, Utreek's men gave a massed shout.

Edgun's line had not fully had a chance to set, to become the unmovable rock the enemy needed it to be. Within moments, they began giving ground. Then, incredibly, Karenna was in the front rank in the middle of the struggle, fighting alongside her men. Her sword flashed as the rain became harder, pelting downward. She carried an ornate shield that matched her armor. Eli had not noticed it before. An enemy to her front went down to her blade.

Opposite from her was Lord Edgun. He had stopped giving orders and was eyeing her with something akin to wariness. Two enemy ranks stood between Karenna and Lord Edgun. Eli could almost sense the tension crackling on the air. Both were representatives of their own gods, and there was no telling how the coming clash would go. Surely it would be a mighty one.

Karenna was confronted by another enemy soldier, who took the place of the man she'd just cut down. He struck at her shield, battering it with his sword. She blocked and struck back, striking his shield with a powerful blow. The man next to her went down, and she had no protection on her right. Eli sucked in a breath as Karenna found herself faced off against two opponents, with a hole in the line to her right and thoroughly on the defensive. Then Utreek was by her side in the line, plugging the hole, struggling with the second enemy, and diverting his attention.

Letting out his breath, Eli recalled his conversation with Karenna.

Lord Edgun's line was slightly longer than Utreek's. And they were beginning to bend around the sides of the rebels' line. More importantly, the end of the line was just yards away.

"I know what we need to do," Eli said. "Rivun, we have to break their line, to roll it up on this end. We do that and Edgun's force will collapse. The whole of the blocking force will unravel. Karenna will be free to face him as was intended."

"Let's get it done, then," Rivun said and, without waiting, sprinted forward, followed by Jit.

"Stay near me," Eli told Mae, looking around at her. "This will be worse than the fight in the fort."

Mae gave a steady nod and drew her sword. Pulling out his daggers, Eli broke into a run. Just ahead, Rivun attacked the side of the line. A man in the second rank at the last moment turned to face the Anagradoom. He raised his sword.

It was a warding gesture, and it did no good. Rivun batted the sword away and, before the man could react, brought his blade inside the other's defense and stabbed him through the stomach. Right behind him, Jit slammed into the next man, jabbing her sword out, plunging it into his middle, and taking him violently down to the ground.

Then Eli was with them, moving past and around Rivun and tearing into the enemy. Moving between the two ranks, he had the flash of terrified faces of the enemy as his daggers slashed this way and that. He brought down two men before a shield bashed him roughly, knocking him aside. Eli tasted copper, for he had bitten his tongue. He turned to face the man who had hit him, prepared to block a follow-up attack, only to have Mae appear from seemingly nowhere. Face set into a snarl, she stabbed the soldier in the side, running her blade deep, screaming wildly as she did it.

Recovering, Eli turned to the next enemy and attacked. He lost himself to the fighting, taking one opponent down after another. With his two daggers, he was performing the dance of death, and on this field, he was the master. He found one enemy, killed or incapacitated him, and then moved onto the next.

He had flashes of Rivun, Jit, and even Mae fighting nearby. So consumed he became that he forgot about everything else. All that mattered was breaking the enemy's line and beginning the process of rolling it up. He was dimly aware of shouting, oaths, yelling, cries, and screams. Blood flew through the air, and spattered him. He fought on, death incarnate.

Then suddenly, there was no enemy before him, no additional opponents. Breathing heavily, confused, Eli stopped, blinking, looking around. Where had they all gone? Sense returned. Friendly warriors who had made up Utreek's formation were rushing by him, pursuing the enemy who had broken and were fleeing. Farther down, the rest of Edgun's scratch blocking line began to disintegrate as the man's soldiers lost heart and gave up the fight.

Eli suddenly thought of Mae. He had intended to watch out for her, and he had not. He glanced around, worried, fearful, feeling guilty. The feeling was like a fist closing upon his heart and he did not like it, not one bit. He scanned those nearest, at first not seeing her. Then he spotted Mae. She was a few yards back, breathing heavily and leaning upon her sword, the point of which was sticking into the ground. As if she had bathed in it, she was covered head to foot in blood. She had a small cut on her cheek and a gash on her right arm.

Mae was looking around in what he took to be shock at the carnage that surrounded them. He could well understand her thinking and feelings. Eli had had similar thoughts after his first true battle, shock at what he had witnessed and done.

Mae's gaze met his and within it he saw her naked relief that he was okay. Eli felt his heart swell for her. He wanted nothing more than to take her within his arms and hold her, to tell her it was okay, that everyone was all right.

Jit was by Mae's side, a wound on her thigh bleeding freely. She was just as bloody as Mae. Jit had lost her sword and held her hand axe loosely in one hand. Blood dripped from it to the ground.

"Look." Rivun was a few feet away. He pointed with his bloodied sword.

Eli turned and saw Karenna confronting an officer standing just before Lord Edgun. A ring of men, about a dozen, had coalesced around Lord Edgun. They were fighting with Karenna's soldiers, who had finally broken ranks to pursue and engage the fleeing enemy. Utreek was amongst them. Glancing around at the rest of the battle, Eli took stock. Edgun's L-shaped battle line still held. The fighting was raging and as brutal as ever. Only the scratch defensive line had been broken. The rest of Edgun's army stubbornly struggled on.

Eli's gaze was drawn back to Karenna and he began moving, closing the distance between them. Rivun, Mae, and Jit went with him.

The officer lunged. Almost as if he were an untrained amateur, Karenna ducked to the side, easily avoiding his swing, and then struck, jabbing back. Her sword pierced the man's thigh.

It was a minor wound, and yet he dropped, as if the strings of his life had been cut, sliced by a pair of shears. Eli's gaze focused upon Karenna's blade and he recalled what she'd said about her sword being the one to kill Edgun and decided it must indeed be enchanted.

Lord Edgun had drawn his sword. The blade was black as polished coal and glistened like it was wet. Karenna stepped calmly by the officer she'd just slain. Immediately all around them, the fighting slacked off, as the men on both sides disengaged and took a step back to watch the coming confrontation. A few dozen yards away, unchecked, the main battle continued to rage.

"I would have expected you to run with your men," Karenna said clearly, her voice seeming to carry.

"Run? Me?" Edgun replied. "From the likes of you? Never."

"Do you remember me?" Karenna asked, removing her helmet with one hand so that he could see her face. "Do you remember what you did to me? To my father?"

Edgun came to a stop. He eyed her for a long moment, then gave a shrug of his shoulders. There was no kindness in his gaze. His voice was gruff and gravelly when he spoke.

"No. Then again, I've had so many tarts. It's hard to recall all of them, especially the ones who do not impress me."

"That's unfortunate," Karenna said with a hardness to her tone. "You caused me great suffering."

"Many have suffered under my hand," Edgun said plainly. "In the end, what does it matter, as long as I serve my lord faithfully?"

"It matters," Karenna said, "to your victims. I am the daughter of Lucius Ren Varreenus and I have come to deliver justice."

"Ah," Edgun replied. "I remember your father, vaguely, but I do not recall you. I guess it comes down to this, then, this very moment. We stand at a fork in the road, a vengeful daughter and a faithful servant of the only god that matters. Whoever wins will be rewarded and our cause advanced."

"Yes," Karenna said. "Those are the stakes."

"Let's get this over with, Child of Mars, for our meeting was destined to occur." He saluted her mockingly and then lunged forward, launching into a furious assault.

She met him and for several moments traded blow for blow, blocking with her shield. The air rang heavy from the clash of steel. Sparks arced out as the two blades came together again and again. It was a titanic struggle related to something larger, beyond the two individuals involved.

Eli could not help but watch, staring in fascination, as the two battled each other, as if possessed by something greater, given strength mere mortals should never have. Edgun's limp had vanished, and he moved as if uninjured.

Both swords came together and locked. For a moment, they struggled against each other, with Edgun trying to overpower Karenna by brute force alone. He could not overcome her. She seemed immovable.

Then, Edgun shifted his stance and stepped forward, knocking aside her shield and lashing out with an armored hand, striking Karenna hard across the cheek. Surprised and clearly stunned, she stumbled back and tripped over a body, falling, losing her shield.

With a look of incredible triumph, Edgun advanced, standing over her. He raised his sword, prepared to deliver the final blow. The blade in his hand burst into black flame.

Before Eli could react and try to intercede, there was a primal shout of rage. Utreek threw himself forward and met Edgun's sword with his own. The blades came together with a ringing clang.

Surprised, Edgun took a step back and away. Utreek swung his blade, aiming for Edgun's exposed leg. The lord of the Castol blocked, then forced Utreek's sword aside, as if a mere child swung it. With his free hand, he pointed at his opponent's chest and, incredibly, Utreek was flung back, as if by some invisible force. He landed hard five feet away and did not stir. Steam rose from his body.

"No!" It was a scream of rage mixed with fear and pain and it came from Karenna. She was back on her feet. Overhead, lightning flashed across the sky and the resulting thunder cracked around the valley, earsplitting in its intensity.

For a moment, no one moved. In abject horror, Karenna gazed upon Utreek's unmoving body. She seemed frozen, stunned to immobility, then she turned her gaze upon Edgun and in it Eli saw grim determination and the heart-wrenching pain of loss.

"You have taken everything from me, spawn of Valoor," Karenna said through bared teeth. "Now, I will take everything from you."

"I think not." With an evil grin, Edgun raised his finger and pointed it at Karenna, like he had with Utreek.

Nothing happened.

The smile slipped from his face as Edgun jerked his finger again. A glowing blue halo of light shimmered into existence around Karenna. It grew in intensity with each heartbeat.

"Your evil magic does not work upon me," Karenna said. "By coming north, Valoor has grown bold and overstepped himself."

"And what would you know of my god?" Edgun snarled.

"I know enough. You have shown me his callous ways. And now, it is time to end the cycle of rebirth for you. That is what I have come to do, to end you, here and now, this day, in the Valley of Tears."

"You don't have that power." Edgun's gaze narrowed. He took an uncertain step back as Karenna raised her sword and advanced. He glanced to the left and right as his men, who were standing in a near circle with hers, simply watched. "Valoor is all-powerful. He is the one true god."

"He is but one of many," Karenna said as she advanced. "Mars, I beseech you to lend me strength."

Edgun took a step to the right and she to the left. Karenna's attack, when it came, was furious and savage. It was born of a life of suffering, reinforced with the loss of her husband. Tears ran down her cheeks as she fought. They traded several sword strokes, then separated, circling each other. Edgun did not appear as sure of himself as he had earlier. In fact, he seemed quite hesitant.

"Kill her," Edgun roared at the nearest of his men. A bubble of calm had formed around the two Champions. Beyond the bubble, unchecked, the battle for the valley still raged. Edgun looked savagely at his men. "I said kill her!"

No one moved. It was as if they had all been rooted to the spot upon which they stood.

Karenna did not hesitate. She continued forward with her attack and Edgun gave ground as she pressed him. Then Edgun stopped retreating and, grim-faced with resolve, struck back. Karenna countered. The light around her had grown in intensity, becoming almost blinding. Eli raised a hand to shield his eyes as the two battled each other. Edgun made a slashing attack; Karenna dodged back, allowing it to sail wide, then she struck, lightning-fast, jabbing out at him.

Edgun screamed as the tip of her blade sliced into his exposed arm. It was a tortured scream, filled with intense agony. There was a brilliant flaring of light and a cracking sound followed by a deep humming. It drowned out all other sounds on the battlefield. Eli forced his eyes closed against the brilliance and covered his eyes with his hands. Still, he found he could see the light as if his eyes were open. It was intense and painful.

When the light faded after a few heartbeats, he looked, blinking. He was able to focus and found Karenna standing as the victor. Lord Edgun lay slumped at her feet, lifeless, a shriveled husk, a mockery of what the man had looked like in life.

Silence reigned upon the entire battlefield. The fighting had stopped. Several of those nearest dropped their swords and ran. Then all of the enemy who had watched the combat broke, running for their lives. A collective groan came from Edgun's men all across the battlefield. A heartbeat later, the army began to disintegrate, first in ones and twos and then in a great mass, as much of the army started running.

Karenna ignored it all.

The light around her had faded away. She dropped her sword to the ground, turned away, and walked almost woodenly over to Utreek. She gazed down upon him, and Eli felt his heart break at her loss, the agony that was plain upon her.

Weeping, she sat down by his side and placed a hand upon his chest.

"I am sorry," Karenna said to her dead husband. "I am so sorry."

Eli took several steps nearer, prepared to offer what comfort he could. He hesitated as she bowed her head in what he took to be prayer. Her lips moved silently, tears rolling freely down her cheeks.

Utreek was pale, lifeless. Ugly black lines crisscrossed the skin of his face, arms, and neck. Karenna continued to pray. Eli felt a surge of something, of what he wasn't quite sure. With it, his hair seemed to stand on end.

What was happening?

Incredibly, Utreek gave a gasping breath and, blinking furiously, opened his eyes. Eli gave a start. The black lines had disappeared, and the color returned to his skin. Breathing heavily, as if he had run a long distance, he gazed up at her, eyes incredibly wide.

"You brought me back," he gasped. "I felt it, as I was crossing over. It ... it ... you ... you and Mars reached out ... pulled me back."

Karenna gave a wrenching sob of joy and hugged him, kissing him.

"Well," Rivun said, at Eli's side, "that was something to see."

"It seems she is a paladin after all," Eli said to him as she helped Utreek sit up. All around them, the nearest of her warriors fell to their knees, clasping their hands before their chests.

Karenna looked over at Eli and then at those nearest, especially those kneeling. She raised her voice so all could hear. "I am no paladin. I am only a humble servant, faithful to my lord. Rise, my friends. Do not worship me. Honor your own gods, for that is how things are meant to be. I was sent to right a wrong, to help free you and defeat a terrible enemy. That is all. Show me the honor of standing, please, I beg you. I deserve not your worship."

Slowly, one by one, the men stood. Each touched a hand to his forehead in respect. With that, Karenna returned her attention to Utreek. She put her head against his. It was an intimate gesture, one born of love and joy. Deciding to give them their privacy, Eli moved away a few yards.

"Do you see Mik'Las and the Atreena?" Mae asked, coming up as she scanned the battlefield. Thousands of Lord Edgun's soldiers were running, climbing the ridge and seeking escape as Karenna's warriors pursued them, killing all they managed to catch. Not all of the enemy were running, though. Scattered across the field, there was still some bitter fighting. "I don't see him."

Eli felt a stab of disappointment and regret at not being able to catch the criminal. He glanced over at Karenna. Still, they had done some good today and set things right. Mik'Las could wait, at least for a time.

"He's likely run for it," Eli said, not even bothering to scan for Mik'Las. He felt thoroughly drained, and it was beginning to grow dark. Not only that, the rain was falling once again and more strongly than before. He was soaked. But more importantly, he needed a rest. They all did.

"If I was him," Rivun said, "I would have run for it and been long gone."

"There's no point in going for him tonight," Eli said. "We have no idea which way he went." Eli let out a long breath. "He will cover his tracks well. It is going to take some effort to track him down. We can start tomorrow or maybe even the next day."

Mae gave an unhappy nod. She looked over at Rivun and Jit. "Will you be joining us? Will you both help us catch him?"

Rivun shared a long look with Jit. After a moment, Rivun spoke. "I would love to, but no. As much as it pains me to say this, Mik'Las is your problem, your mission. I promised Jit we would do something first and I mean to see that through. I also have something personal I need to attend to." He looked over at Jit with feeling. "And I always keep my promises. After that, who knows?"

"He is going to help me find my son," Jit explained. "He was taken from me and brought north."

Eli gave a weary nod. There would be no changing Rivun's mind. As he was in love, he was now bound to Jit and would do everything within his power to help her. Eli glanced over at Mae. He did not begrudge Rivun that, not at all. Besides, Eli knew he could catch Mik'Las on his own, and he would do just that.

"I wish you luck at finding your son," Eli said.

"Thank you," Jit said.

Rivun glanced around, studying the remains of the battlefield. There were still pockets of active fighting, where entire enemy companies were withdrawing in order, along with hundreds, if not thousands, of wounded and dead scattered all around. This was particularly true where the battle lines had been. His gaze fell upon Karenna and Utreek. She had gotten him to his feet and, with an arm about his waist, was helping him away.

"I think," Rivun said, "we will remain here for a few days and render what aid we can. I will send a message to Si'Cara and bring her up to date on matters here. I am certain she will be very interested."

"You have a means to reach my mother?" Mae asked.

"I do," Rivun said. "There was a time when she listened to my council. Maybe, just maybe, she will listen again and offer these people some help."

"Mother always spoke highly of you," Mae said. "I never heard her utter a cross word. Speak true and she will listen, and if she does not, let me know."

"You are very much like her," Rivun said and then his expression became one of sorrow, "and your father. I can see them both within you."

"My father?" Mae asked, blinking furiously.

"That's right. Your father would be proud of the ranger you have become. Trust me on that."

"My father?" Mae whispered again.

"Tal'Thor was one of the best of us," Rivun said. "Never doubt that, no matter what anyone says of him."

Eli glanced over at Mae, troubled by her reaction. Her father had never made it to Istros. He did not know the full story, but what he had heard had led him to the understanding that Tal'Thor had made the ultimate sacrifice for his people. But something else had happened that the elders would not speak of, even Eli's father. A cloud of some kind hung over Tal'Thor's head. Perhaps one day he would learn the truth. Until then, it was just one more mystery that required solving.

Eli felt a wave of exhaustion. He saw a large log a few feet off, moved over to it, and sat down. Despite the rain, a smoldering campfire lay next to the log. It provided some warmth. A collapsed and trampled tent was a few feet away. Mae sat down next to him.

She reached out and took his hand, which had begun to shake. Whether it was from exhaustion or nerves, Eli did not know. Both of them were covered in blood, gore, and mud. She leaned her head against his shoulder. Having her there felt right and good.

"When I speak with your mother," Rivun said, "I will omit what is growing between you both. That news is better served coming from you and not me."

"Thank you," Mae said.

Eli was too tired to reply. He just gave a nod. With that, Rivun walked off. Jit trailed after him.

Eli and Mae sat there together for a time. He turned his head and kissed the top of hers.

"I do not want this moment to end," he said softly to her, enjoying her closeness and the feeling that they had both survived.

"Neither do I," she replied. "I want it to last for eternity."

Eli closed his eyes and, thoroughly exhausted, enjoyed the moment.

EPILOGUE

Eli tied his bag closed and stood. Mae was finishing up securing her things. Thunder rumbled off in the distance, presaging another rain. The fire provided the light by which they worked, for dawn had yet to arrive. It was still several hours off.

They had stayed two days after the battle, not only to recover, but also to help tend to the wounded. There had been many who had fallen in battle and even more injured. Now it was time to leave, to continue the hunt for Mik'Las. Eli checked his bundle of arrows. It was tied tight and secured to his pack. He had retrieved several extra arrows from the battlefield. At some point he would have to make more.

He straightened and scratched an itch upon his arm.

"Are you ready?" he asked, softly, so as not to disturb those sleeping in the nearby tents.

Mae looked up. "About ready."

Then her attention drifted off to the left and he saw her stiffen. Rivun was approaching with Karenna. She was no longer wearing her armor. She wore a simple homespun gray dress and looked relaxed and at peace.

"I thank you again, ranger," Karenna said, by way of greeting. "You made the difference and ensured my moment with Edgun was possible. For that, you have my gratitude.

You all do." She glanced over at Mae. "And now, you must leave us, yes?"

"We have a mission," Eli said.

"To capture a criminal," Karenna said.

"Yes," Eli said. "What will you do now?"

"Now?" Karenna's gaze became distant for a moment. "Now, I will put fighting behind me. My days as a warrior are done. I will step back from the sunlight and spend time with my husband and live my life. More importantly, I will be returning home to my family. If I am lucky, raise a family too. I think I would like daughters, several."

"Really?" Eli found himself surprised. "You are going back to the empire? What does Utreek say to that?"

"We have talked it through," she said. "He will go where I go, where our god wishes us both to go."

"I see," Eli said. "Are you certain you are not a paladin?"

"A paladin, no," Karenna said, "a priestess, yes."

Eli bowed his head respectfully, for she indeed had a god's favor.

"Edgun named you a Child of Mars," Eli said.

"I am so."

"The god of war and guardian of agriculture," Eli said. "You have served him well."

"I have a favor to ask," Karenna said, "when you return this way, when your mission is complete."

"If it is within my capacity to deliver, I shall see your favor done."

"My armor," Karenna said, "I only borrowed it. My god would like it returned. I will leave it with the caretaker. Will you give it to the warden? It belongs to her, and your people."

"I will," Eli said.

"Thank you." Karenna looked over at Rivun. "I hope my efforts here build something lasting—a peace amongst the tribes and forest people. I will help begin that effort, but I will not see it through. Others will, and Rivun has offered to help us make a start at that, especially if the king is in a forgiving mood."

"With some fortune and convincing," Eli said, "the warden will lend you her support. I am sure of it."

"And when that's done," Rivun said, "I might even see what I can do to help the king and his son."

"The king of the Castol?" Eli asked, surprised by that. "I thought you were committed to helping Jit?"

"I am and will. I believe I can get two birds with one stone."

"I see," Eli said.

"I also doubt the warden would enjoy seeing the kingdom devolve into chaos," Rivun said. "That is surely where things are headed if they remain as they are. I intend to trade with Si'Cara, a semblance of stability along her border for her support with Karenna's people."

Eli became amused. "I am certain an old Anagradoom can do anything he puts his mind to."

Rivun started to turn away, clearly intending to leave. He stopped. "Old? Did you really just call me old?"

"Did I say old?" Eli kept his face a mask of innocence. "I meant ancient."

"You are a real pain in the ass, literally," Rivun said, "but I enjoyed finally meeting you. When you see Garus next, tell him I said hello."

"I enjoyed meeting you too, Rivun." Eli stepped forward and they clasped arms.

"One day, I hope our paths cross again," Rivun said. He looked at Mae. "That goes for you too." He paused. "You are both meant for each other. Take my word on this...do not waste the time you have, for it is precious."

With that, and one last look, he stepped away from the fire and was swallowed up into the darkness.

Eli shared a look with Mae.

"There is one more thing," Karenna said.

"And what is that?" Eli asked.

"There is someone here to see you."

Eli glanced around. No one else in the camp was up. Most were sleeping. Mae had gone still. Her gaze snapped to Karenna.

"Who?" Eli asked, suddenly on guard. "And where is this person?"

"As to who," Karenna said, "it is not my place to say. The caretaker has arranged this meeting." She turned and pointed to the east. "You will find him in a small clearing, a mile past the top of the ridge, over that way."

"I am not sure I like this," Eli said. "The caretaker made this possible?"

"He did and there is nothing to fear, but you need to go," Karenna said. "With that, I will take my leave. I wish you both well, and again, you have my thanks."

With that, she turned away and left them, walking off into the darkness. Eli watched her for a moment, his curiosity on fire.

"Let's go find out who has come to see us," Eli said to her.

"No," Mae said. "I am not going."

Eli looked over at her, surprised. The haunted expression had returned.

"This is not for me," Mae said, in a whisper, "it is for you, and it will mean we will need to ultimately put our happiness aside—for a time, maybe forever."

"What are you talking about? I—I do not understand."

"You will." Mae sat down by the fire and threw another branch upon it. Sparks flew up into the air. "You will."

Eli hesitated. He was about to speak when she beat him to it.

"You might recall you cautioned me not to reveal what I saw at the Pool of Reflection. I have decided to take that advice to heart, even though it may ultimately break it."

Eli went cold at that.

"Get going," Mae said, her tone hardening. "I will be here when you return." Her voice became a whisper again. "I will be waiting."

Eli swallowed and then turned away. He started out, heading eastward. Warriors were sleeping everywhere in tents and out in the open. So too were women and children. He moved silently and quickly around them and soon left the camp behind. He climbed the ridge. In the darkness, guided only by a weak moon, Eli made his way east. After a mile, he smelled woodsmoke and then saw the faint glow of a fire.

Slowing as he neared the fire and scanning in all directions, Eli moved carefully forward. There was no one about, at least anyone he could detect out in the darkness. As he came to the edge of the clearing, he crept forward as silently as he could.

With his back to Eli, a solitary man wearing a gray military-style tunic sat before a campfire. The cut of the tunic reminded Eli of a legionary's. The man was gazing into the depths of the fire, seemingly absorbed in thought.

After several moments, he shook himself and reached into a leather pack that sat by his side. He pulled out a blanket and made a disgusted-sounding grunt. The man stood and shook the blanket vigorously several times. Silhouetted against the light of the fire, thick, chalky dust flew up into the air from the blanket.

"Fool gnomes and their volcano," he grumbled in Common, sitting down again and wrapping the blanket around his shoulders. Thunder rumbled off in the distance. "Just great, more rain. I've had enough of that too. Bloody gods, I don't think I will ever warm up."

Besides the pack, the man was armed with a sword, which was sheathed, though from his angle, Eli could not see what kind of blade. The weapon lay within reach and next to the pack. A second sword, a short sword of some kind, was leaning against a tree at the edge of the clearing. He was an imperial. That much was certain from his accent.

Eli remained there and watched as the man settled down before the fire again, returning to staring into its depths. After a time, the man's head came up and gave an almost knowing sigh, followed by a low chuckle.

"Won't you join me?"

Eli had no idea how he had been discovered. It should have been impossible for an ordinary human to know he was there. Given a similar situation, most elves would never have discovered his presence, even some rangers he knew.

It was time to find out who this man was and what he wanted. Stepping forward and into the clearing, Eli moved around the edge to the other side of the crackling fire. The man looked up at him as Eli stepped into his visual field. He was clearly a warrior, for his arms were muscular and heavily scarred, particularly the forearms. There was a vicious scar on the man's upper left cheek, giving him a sort of perpetual sneering expression.

"It is good to see you again, my friend," the man said, his expression cracking.

"Do I know you?" Eli asked.

"Not yet, but I know you."

Something large shifted out in the forest. The ground trembled and a tree came crashing down, a large one from the sound of it.

"What was that?" Eli asked, alarmed.

"My ride," the man said, drawing his attention again. "Eli, my name is Ben, and I've come a long way to see you—a long way—just so we can talk for a few hours before I must take my leave. I also have something for you, a gift." He gestured at the short sword leaning against the tree. "Trust me—we have a lot to discuss."

The End

Eli and Mae's adventures will continue in 2022. Look for Book 2 of a Ranger's Tale. Rivun and Jit's journey will also continue, sometime in the future.

Important: If you have not yet given my other series a shot, I strongly recommend you do. Hit me up on Facebook to let me know what you think!

You can reach out and connect with me on:
Patreon: www.patreon.com/marcalanedelheit
Facebook: Marc Edelheit Author
Facebook: MAE Fantasy & SciFi Lounge (This is a group I created where members can come together to share a love for Fantasy and Sci-Fi)
Twitter: @MarcEdelheit
You may wish to sign up to my newsletter by visiting my website.
http://maenovels.com/

Or

You can follow me on **Amazon** through my Author Profile. Smash that follow button under my picture and you will be notified by Amazon when I have a new release.

Reviews keep me motivated and also help to drive sales. I make a point to read each and every one, so please continue to post them.

Again, I hope you enjoyed *Eli, A Ranger's Tale* and would like to offer a sincere thank you for your purchase and support.
Best regards,
Marc Alan Edelheit, your author and tour guide to the worlds of Tannis and Istros.

Printed in Great Britain
by Amazon

83441887R00171